THE COTTAGE IN THE CLOUDS

CAROLINE YOUNG

Storm
PUBLISHING

Ebook ISBN: 978-1-83700-360-0
Paperback ISBN: 978-1-83700-373-0

Cover design: Emma Rogers
Cover images: Shutterstock

Published by Storm Publishing.
For further information, visit:
www.stormpublishing.co

To my dear Aunty Maggie, who, like Anwen, celebrated the beauty
of North Wales in her art.

And in memory of Ann, a dear friend, who treasured words as much
as I do.

ONE
LONDON, OCTOBER 2024

That Tuesday morning was no different from hundreds, thousands, of other mornings for Elin Pugh. She was sitting at her desk in the office she'd worked in for seven years, looking up at the sliver of grey sky between her building and the one next door and longing for a pair of wings. She had a deadline for writing an article about new trends in interior design, but all she had thought about all morning was what to get for lunch. These days, that was now the most important decision of her day, and by far the most interesting.

When her phone buzzed and she saw "Mum" flash up on the screen, she groaned. If she didn't pick up, Barbara would either be offended and not contact her again for weeks, or panic, as she regarded London as a lawless pit of barbarity. Most of her mother's life had been spent on a remote farm in North Wales, so she had no idea how cities worked, having never lived in one. Elin understood all this, but she still had to take a very deep breath before answering the call.

"Mum, sorry, I'm at work. Can't really chat right now."

"I know, dear, but I've got some news I thought you might want to know," her mother said. The unusual, breathy excitement in Barbara's voice was vaguely intriguing, but Elin knew that her mother could get excited about a new hand cream, or a plot development in a TV soap.

"OK, but if you can tell me this news fast, that would be great, otherwise we'll talk tonight. I really am busy right now, and Sadie's on the warpath."

A familiar, offended pause. "Right, well, in brief, I'm getting married again in the spring."

For a few seconds, Elin was lost for words. When she found them, she hissed, "What the hell? Or rather, *who* the hell?"

"Mind your language, please," her mother replied.

"I minded it. But you can't blame me for being a bit *surprised*." Another icy pause before Elin blurted, "Oh, Mum, just tell me who you're marrying, for goodness' sake."

"Elin, *please*," Barbara replied. "I refuse to speak to you when you're like this. I'll ring back at 1 p.m., which I assume is your lunch break." And she hung up.

Elin sighed. It was useless trying to ring her mother back and protest. This was the game they played, and breaking the rules would only make things worse.

"Looks like the 'comfort' rather than 'healthy' lunch option today," Elin muttered, wishing she still smoked.

They were mother and daughter, but they were so different that Elin had long since decided that they shared nothing apart from their genes. As soon as she had graduated from art school in London, she had not returned home but travelled all over Southeast Asia for much of her twenties, earning money drawing portraits at tourist resorts, doing bits of freelance illustration and working in hospitality if she was desperate for cash. She had come back to the UK to support Barbara when her father Llion fell ill with pancreatic cancer, but also to lick her wounds after a nightmarish break-up with Antoine, the man who had jettisoned her for a better option once she sailed into view. Elin and her mother had stayed by Llion's side for his final, terrible months and she was unable to go further away than London after his death, paralysed by both grief and self-loathing.

Having assumed her father would always be there, as permanent as the mountains they had lived amongst, Llion dying had left Elin unsure of almost everything, especially herself. Her confidence had gone – Antoine had seen to that. More solo travelling seemed impossibly daunting, so she'd done a short course in copywriting and picked up assorted jobs on the back of it, but had never intended to be treading water like this for long. And yet for seven long years, she had lived with her cat, Mouse, in a rented basement flat in Tooting, a space so dark that all her plants died within weeks and her skin had a pallor that reminded her of the waxworks in Madame Tussaud's. While her small group of friends from school married and began to have children, Elin was single, childless and bitter at thirty-one. She felt herself adrift, being carried further and further away from the life she had hoped for, a home filled with the chaos and chatter of the family life that her own had so palpably lacked. Instead of love, hers had been a childhood steeped in disappointment.

Wern Farm, the rambling stone farmhouse she had grown up in, was sold within months of her father's death, and with it, the carved, dark oak chest he had so treasured, the countless boxes of vintage opera 78s and the copper pans Barbara had reluctantly polished each week because he'd told them both they were valuable heirlooms. They had all fetched pennies at auction or ended up in a skip. Barbara had always pined for Shrewsbury, the safe market town she'd grown up in and desperately wanted to return there when she was widowed, but the farm had accrued such huge debts that they, and death duties, meant that she lacked the capital to do so. Llion Pugh had farmed the unforgiving land of Eryri all his life, as his father and grandfather had before him, and the unique energy of its rocky slopes and windswept crags ran through his veins. He had loved it with his whole soul, but Barbara had spent the thirty-five years of their marriage under sufferance in their damp, draughty farmhouse. It was this sense of a life half-lived that filled each room and hung over the family like a pall of gloom.

When Elin, an only child, won a scholarship to a prestigious boarding school in Cheshire at the age of eleven, Barbara was delighted and Llion resigned to her departure, but Elin fought against her fate as hard as she could.

"I want to go to school here, with my friends. Why do I have to leave my home?" she had wailed.

"Because you *can*," her mother had replied. "This is your exit strategy, don't you see? I only wish I had one."

At this point, Elin had flounced out of the room and dutifully slammed the door.

However she tried to deny it, to unsee it, Elin knew how much Barbara hated her life. It was worlds away from the neat redbrick semi she had left after a chance encounter with a handsome young farmer at the livestock auction in Shrewsbury. At thirty, Barbara had almost resigned herself to spinsterhood, but when Llion Pugh seemed to offer her the status and respectability she craved, she had jumped at it: it was the first and last rash decision of her life. The austere grandeur of the Welsh landscape was a universe in which Barbara did not belong, making her lash out like a cornered animal at home, where no one could see or judge her. All this, in retrospect, Elin could now understand, if not forgive. She was no stranger to frustration or unhappiness. The only thing that still made no sense to her was why her mother had stayed at all.

When she had left Wales for art school, Elin did so in the knowledge that she could always return if she ever wanted to, so when the farm was sold, she felt as if a part of her soul had died. She loved the ever-changing moods of the hills as much as her mother hated them: they had been her and her father's shared paradise, where both had forgotten the constraints of everyday life. At art school, her final piece had been a large gouache painting of Nant Ffrancon, a spectacular valley carved out of the mountains by a glacier, and in which their home nestled, its only shelter from the elements being the walls of rock around it. Her tutors had said it showed a raw energy, but the first-class degree and career as an artist she had hoped it would secure did not materialise and she was left feeling ashamed for ever daring to believe it could.

As the clock on her office wall inched towards lunchtime, and Elin braced herself to talk to Barbara again, she looked out of her rain-streaked office window and remembered that ice-carved valley. Since Llion's death, Elin had avoided returning to Wales for fear that the emotions this would release would finally drown her. She had promised her dying father that she would never forget his family's struggle to hew a living from the harsh mountainsides, or the land she had come from, but she had not been able to go back to visit Llion's grave since the day they'd buried him, and suspected that Barbara seldom did so. Unbeknown to Elin, the only person to go regularly was a white-haired woman carrying daffodils in spring, lilac in the summer and a small circlet of holly at Christmas, which she placed on the flat slate stone and on another one, near it.

TWO

At 1.03 p.m., just as Elin had taken one bite of the cheeseburger and fries she'd ordered in for lunch, her mother called back.

"Are you available to talk now?" she said.

Desperately trying to chew and swallow the soggy bolus of bread and meat, Elin replied, "Sorry about earlier. Yes, I am. I'm eating, but fire away."

"As I was saying, I am getting married again. It's all very exciting, and not what I'd expected at *all*," Barbara said. Elin could tell that she was settling down for a slow reveal that would last for her whole, precious lunch hour. Swallowing quickly, she swilled the food down with a gulp of sugary drink.

"That's great, Mum, but are you going to tell me about the man in question?"

"Of course! What do you want to know, dear?"

"Look, I don't want to know about his prospects, Mum, but his *name* might be a good place to start," Elin said, adding, purely to tease her, "And his inside leg measurement, perhaps."

"Very funny. He's called George Hastings, and he's a very respectable man."

Elin rolled her eyes. Her mother's idea of "respectable" would probably mean someone who smoked a pipe, wore a tweed cap and drove a vintage Jaguar, as her points of reference would be daytime TV reruns from the 1980s.

"So, you mean he's English and well-off? But is he *kind*?"

"Yes, he is. Very nice, and very kind, *and* he's a retired bank manager," her mother said gleefully, as if this far surpassed any other quality in a prospective husband. "Aren't you going to congratulate me?"

"Yes, sorry. Congratulations. It's, er, great, but it's all a bit... out of the blue."

"Yes, I suppose it is, but sometimes love intervenes and you just can't help yourself. You'll understand that, sadly," Barbara said. Elin refused to embark on a discussion of Antoine and how he had gulled her so entirely.

"Tell me more about George Hastings," she said, looking at her watch. Her burger was cooling rapidly, globules of fat congealing on its moonscaped surface.

"So, George is a widower, very charming, and he has a large, detached house in Bath. He was up here with ex-university chums for a walking holiday when I met him in the supermarket in Menai Bridge, of all places." She giggled girlishly.

"A detached house," Elin repeated with a sigh. Like "respectable" and "nice", this word also had particular significance for Barbara. She'd hated having to lower herself to a dark terraced house in the small town of Bethesda once the farm had sold, and Elin had witnessed her distress as next door's TV blared through the living room wall. Her mother was a complex woman, but perhaps this was her last chance to be happy, so who was she to spoil it? She should be congratulating her wholeheartedly. But suddenly, dread flooded Elin's body as she realised one bald fact: her mother was about to pull up the drawbridge on her past life, all the history they had shared and any possibility of her returning to the farm. She would be selling up and leaving Wales for good.

Without thinking, she blurted, "But Bath is so far away from home, Mum. And how can you bear to go so far away from Dad's grave?"

A long silence followed, in which Elin felt her mistake keenly. She remembered the silent house, the separate bedrooms, the frosty greetings each morning. Her mother would be very defensive now. Indeed, when she spoke, Barbara's tone was as tart as vinegar.

"Elin, your father is long gone and I was loyal to him, as you know, but now I have to get on with my life. I have never liked North Wales, and I am looking forward to leaving it, to be honest. It doesn't agree with me and never has."

"I know that, Mum," Elin said quietly. "I have always known it."

When another silence greeted this comment, Barbara went on in a slightly gentler tone.

"Look, you left home years ago and never came back, dear. Leave the past behind – it's the best place for it. I may not sell this house for a while if you feel a yen to go back to North Wales, so you can always stay in it."

"I will, Mum. I want to... take lots of photos of it, perhaps even paint it, to fix it in my mind before I lose it forever," Elin said, on the verge of tears.

"I know how you loved your painting," Barbara said soothingly. "You could go on an art course up here, a retreat, or become an eccentric artist, like the woman your father used to take you to visit up in the mountains."

Memories, deeply buried, stirred like the worms in the mudflats where she and Llion had dug for fishing bait. "Yes, I remember that."

"She filled your head with ideas of painting your way around the world. Silly idea, irresponsible of her," Barbara said, clearly keen to move on.

But Elin was not. Her skin was tingling, her breathing stilled. She put her burger back in its box and closed it. "What was her name?"

When Barbara replied, there was a catch, a hesitation in her voice. "Anwen Jones. An old childhood friend of your father's. He took you to visit her quite often when you were little, but once you got older, you went less and then, well, your father stopped going to see her."

"Why?" Elin blurted.

A pause, in which several possibilities lurked.

"I don't know, not really," Barbara replied in a rare, sombre tone. "I wasn't there."

Elin closed her eyes as a series of images, moments, flashed in her brain like firecrackers. She remembered shouting, her father wagging his finger and a crash of crockery. "I think there was a quarrel, but yes, I remember her."

She saw herself, a little girl, being led up a slippery, rocky path to a small, stone house, holding tightly to her father's hand. She could almost hear the constant murmur of the river running down the steep slope behind and alongside the saggy-rooved outbuildings. She could also hear a woman with wild hair telling her in a low, gentle voice that the water "ran in through the back door and out the front door" when it was in full spate in winter.

Elin pictured a small, cramped room that smelt of cigarette smoke, cat piss and oil paint. When she was little, whenever they visited, she had wondered if this woman was a witch like the one who had lured Hansel and Gretel into the forest. The rooms were dark, the windows rimed with blackened condensation and thick cobwebs festooned every ceiling like a huge bridal veil. Elin had half expected to see a cauldron bubbling on the range and a broomstick behind the door, and yet, even as a child, it was a place she'd always felt comfortable, as if she was welcome there. There was no sense of dread, or even gloominess – but just an atmosphere radically different from that at home. Her father had told her that Anwen was a great artist, whose works sold for a fortune around the world. The little girl had believed him, as there were dust-encrusted paintings on every inch of every wall and Daddy did not lie. But secretly, she had wondered how anyone could create anything great amidst this litter of cigarette butts, old newspapers and mouldering fruit.

"Yes, she and your father fell out. She was very selfish, with a sharp tongue," Barbara said. "Your father never forgave her for, well, what she wanted to do, especially after everything we'd done for her."

These were murky waters, churning with questions, but the one Elin actually asked, surprised her. "Why didn't you ever come on those visits?"

"Oh, it's all water under the bridge," Barbara said quickly. "I haven't given her a thought for years and neither should you."

As her mother launched into a familiar spiel about Wales and how narrow-minded the people could be, Elin allowed her memory to drift over the past, and what she remembered of Anwen Jones. She had never seen her father as relaxed as he had been in that cottage when the two childhood friends had spoken Welsh with a musicality that matched the river's undulating rhythm. She had sensed that they shared an unbreakable bond, and she wondered if Barbara might have been jealous of that, which had caused the final falling out. Llion was truly himself with Anwen, but not with her.

No, she had never forgotten that remarkable woman, however deeply she had buried her memories of her. A face, clouded with the residue of years, floated into her mind, with a halo of spiky hair, a paintbrush in one hand and a burning cigarette in the other. A woman who had both shared, and recognised her yearnings and encouraged her to create, to experiment and to believe in her ideas as Barbara had never done.

"She used to ask me questions," Elin murmured, unaware that her mother was still there. "And she always used to ask me if I was happy."

"What a strange question to ask a child," Barbara said with new sharpness.

"Really? You think so?" Elin said. To her, it seemed a remarkably astute question to have asked her. Anwen had sensed that Elin, a lonely, only child, already set on a path she had not chosen by being sent away from home, was very far from happy, but that nobody had ever really noticed. And yes, it was Anwen who had told her to travel, and to take her art with her wherever she went as a ticket to the freedom she yearned for. She had recognised a fellow seeker, as nobody else had done before or since.

"Elin, are you still there, dear?"

"Yes, sorry, just... thinking. I hadn't seen her for so long, for years and years in fact, but she was at Dad's funeral, wasn't she? I think we even had a conversation about... oh, some crisis I was having." Elin blushed as she recalled herself, several glasses into a bottle of wine, telling Anwen how much she admired her for daring to do what she really wanted to despite what the world thought, and about how miserably she had failed in her own attempt to do so, and about Antoine, who had taken, and then broken, her heart.

"Did you, dear?"

"Yes, and I told her how much I'd loved going up to her house. She used to let me feed her chickens, knead the dough for bread and she even let me use her charcoal and artists' crayons and draw whatever I wanted to. I even drew a portrait of her once, and she said it was good – very good, in fact."

"That was nice, but you can't deny that she was... a rich diet, as my mother used to say. I suppose artists feel they have to be," Barbara said. "She was your father's friend, and had a good heart I suppose, but not my cup of tea at all."

"No, I'm sure. I liked her, though, back in the day," Elin said, tapping her fingers on her desk in her impatience to think, to remember. Hadn't the old woman whispered a few words in her ear before leaving the funeral wake? What on earth had those words been? Sadly, wine, sadness and time had erased them.

"She was a real rebel in her younger days, you know," Barbara said. "Went off the rails, travelled around Europe, getting up to who knows what with nobody knows who."

"That was very brave," Elin said, recognising her own behaviour. There was so much she could never tell her mother about her nomadic years alone.

"Hardly. She broke her mother's heart with all her carryings-on," Barbara said, adding more softly, "and several other people's hearts as well."

"Well, I wish I'd kept on visiting her, however weird she was," Elin muttered. "I remember her taking me out into the hills and encouraging me to try out her watercolours a few times, telling me to 'fill the space with colour'..."

"I never liked her pictures myself," Barbara said. "All grey rocks and rainy hillsides – though I suppose that's pretty accurate for North Wales now I think about it. Thank goodness you didn't pursue a career in art after you left college. London must be full of opportunities and copywriting is much more *you*."

"Is it, really? It doesn't feel like it," Elin muttered. How could a mother know so very little about what made her own child tick?

As Barbara began to talk about wedding plans, Elin let her thoughts drift once more. The acute sense of failure, of creative frustration and disappointment in herself that threaded through each day was sometimes so great that it caused her physical pain, a pain she had numbed with wine and disastrous love affairs. How had she allowed this zestless life to become hers in a city she had always hated? Perhaps her mother's news was what she needed, a catalyst to cut free of the snares of the past and start anew? But hadn't she tried that before, in trusting Antoine? It had not ended well...

"Oh, George and I are off to Tuscany for a few days tomorrow, but I'll be in touch. Just keep March free, dear. Oh, and of course, I'd like you to be one of my bridesmaids, and I was thinking peach tulle for your dress..."

Elin winced. *Tuscany? Peach?* Was this how it was going to be from now on?

"Who's the other one?" she blurted, hurt, despite herself.

"George's daughter, Harriet. She's stunning, and a top PA in the City. He has a son too, Rufus. You'll all get on fine, I know it."

Elin doubted it very much and wanted this conversation to end immediately. "Got to go now, but all very exciting and we'll talk soon. Bye, Mum, and congratulations."

After she had hung up, Elin took some slow, deep breaths. Her mother's taste was not hers, and she was maddening at times, but nobody deserved a lonely old age. Tuscany and peach it was, if that's what Barbara wanted. Elin just needed to find out what *she* wanted.

That evening, she opened a bottle of wine and toasted her mother and George's happiness. Closing her eyes, she sank into the sofa and felt the tension in her body loosen and her whirring thoughts begin to settle, like starlings on an autumn evening. Only when she had completely relaxed did Anwen's parting words at Llion's funeral return to her.

"I'll be waiting for you, Elin, when the time is right."

THREE

In the days that followed Barbara's news, Elin felt as if everything was poised on a set of scales and that the tiniest of movements, or changes of mood, could upend the balance and send her life spiralling into chaos. She brooded, trying to identify the wrong turnings that had led her to where she was now: lost, frustrated and lonely. There were options, one of which was to make the best of the life she had carved out in London, and her loyal group of old schoolfriends. The other was to go back to Wales and see Anwen again, if only to get answers to her questions and silence the growing din in her head. Had Anwen seen something in her as a child that had been buried under years of rejection and self-doubt, or was she just being kind? Would meeting her again free her from the huge weight of disappointment she now felt every single day?

Images from the past began to trouble her dreams at night and her sense of restlessness, of somehow being in the wrong life, grew even stronger. Some of these memories were so vivid that she awoke convinced she was back in her bedroom in the farmhouse with the gnarled old apple tree outside the window, its branches creaking in the chill breezes that filled the night. Allowing these wisps of memory to coalesce into events, feelings, experiences she recognised was a difficult, often painful process, but resisting would be even more so. Before going forward, she knew she needed to go back.

The rambling, low-roofed farmhouse her parents had shared for their whole married life often always felt more like a battle zone than a home. In lambing season, her father spent long nights out on the *ffriddoedd*/mountain pastures, helping ewes deliver in often brutal weather, and then collapsing into bed for a few hours before going out again. Barbara was always present, feeding him, putting his boots by the range to dry and washing his filthy overalls, but Elin could not remember any chat, or signs of fondness. They did not shout or rant or weep, but their marriage had seemed like a loveless, profitless business that had bankrupted both of them.

Other memories lurked on the periphery of life at the farm-house, mere shapes and shadows, but Elin clearly remembered another face hovering above her, smiling and singing to her. Her *Nain*/grandmother Nesta Pugh had died when she was a toddler, so perhaps this kind face aglow with love had been hers... but who could she ask?

There were some happy memories too, she reminded herself. Each spring, she was given the task of feeding the orphaned lambs and ensuring they thrived: she whispered her secrets into their warm, soft ears, confident that they would never betray her. But at home, her mother's mood could change in an instant and her father retreat into sullen silence. Plump, shy and spotty, at school she sought solace in drawing and painting and spent every free moment in the well-equipped art rooms, trying to make sense of her world on paper or on canvas. At night, she devoured novels under her blankets. No matter what Jane Austen had written on the subject, neither love nor marriage seemed worth aspiring to, in Elin's experience. The noble, strong heroines of the novels by George Eliot – Dorothea Brooke and Maggie Tulliver – who yearned for more than marriage, were the sort of women who inspired her. As an awkward teen, how she longed to have said of *her*:

"She was not a woman to be spoken of as other women are."

For Elin, the only real warmth in the farmhouse she had grown up in was her relationship with her father, though she could not help but sense his disappointment that she was not a son, however well he tried to hide it. His face lit up whenever he saw her, and his voice, low and gruff from barking orders to animals or farmhands, became soft and loving whenever he spoke of his *hogan fach*/little girl. Three years after his death, Elin still missed him, but amidst the images of a fond, caring father, she saw herself trotting behind him as a small child, breathless and slightly scared. Like a faithful puppy, she had followed him wherever he went and listened as he ranted aloud to the air or slammed sheep pens or farm gates. She had seen his frustration as gruelling day followed gruelling day, and the weight of his responsibilities was too great to conceal from her. One day, she learnt that there was more behind his pain than even she had guessed.

Elin had been almost eleven, and it was her last year at home before being sent away to school. Llion had taken her with him up onto the *ffriddoedd*/mountain pastures to check on the sheep, who were all within weeks of delivering their lambs. As they scrambled up paths that were only reachable on foot, the mountain air was so cold and crisp that breathing almost hurt, and their heads were surrounded by shimmering clouds of exhaled air.

"We're breathing fire, Dad," she'd said. "*Fel draig*/like a dragon."

And Elin had heard him laugh, long and loud, producing a cloud which had obscured his face, but when the air cleared, she saw a different man altogether. He was standing atop a rocky outcrop, looking into the distance, and tears were rolling down his cheeks.

"Dad, what's wrong?"

He had shaken his head, his face screwed tight. "I never wanted this, you know. This was supposed to be my brother's lot, my brother's life, not mine. I hate it, every second of it."

Frightened, Elin had moved nearer to him and wrapped her arms around his waist. If her father was not the strong, invincible hill farmer, who was he? And who was this brother, this uncle, she had never even heard of?

"Why do you hate it, Dad? Tell me, and tell me about your brother," she'd whispered, wanting, and not wanting, to know.

Llion sighed, wiped his face roughly and sat down, bringing his daughter gently down to sit alongside him.

"O *cariad*/oh darling, it's too much for you to hear."

She looked up at him and saw such pain etched on his weathered face that she had no choice but to offer her help again. Could he trust her?

"It isn't too much," she whispered. "I didn't even know you had a brother."

Her father took a deep breath and met her gaze.

"I haven't, not anymore. He died. He died, because of something I did."

He pointed the binoculars he always carried to the distant peak of Tryfan, one of the tallest mountains in the range, two tall columns of grey rock standing like lonely figures at its summit, and he then showed his daughter.

"Adam and Eve, those rocks are called. Can you see them?" Llion whispered. "It was a dare most boys tried, to jump from one to the other. A rite of passage, you see."

Elin squinted up into the wintry sunlight. "I see them, but it's so high, and if you fell, you would certainly... die."

Llion looked at his daughter once more, his eyes brimming with tears. "Yes."

Neither spoke, as there was no need of words, but both looked up to see a buzzard circling above them, slow and silent in its lonely orbit. Its pitiless gaze was focused on its tiny prey far below, as it tried to hide in a landscape that offered little shelter. When, a few minutes later, the bird dived, arrow-sharp, only a tiny, helpless squeak marked the end of a life, a small victim of this unforgiving place.

"My brother wanted this life, not me. Much as I love the land, our animals, grubbing a living from these mountains was not my dream, and it certainly wasn't your mother's."

"I know. She hates it here," Elin replied, totally matter-of-factly as children often do. "But what did you do, to make your brother fall?"

Llion winced. "I can't tell you what happened that day up there, but I didn't murder him, if that's what you're thinking. It was a stupid accident, a dare that went very wrong. It should never have happened."

"But it must have been awful for you," Elin said. "It might help to confide in someone. Don't you trust me enough to tell me, Dad?"

Her father got up quickly. "It's not about trust. It's that some things are best forgotten, along with everything else I hoped my life would be."

They began the long descent down to the farm in silence and Elin never heard her father mention his brother again.

FOUR

"Have you actually *started* the copy for that feature on ambient lighting?"

Elin jumped violently. She had not heard Sadie, her managing editor, approaching her desk early enough for her to look suitably busy. The look on Sadie's face said it all: she was furious.

"Er, I have, yes, but it's still in pretty first draft form at the moment..."

"Well, it's needed in final draft form by close of play today, as you know," Sadie said. "I really need your full commitment here and I don't feel I'm getting it." She leant right over Elin so the wafts of sweet, musky perfume from her cleavage almost made her retch. "We've talked about this before: this has to be the last time we do, right? There are people queuing around the block for your job, Elin. Am I making myself clear?"

Elin nodded that she was.

"In my inbox please; 5 p.m." And Sadie sashayed away, her fake Jimmy Choos click-click-clicking on the laminate floor all the way back to her desk.

Burying any thoughts of her father, Elin began typing straight away. She had an extortionate rent to pay on her grotty flat in Tooting, and these upsetting trips down memory lane were unhelpful. Biro between her teeth, she typed:

Creating the right mood in your living space is easy when your lighting does the work for you. Go for soft-light bulbs, smoky-hued lampshades and natural lamp bases to conjure up an oasis of elemental calm in your home, a sanctuary from the hurly-burly of everyday life.

An hour later, she had somehow written the requisite number of words and fulfilled the brief. Finally, she browsed some websites to find photos of lamps that might illustrate her vacuous points, screenshotted a few lit candles as a smaller image to have to the right of the main title and at 4.55 p.m. exactly, pressed 'send'. Watching a hungry lamb emptying a bottle of milk had been infinitely more satisfying, she recalled, but she shut that flash of memory down fast.

"Oh well. There goes another load of absolute crap," she muttered, glancing at the clock to confirm she had sent it off in time. As she began to shut down her PC, an email from Sadie pinged onto her screen.

"Thanks, Elin. Can you look at non-slip rugs tomorrow? About 2K words. S."

Elin sighed, and watched her PC screen go dark. "Can't bloody wait."

That evening, she resisted her usual urge to down a large glass of Sauvignon Blanc before she'd even taken her coat off. Instead, she fed a miserable-looking Mouse, made a cup of tea and sat quietly in her living room listening to the sounds of the city as it prepared for the end of another day. Electric buses stopped outside her flat, their doors whooshed opened and then closed before they smoothly whirred off into the distance; the drone of car engines was constant, punctuated by the occasional screech of tyres or parp of a horn, as was all the muffled chatter of people making their way to wherever they were going. These sounds formed the backdrop to Elin's thoughts as they ranged over her life, her past and into imaginings of her future. Was she, like her father, trapped in the wrong life or were all her tomorrows to be filled with a heady mix of non-slip rugs and Sadie's sickly perfume and palpable dislike?

As the room descended into blackness, she could see *Wern Farm*, the valley, the mountains wreathed in mist and mystery, her father's sheepdogs streaking up and down the slopes to corral the flock into order, but now she could also see Anwen and her cluttered, chaotic cottage. Those memories had been clouded by time, buried, but that night they emerged vivid and clear, like colour heightened on a screen. Clearly, the very last thing her mother would want her to do was to visit Anwen and talk to her again, but for Elin the urge to do so was becoming irresistible.

Finally, at almost 11 p.m., the hum of traffic dwindled and the chatter of voices hushed to the occasional yell or cheer. Elin got up, turned on the main light and went over to a painted wooden blanket chest she had picked up in a charity shop years earlier as it reminded her of the traditional dark oak one her father had so cherished. Opening the lid, she rifled through the sleeping bags and blankets she kept for unexpected visitors and pulled out a thick A4-sized sketchbook, its pages yellowed with age. Anwen had given it to her when she had first started visiting her with Llion, and she had used it every time she had been there and kept it all these years. It chronicled her childhood away from the unhappiness of her home. Nervously, she flipped it open.

The first few pages held no surprises: basic sketches of lambs, clumsy watercolours of *Llyn Ogwen*/Lake Ogwen surrounded by solid, towering rocks on all sides, with no subtleties of shade or shafts of light; these were the efforts of a young child. But as she turned more pages, the skill on show grew until she reached her painting of a beach that seemed true to the wildness of the North Welsh coast with its limited, but distinctive, palette of colours. There were gold-tinted sand-dunes, pine trees and she could almost feel the wind in the silvery marram grass as it blew off the sea, carrying the smell of salt and seaweed. The memory tantalised her, but she could not remember the name of the place she had captured. She took a photo of her painting, in case it came back to her, as things often did in her dreams, or when she looked at them again with a fresher eye.

Towards the end of the sketchpad, when she must have been in her teens and home for the school holidays, one small pencil sketch made her gasp. A woman's face looked out at her, eyes meeting hers, a wisp of hair across her forehead and a mouth with wide, plump lips. Anwen Jones, her hair a mousy brown but flecked with grey, her forehead fretted with wrinkles, smiling at her. Finally, Elin knew what she had to do.

"The right time is now, isn't it, Anwen? I need to come and see you again," she whispered.

Opening her laptop, she booked a return ticket to Bangor in North Wales for 6 a.m. the following morning. Having texted her neighbour Yan in the flat above to ask him to feed Mouse once a day, she emailed Sadie:

Sadie, sorry, but I need to take a few days off.

How could she sweeten the pill? Losing her job would be disastrous right now, with rent to pay and spiralling credit card bills. Sadie was not a fan of self-care in her employees, but Elin would have to gamble on her sympathy.

I know I haven't been firing on all cylinders lately. When I come back, I will be. Lots going on, and lots I need to sort out in my head. Thanks, Elin.

She read it through once, and pressed send.

FIVE

It was only when the train pulled away from Euston early the next morning that Elin wondered for the first time how this grand plan was going to pan out. She had nowhere to stay, her mother was away, and she didn't trust her neighbours enough to have left a key with them. She also had no idea what Anwen's address was and had risked losing her job if Sadie was having a bad day when she read her email at 9 a.m. And yet, despite all the above, she had never felt more sure that she was doing the right thing.

At 9.10 a.m., she received a terse response from Sadie:

Hi. Unless you're ill, this will have to be unpaid leave. Will expect you back next Monday at the latest. S.

A part of her wanted to send a similarly terse reply, telling Sadie that normal people have lives and problems and *feelings*, but she resisted. For the moment, she needed to afford to *live*. Her mother might still be in bed with George (something she did not want to visualise), but she messaged her anyway. She would want to know her plans, whatever she thought of them.

> Mum, I hope you enjoy Tuscany. I've decided to go back to Wales and see if I can find Anwen Jones. Feel I need to talk to her. Have you still got her address anywhere? E. XX p.s. I'll find a hotel to stay in.

Treating herself to a ludicrously expensive cup of coffee from the buffet car, she sat back and watched the scenery flash past as she waited for Barbara to reply. Her mother would either be hurt, irritated, confused or all three, but if she had Anwen's address, she knew she would send it. As the train inched past Nuneaton, Barbara proved her right:

> Elin, I have no idea why you're doing this, but Anwen lives up in the hills near Lake Padarn. I can't remember the name of her cottage, but everyone knows her and will tell you where she is. I'll call you from Tuscany. Take care. Mum x

Elin closed her eyes and felt a wave of fatigue wash over her. She had slept badly and got up before dawn to pack before getting the Tube to Euston. *What* she had packed, she had no idea, but she knew her antidepressants were her only essentials and they were definitely in her bag. Anything else, she could buy when she arrived. Her hand had hovered briefly over the sketchpad, but she decided against it. Anwen was unlikely to want to look at a child's decades-old doodlings, however kind she had been about them at the time.

After changing trains at Chester, the overpowering heat in the train carriage and exhaustion finally overcame her, and Elin fell asleep. When she woke and looked to her left, the railway line was so close to the sea that spray had coated the windows of the train with salt. The weather in London that morning had been nondescript, but here, the wind was whipping the water into waves that battered the shore with a power Elin only wished she could feel and hear. She sat upright and looked beyond, at the horizon, where the soft outline of the little island of Anglesey lurked with a small black and white striped lighthouse at its tip.

"Oh, my goodness, Dad took me there," she murmured. "I remember sitting on a blanket while he did some fishing, and I had some grapes to eat... and there was someone else there with us too, a woman."

Had her mother come too? It seemed unlikely that Barbara would have braved the inevitable wind at such an exposed spot. Elin did not need to say her name aloud to trigger the realisation that it was almost certainly Anwen Jones, her father's dear friend, who had come on that precious day out. She shivered, as she dreaded the uncomfortable possibility this suggested: had Llion Pugh, her strong, noble-hearted father, been unfaithful? If so, Barbara had every right to despise Anwen, but Elin did not feel it could be true. Her parents had co-existed in an uneasy truce that neither had ever risked breaking, though what had bound them, she could not fathom. Now, her father was gone, and Barbara was reluctant to revisit the past, so the only person who could answer any of her questions was Anwen. The fact that that woman seemed to be at the centre of so many memories made her mission all the more urgent.

When the train pulled into Bangor, a dribble of people disembarked and rushed, collars up, into the icy wind that blasted down the platform. Elin had found a car hire company online and booked a small car, but it was not available until 2 p.m. Places to stay in the area off-season seemed limited and the best she could book was a so-called boutique hotel in Llanberis, a village at the base of *Yr Wyddfa*/Snowdon that she did not know well but was near where Anwen lived. The place looked more like a pub to her, but most rooms overlooked *Llyn Padarn*/Lake Padarn, "a stunning glacial lake renowned for water sports, wild swimming and its healthy population of Arctic charr, salmon-like fish who like very cold, very clean water", or so the website ran.

"No chance of my going in for a dip," Elin muttered. "I'm a hot tub girl."

With an hour or so to kill, she walked into the city of Bangor, though she soon decided that calling it a "city" was somewhat optimistic. The small cathedral squatted at one end of a long, narrow high street, and some grandiose university buildings were perched up on a hill above it. Vape shops, charity shops and estate agents were interspersed with discount stores and takeaways, but the many boarded-up shopfronts told a mournful tale of decline, deprivation and neglect. Urban planners had tried to inject some colour with large planters full of rather wind-battered dahlias, but the contrast with the sleekness of life in London was unsettling. An elderly busker sitting on a plastic bag and producing the same, repetitive phrase on his tin whistle smiled up at her, so she dropped some money into his hat.

"Have a good one, sweetheart," he said, and his cheeky wink made her blush like a teenager.

As she passed the redbrick clock in the centre, Elin recalled coming to Bangor with her mother and the fizz of excitement at trying on clothes in the now-defunct department store. It was different now, and definitely down at heel, but the air was still filled with people loudly greeting each other across the street and gaggles of schoolkids laughing as they ate their greasy bakery haul. Just like in London, these people were going about their daily lives as best they could, but on a smaller, less frantic scale. Elin decided that it was good to be able to make eye contact with those she passed, and often have her shy "hello" reciprocated. She was pleasantly surprised at the price of some of the houses too: she could buy a three-bedroomed home for less than half what the flat above hers in London was going for, should she wish to.

Places in the villages slightly outside Bangor, heading up into the mountains, such Bethesda, Deiniolen and Guerlan, were even cheaper, and once Barbara married George and sold her little terraced house, a little money would be coming her way. Within seconds, Elin visualised herself tossing feed to clucking chickens and tending vegetables in a sunny mountainside garden. When her thoughts wandered towards dogs, husbands and rosy-cheeked babies, she stopped herself.

"Get a grip! Remember why you came here. To find Anwen."

An hour later, she was heading out of Bangor and through the winding, forest-lined road that would take her to Llanberis. When she emerged from the thick wall of conifers, the landscape seemed to open out around her and the sky was wide and flecked with patches of hopeful blue. Ahead, the edge of Eryri loomed, the soft, rolling lower slopes giving little hint of the craggy peaks beyond them. It was breathtakingly beautiful. On either side of the road, marshy land was peppered with cottages, slabs of exposed rock and slate and some tough-looking sheep doggedly grazed on scrubby grass and thistles.

Winding down her window, she shouted, "Well, sheep, there may be no shops here, but the views are fabulous!" They ignored her.

The boutique hotel was indeed a pub with rooms, but it was perfect, and the owners, Emlyn and Gwenda Rees, were friendly and welcoming. Sitting on the armchair in the window looking out over the lake, Elin watched a few paddleboarders set out, and marvelled at the group of women in neon hats who dived off a pontoon and headed for the other side, their pale arms lifting above the dark water as they swam. Further down the lake, she glimpsed the endless walls of slate, quarried for decades and exported all over the world. These works looked like an exposed wound somehow, brutally stripped of any trees or vegetation. They told their own story, as everything in this landscape did, and the golden light of the setting sun gave it a beauty all of its own.

Barbara had told her to *ask people* where Anwen Jones lived. If nobody in fact knew, Elin had no plan B. Luckily, Emlyn Rees proved Barbara right.

"Yes, of course I know where she lives. Everyone does, but she's not fond of visitors, mind," he said, shaking his head. "Her scowl could melt glass if she takes against you."

"I, er, hope she won't. I knew her when I was a girl, as my dad was a friend of hers," Elin said, adding, "Llion Pugh, though I don't suppose you..."

"*Arglwydd mawr*/Great God, you're Llion's girl? That's incredible," Emlyn replied. "A good man, he was. You don't look much like him, though – more like his brother Dafydd, you are. He had finer features than your father, so you 'lucked out', as my kids would say."

Elin smiled, both at this flattery, and at the incongruous phrase. No, it was true that her father had not had "fine features", but she was delighted that Emlyn remembered him as a good man despite his rather squashed nose and craggy chin. She was also glad to learn her late uncle's name at last: Dafydd Pugh, probably as Welsh a name as it was possible to have.

"Could I ask you exactly where Anwen lives, please? I can see her cottage in my mind's eye, but I have no idea how to get there," she said.

And as Emlyn patiently gave her directions, telling her that she could walk to Anwen's cottage but it was a steep climb, his wife Gwenda joined them, grunting as she carried a washing basket full of folded towels.

"*Dyma ferch Llion Pugh*/This is Llion Pugh's girl," Emlyn said, adding, "Oh sorry. You don't speak Welsh anymore I expect."

"I used to, but I think it's all gone," Elin replied.

"It won't have gone. It's all there, like a seed waiting to be watered," the woman said. "And kindly take this heavy basket from me, *twmffat*/idiot!"

They all laughed, as Emlyn did as he was told.

"Elin wants to visit Anwen Jones," he said, and Gwenda grimaced.

"Really? She's not a fan of visitors, you know."

"I just told her that." Emlyn said. "I have no idea if she has a mobile, or how to contact her to let her know you're coming. Good luck, I say."

"She's not that bad. But I do advise taking cake. She likes cake, does Anwen."

"Then I'll take some, though I have no idea where to buy any in Llanberis."

"We may not have fancy shops, but we do have a Spar," Emlyn said.

"Sorry, of course," Elin replied, embarrassed. "And I'm not a fan of fancy shops anyway."

Cake duly purchased and a dinner of steak and chips devoured, Elin felt as ready as she ever would to meet Anwen the following day, but alone in her room, she was nervous as she tried to sleep. It was so very dark outside, and all she could hear was the occasional cry of a bird out on the lake. Although she still had memories of the soundscape of her home, of a darkness like no other, they were faded and unfamiliar now, replaced by noisy, street-lit city ones. As her body gradually relaxed, a persistent belief that she was doing the right thing dispelled her nerves about what tomorrow might bring. What was the worst that could happen, after all?

SIX

Elin woke very early, ready to face whatever the day held, but her heart sank when she pulled back the thick velveteen curtains in her room. It was pouring, the sky a sheet of steely grey and her view of the lake was now in soft focus through very rain-streaked windows. Of course it rained a lot up here, and she remembered days spent reading in her attic bedroom as rain drummed on the farmhouse roof, but today of all days, she had hoped it would be dry. The path around the lake that led up to Anwen's cottage was rocky, and went through thick woodland, Emlyn had told her. It would be even more difficult to follow if it was still pouring and the ground slippery. She had brought her cracked leather walking boots, but had not walked somewhere so wild for a long time.

Emlyn and Gwenda were waiting for her in the old-fashioned dining room, and both beamed when they saw her crestfallen face.

"*Bore da*/Good morning," Gwenda said cheerily. "And don't let a bit of rain put you off, love. It's due to stop later anyway. Need to borrow some waterproofs? You're pretty small, but our eldest Esyllt was about your size as a teenager, so why don't we see if her kit fits you? After four kids, she's a heck of a lot bigger now!"

In half an hour, Elin left the pub wearing a lightweight purple waterproof jacket and matching trousers that she was assured would keep her warm and dry whatever the sky threw at her. Gwenda, misty-eyed with memories of a younger, slimmer, Esyllt, was delighted, but she had a word of warning:

"Don't expect too much of Anwen, will you? She's always followed her own path, so she may not be as you expect, or want her to be."

"I know," Elin said. "We met a few years ago at Dad's funeral, but before that, she might not remember me visiting her as a child, and what, well, what she meant to me."

"Oh, she'll remember all right. She remembers everyone and everything. Like a bloody elephant, she is."

"Don't you like her, Gwenda?" Elin asked, slightly rattled.

At this question, Gwenda folded her arms over her ample breasts, and looked directly at Elin before replying in a firm voice:

"*A dweud y gwir*/To tell the truth, I don't actually know anyone who does."

As soon as Elin started walking around the lake, she had a very strong sense of *déjà vu*, as if she had come this way in a previous life – which, in many ways, she had. The first surprise of the day came when a herd of about ten horned mountain goats made their way down the small road that led up towards the woods. Elin stood aside and watched as their hooves clattered past, amazed at the way they streamed around a car that had stopped for them without any hesitation. They had right of way here: the mountains were their domain.

As Emlyn and Gwenda had predicted, the rain eased off just as she skirted the slate museum and passed the old railway and the crumbling quarry workings. Shards of slate and tangled tree roots made some parts of the path difficult, but she felt herself begin to find an easy, walking rhythm and her body felt more attuned to what she was doing than it had for a very long time. The air was crisp, and her in-breaths were damp, but with each one she took, she felt more invigorated. When, after half an hour or so of steep ascent, she reached more level ground, she began to notice small changes in everything around her. Now, the walls were drystone rather than slabs of slate, and a grass-fringed road replaced the rocky path, which she assumed led up to the few scattered houses hunkering down amidst this ancient woodland. Birds, unseen, sang from every tree, telling her that she was far from alone. Some of their songs she recognised from childhood, when her father had always named each bird as they heard them. The names, too, came back to her unbidden:

"That's a willow warbler."

"There's a blackbird, and he's a bit worried about us."

"Just listen to that wren, singing its little heart out."

How quickly the past joined the present, as if grafted onto it to form one continuous, seamless whole.

She remembered that her father had always parked somewhere lower down the hill, and then they had climbed up a tiny path to see Anwen, as if doing so was part of the experience. They were visiting another world from the humdrum farming life he was shackled to almost every day of his life, and it was important to him that they approached it with reverence. The last part of the route remained unchanged, but the path was more overgrown and there was no clear way ahead. A slab of slate at the bottom of a footpath with some words roughly painted on it was the only indication that there was a house hidden at the end of it at all:

CÂN Y MYNYDDOEDD.

"Song of the mountains," Elin translated aloud without thinking. "What a truly beautiful name."

She began to climb up the mossy path, glad of her faithful old walking boots, and with each step she was almost tempted to stretch out her hand and feel for her father's because the memories of having come here with him were so vivid. It amazed her that her young legs had managed this arduous route, but Llion had never, ever offered to carry her or give her a piggyback. She could almost see and hear him, striding ahead, refusing support or sympathy as she puffed and panted, and him telling her to be a *"Cymraes fach go iawn"*, or "real little Welshwoman" and get on with it, as he had had to do as a boy.

"You were sometimes as tough as you were kind, Dad, so perhaps it was good for me and made me stronger now. I hope so."

She remembered a quote she had loved during her years of teenage angst, from her favourite author, George Eliot:

"It would be a poor result of all our anguish and our wrestling if we won nothing but our old selves at the end of it."

"Refinement through suffering, wasn't that her doctrine?" she muttered. "Not sure I buy it anymore, sorry. More like *minced*, in my case."

Just as her glute muscles were burning almost too much to bear, a large stone cottage loomed out of the gnarled and scrubby trees. At this altitude, few grew tall, as they had to endure the bitter gales of winter and weeks of snow. The front of the house looked just as Elin remembered it – solid stone blocks, a slate roof and a large front door, painted black. The windows, small and streaming with condensation, had wooden frames that were urgently in need of painting, if not replacing, and the cottage had an overall air of hopelessness, as if it had been allowed to sink into disrepair but couldn't care less. Elin shivered. She had expected to feel the same frisson of excitement she'd had as a child when she arrived here. Instead, she felt only sadness. Approaching the front door, she noticed another painted sign on the ground, slightly to the right. This one was in English first, and then Welsh, which Elin guessed was to deter walkers, or anyone at all, in fact.

ARTIST AT WORK. GO AWAY./*ARTIST WRTH EI GWAITH. EWCH I FFWRDD.*

For the first time, she felt a quiver of real fear. What was her reception going to be like if this was how Anwen greeted anyone approaching her house? She had not been able to let her know in advance that she was coming, which many older people would see as rude. Barbara certainly would have done.

Gingerly, she picked up the brass door knocker and let it drop onto the wooden door, sending a loud *thump* into the air that ricocheted off the walls like the knell of doom. For a full minute, there was silence, before she heard a shuffling sound and then the slow screech of the drawing back of one, two then a third bolt. When the door slowly opened, Elin looked down to see a tiny, white-haired woman blinking up at her with watery blue eyes that had clearly not seen bright daylight for a long while. She was probably in her mid-seventies, Elin decided on sight, but she could not be sure as her life must have been a hard one up here on her own. Suddenly, a black and white dog shot past them both, peed on the path and then scampered off into the bracken, fringed tail wagging. A Welsh collie, and a young one.

"Looks like she needed that," the old woman said, her eyes totally fixed on Elin's face. "Can't you read?" She pointed a finger at the sign by the door. "I even translated it, in case of ambiguity. You still understand Welsh?"

Elin struggled to make her mouth form any words in response. The only sound produced were mumblings, as she felt as if the unrelenting gaze of the older woman was boring into her like a laser, paralysing the muscles of her face and mouth. Perhaps she wouldn't remember her at all? Their chat at the funeral was probably as wine-fuzzed for her as it had been for Elin. Her reception thus far had been very far from friendly, and she already had the distinct sensation she was being tested to see if she passed muster.

"I'm sorry to disturb you. I'm Elin, Llion Pugh's daughter. We spoke at my dad's funeral, and I used to come here and..."

"I know who you are! I would have known you anywhere, from your eyes," Anwen said. "Windows to the soul, eyes are. Either Cicero or Shakespeare said that. Doesn't matter which."

"You can see into my soul?" Elin blurted.

"Not much to see at the moment, is there? The funeral was

three years ago, so what have you been doing all this time, you silly girl?" came the brusque reply.

Elin bridled. "Silly" was the word she had used about her schoolmates, who didn't understand her need for more than discos and dating. Again, she could not find words to reply at first.

Anwen examined her very closely now, tilting her small head to one side like a curious robin. "I told you I'd wait for you to come, but it's been too long and you're too late. Goodbye." She closed the door but did not slide the bolts into place.

"Anwen, please!" Elin cried. "I came as soon as I could, as soon as the time was right, just like you told me to!"

A long, long silence followed. Elin listened for steps going away from the door, but she heard none. She suspected that Anwen was on the other side, also listening, waiting for something. So she stood, unmoving, on the doorstep, as the dog nuzzled at her left hip. Its liquid brown eyes spoke of love and loyalty as all dogs' eyes do. She reached down and stroked its head gently.

"Hello, gorgeous. Are you sure you want to go back in there?"

The door then flew wide open revealing a furious Anwen with a very dark hallway stretching back behind her. The dog slipped past Elin's legs and into the house.

"Yes, she does actually, because she lives here, don't you, Smot?" Anwen snapped.

"Sorry, I..."

Anwen tutted and said with a sigh, "*Tyrd i mewn os ti'n dod.*/Come in if you're coming."

Warily, and with a racing heart, Elin followed her into the darkness.

SEVEN

For almost a minute, Elin could see nothing at all. The house was very dark inside. The windows were small and grimy, admitting little light, so she had to rely on her other senses. The sound of Anwen's shuffling footsteps were her only guide until they reached what was obviously the kitchen. Elin could smell overripe apples, cigarettes and burnt toast. Immediately, she was a young girl again, visiting with her father.

"Sit down. I'll make us a *panad*/cuppa," Anwen said from somewhere in front of her.

Sitting down involved Elin having to feel her way around the room before lowering herself very slowly onto what she assumed was a chair but proved to be a cat. When it yowled, and streaked out of the room, Elin leapt up and screamed.

"Ha! Merlin likes to sleep in awkward places. Don't worry."

As her eyes became accustomed to the murk, Elin remembered why she had wondered if Anwen was a witch when she had come here as a child. Having a cat called Merlin intensified that feeling even to an adult, and as the blackened kettle began to boil on the old range, it was all too easy to imagine this woman casting spells and tossing in grisly ingredients for potions. Luckily, Anwen's next words were so prosaic that this dark fantasy ended in an instant.

"I hate visitors."

Taken aback, Elin decided it was safest to meet frankness with frankness. "I gathered that, but you let me in, so thanks for that."

"You are always welcome here. Always will be."

The old woman grunted as she prepared their tea, scooping tea leaves and pouring the boiling water into the pot so slowly that Elin had time to look around her. Every surface was completely covered with dishes, cups, newspapers or glass jars filled with murky water. One end of the kitchen table was strewn with mud-encrusted potatoes, and the other with a basket of crumpled clothing. The foisty atmosphere in the room made it likely that they were washed but not yet dry. Weedy house plants yearned towards any thin source of light and spiders' webs formed a delicate film over every windowpane. Looking up at the ceiling, Elin saw a mesh of thin-twigged branches suspended from the beams with bunches of drying herbs, threaded seashells and bracts of dry, brittle heather hanging from them. The overall effect felt like a combination of being inside a finely spun cocoon and beneath a magpie's nest, and yet Elin felt the same chaotic *comfort* here as she had as a child.

By the time Anwen had made and brewed the tea, the cat was back and purring on her lap, so Elin felt much calmer and more prepared for the conversation that lay ahead as to why she was here. She waited until the old woman sat down, noticing that Anwen was not looking at her now, but down at her feet where Smot, her dog, was curled over her slippers. Was she perhaps a little nervous too?

"So, here I am. You remember me, and my father, Llion? We came here a lot when I was little, didn't we?" Elin began nervously.

"You did indeed. And then you didn't, because your father felt he couldn't come anymore."

Elin tried again. "I remember that, yes, but I remember you showing me how to draw, and letting me use your watercolours. I wanted to be an artist, like you."

Anwen lifted her head and met her gaze head-on.

"So, why aren't you one?" she said.

Elin's eyes brimmed with sudden tears, but she held them back. That arrow had hit its target.

"I don't know," she said quietly.

Anwen shuffled in her seat and then winced. "Love, I expect. You told me about some Frenchman when you were drunk, at your father's funeral. Said he had broken your heart."

"He did, yes. And I lost so much because of him. The life I had imagined, my dreams, a future in which I was important, because..." She stopped, tears brimming.

"I don't need to know details," Anwen cut in brutally. "We have all had our dreams shattered. Your mother is particularly fond of self-pity in that regard, I recall."

Stung, Elin sipped her tea to calm herself down. Strong and bitter, the globules of milk floating on the surface made swallowing it difficult.

"Why did you come here, Elin?" the old woman asked, her voice softer, lower and her eyes now scanning, analysing every detail of her face once more.

Taking a deep breath, Elin tried to answer.

"I'm not sure, but it felt like I was *called* back, and that seeing you again was something I had to do before I decide what to do with my life."

Anwen nodded thoughtfully. "So you're still not sure? You were so certain, as a child."

Elin shook her head. "I know. But now, I never do anything creative, Anwen. I hate my job, I hate my life, I hate living in the city..."

Tears trickled down her face as she released them, and her true feelings, but Anwen simply stared at her, saying nothing. Elin, who had been hoping for sympathy at this point, began to panic. This was not going well at all.

"And now my mother is leaving Wales as she's getting married again to some rich man in Bath! What will I do then?" she pleaded.

"Well, I can't say I'm surprised she's leaving," Anwen said with a snort. "Barbara needs to be spoilt, cossetted, like a small child.

Llion couldn't offer her that, on the farm. He had neither the time nor the energy."

This was rude, but Elin did not retort angrily as she knew it to be true. This woman understood things it had taken her a lifetime to grasp, and yes, Barbara was both childish and selfish at times. She remembered how openly her father had talked with Anwen, how close they had seemed, and how much history they must have shared over the decades. Yes, this woman had probably known more about what Llion thought and felt than anyone did before they argued, and parted ways forever. *Why* that had happened, she had yet to find out.

"Yes, I think you're right. I grew up in a safe, if not a happy home. There was no cossetting there, that's for sure. Mum made sure of that."

Anwen's face clouded, as if a sad memory had intruded into the present. She nursed her tea as rain began to patter on the roof, making the metal guttering ring – another childhood sound that Elin only now remembered.

"I'm here for a week. I'd like to spend some time with you if that's OK," Elin said, feeling as if she was casting a rod out over deep, deep water. Would this fish bite?

"Why?" Anwen snapped, startling the dog who jumped up and looked at her anxiously. "What do you expect me to do for you?"

Elin found she had no good answer to give to this question. At that moment she was not sure herself.

"I don't know, but it felt like the only thing I needed to do."

A pause. "I see. Well then, come again if you want, but now, you'd better go," the old woman said. "The rain's getting heavy again, and streams become rivers quickly enough."

"And they can run in the back door and out of the front," Elin whispered. "I remember you telling me that."

Anwen smiled, and her face knitted into a web of wrinkles. As she got up, she winced again.

"Are you in pain?"

"Always."

Elin felt she could not ask why, so she stretched out a hand instead: a hug was a rare and dangerous a thing to offer too soon, in her experience. Anwen grabbed the hand and wrapped both her own hands around it. Roughened, icy-cold and gnarled with arthritis, each joint looked like the hard, round gall from an oak tree.

"Your hand is so warm, and young," she said with unexpected tenderness. "There are so many things you will do with it that you know nothing about."

She let Elin's hand go slowly and with evident reluctance. "Time to go."

The moment Elin was through the door she heard Anwen slam and bolt it, once, twice, three times as if bidding her good riddance. This could have hurt her feelings, but the old woman was nothing if not unpredictable. In truth, Elin was already beginning to think that, like a hedgehog, Anwen's spikes were for self-defence rather than attack.

Picking her way through the dripping trees and down the slippery path, the leaves around her murmured as a slight breeze disturbed the wet branches. She was sheltered from the rain by them, and thankful for that. Below, on the lake, the sound of ducks quacking happily reverberated off the surrounding crags, making ten birds sound like a hundred. For the first time in years, Elin felt enveloped by a world that aimed to comfort, not to crush her.

EIGHT

Elin was exhausted by the time she reached the pub, so she snuck past reception and up to her room rather than run the gamut of Emlyn and Gwenda's questions. As soon as she came down an hour later, Emlyn pounced, but instead of grilling her about meeting Anwen, he surprised her.

"Are you going to join us later for the *Noson Lawen*?" he asked, pointing at a hand-drawn poster taped to the front of his desk. "Starts at 7 p.m. prompt."

Elin scanned it quickly. It made no sense, and she needed to eat, urgently.

"I may do, yes, but I'm hungry now," she replied.

In the dining room, she wolfed down an early dinner of chicken pie, peas and mashed potatoes almost without tasting it. Then, she googled *Noson Lawen*, which defined it as meaning "a merry or joyful night", and one "which may include singing, dancing, comedy and/or poetry recitation". She was very tired, but both Emlyn and Gwenda were at the reception desk when she left the dining room hurriedly, looking forward to a hot bath and an early night. Disappointing them when they had been so kind to her would be hard, if not impossible.

"So, will you come? Please do. Should be a good night," Emlyn said, his expression so hopeful that his eyebrows went up inches and his glasses followed them to his hairline. "We'd really value your support."

"Emlyn, *cae dy geg*/shut up," Gwenda said, digging her husband in the ribs. "How did it go with Anwen, *cariad*/love?"

Elin hesitated. All the way down from *Cân y mynyddoedd* she had been trying to process her meeting with Anwen, from her initial hostility to the way the old woman had clung onto her hand before she'd left. It was not easy to give a simple answer to Gwenda's question, so she went with total honesty.

"I'm not sure. Good and bad bits, I guess. She's a one-off, isn't she?"

"Always was," Emlyn said. "*Diolch byth*/Thank goodness, I say."

"Give her a chance. She might surprise you," Gwenda added. "And do come along later if you feel like it. Your father used to love singing, and his brother too. Beautiful voices, they had."

"Yes, Dad sang to me a lot," Elin replied, but this revelation disquieted her a little. She had always thought Llion's singing was a secret gift, from him to her.

Sitting quietly on the armchair in the window of her room looking out over the lake, she tried to imagine Llion singing in public, with control and confidence, but she could not. Their home had been a place of brittle silence and he had sung to her shyly, and only ever as she'd drifted off to sleep. How on earth had the man she had known sung at lively gatherings like the one that would soon begin downstairs? If he had, it was more than likely he would have done so without Barbara's knowledge or consent, and Elin was away at school for years. She owed it to her father to find out the hidden, happier side of him that she had never known.

"I'll go this *Noson Lawen* thing, but only for your sake, Dad," she murmured.

She did not dress up, as it seemed unnecessary, but she showered and brushed her hair before going downstairs just before 7 p.m. This seemed very early for a gig to begin compared to

London, where nobody went out until 11 p.m., but a bubble of chatter rose up before she reached the ground floor, which was crammed with people. The only language she could hear was Welsh, and Elin's brain struggled to fish what she remembered of her mother tongue out of the silt of years of neither hearing nor speaking it. There was no stage, but only one end of the room was lit and an expectant mike stand waited for the first act. Elin slid into a chair in the back row, suddenly glad of the anonymity. Did she have a right to be here? This was an event for locals, and she had left Wales years ago. Was she a tourist or a cultural *voyeur*, intruding on something she could never fully understand? Again, the questions of who she was and where she belonged nagged at her, and as ever she had no answers.

Elin understood very little of the first few acts as it was entirely in Welsh: a young woman reading a short story she'd written; a group of teenagers singing in close harmony and a spectacularly bearded elderly man singing a folky song had some of the audience dabbing their eyes. When a young girl performed a monologue, her Welsh was more colloquial and Elin began to understand a little more, but, surrounded by people who all knew each other, she still felt awkward, peripheral. Just as she was getting ready to slink out, the last act was announced and a tall, slim young man with an acoustic guitar sidled into the lights, and cleared his throat.

"Hiya. *Dylan Williams dw'i.*/I'm Dylan Williams. *Fel plentyn rôn i'n rhugl yn y Gymraeg, ond rwan...*/When I was a kid, I was fluent in Welsh, but now..." he stuttered, and then stopped. Elin could almost feel the waves of encouragement emanating from everyone in the room: clearly, they all knew him. A burly man near her shouted:

"*Dal ati, boi bach.*/Keep going, lad."

The young man looked at the floor as if lost for any words at all, be it in Welsh or English.

"*Rhaid i mi siarad yn Saesneg, sori*/I have to speak English, sorry," the young man said. "But I can sing to you in Welsh!"

When a roar of approval rang out, the man relaxed and began to tune up. Elin watched his slim fingers skilfully tweak the tuning pegs as his long hair hung over the neck of the guitar like a curtain. He was so tall and so thin that he reminded her of a heron poised at the water's edge on legs that seemed far from sturdy enough to support him. He plucked each string again and again, turning the pegs very slightly, very gently, until he lifted his face, tied his hair up into a messy ponytail and beamed out at the audience.

"*Barod*/Ready," he said.

A ripple of whoops broke out, stopping the second he began to sing, as if a switch had been flicked. Elin sat quite still, unable to leave even if she wanted to, as if his voice had pinioned her to the seat. It was without affectation or training, a pure, soaring sound which stilled the room. People listened, totally absorbed, as the young man filled the air with words and melodies she recognised, ones they had all grown up listening to. Llion had sung these songs to her. He sang, weaving between both languages at times, of the sea, the mountains, the lakes and fields of their homeland with a soulfulness that she knew would be called "*hiraeth*", a Welsh word which has no real translation beyond "a deep longing for home". Some songs were about love and the price of it, which had heads nodding sadly in his audience. When he started to sing the lullaby *Suo Gan*, Elin felt a huge lump in her throat as she remembered her father singing this beautiful song when she was a little girl and could not fall asleep.

As the music washed over her, Elin could almost hear another, softer voice singing to her, rocking her to and fro and holding her close. Barbara never, ever sang, as she believed it was an activity best left to the professionals, so could this also have been Nesta, her long-dead *Nain*/Grandmother? Part of her was relieved when the lullaby ended, with its words of love and constancy, as it was stirring feelings that she had suppressed for years. Love was a hope she had long since buried.

After his set, Dylan was surrounded by people, and Elin heard comments such as "*siaradaist am calon*/you spoke to my heart" and "*roedd hynny'n anhygoel*/that was amazing". Shepherded to the bar, he was plied with pints and backslaps and soon vanished from sight into a cloud of adulation.

It was almost 10 p.m., but there were still a few streaks of faint light in the sky when Elin went outside to get some air before going to bed. The moon, blurred by drifts of misty cloud, was velvet-edged and as she sat on a bench to look up at it, stars began to appear, sprinkling the sky with pinpricks of silver. Here in the mountains, where there was no noise or light pollution, everything seemed sharper, more vivid, and Elin sat without moving for a long time, simply *looking*. Being busy, striving, seeking for something meaningful in life had pushed addressing her sad childhood and other disappointments to the edge of her mind, but now, in this dark silence, they began to surface. Just as she was beginning to feel slightly overwhelmed, she felt someone else right next to her in the darkness. Startled, she stepped back.

"Hi," a male voice said. "A beautiful night, isn't it?"

Elin turned towards the voice, still wary. In London, an unknown man behind you was a very real threat. "Yes. Lovely," she answered nervously.

"Sorry, didn't mean to scare you. I'm Dylan, by the way."

"Oh, the singer!" Elin exclaimed. "You were brilliant!"

"Thanks. Glad you enjoyed." A pause. "So, you are...?"

"Sorry. Elin – Elin Pugh. I would shake your hand, but I can't see it."

A laugh, deep and genuine. "Good to meet you, if not to see you!"

As she felt a hand fumble into hers, Elin laughed as well. This hand was soft and warm, there was no threat here.

"Your name sounds as Welsh as mine. Do you come from around here as well?" Dylan went on.

Elin hesitated. This was a moot point. "Well, I grew up near here, on a farm in Nant Ffrancon, so I suppose I do, yes. I'm visiting an old friend right now, but I'm based in London."

"Ah, I get it. So, how's your Welsh? As you heard, it's probably better than mine."

"Much worse, actually. Considering I was fluent until I was eleven, it's weird how it's all just gone. It's as if someone's pulled the plug and it vanished down the sink," Elin replied.

"It'll still be there, lurking," Dylan replied. "I find it comes out when I try to speak a bit of French, which is not very helpful!"

Elin laughed again. She liked this man's willingness to mock himself. Considering his talent, and the reaction of his audience, it surprised her.

He cleared his throat. He was nervous. "So, what about you? Do you still live here?"

"No. Similar story to yours in many ways. Grew up here, on a smallholding not far from Bethesda, sentenced to endure my parents' dream of self-sufficiency. They opted out, moved up here from Surrey when I was three, expecting 'the land to succour them'. It chewed them up and spat them out, and my sister and I paid the price for their failure, in different ways." He paused, and cleared his throat again. "As soon as I could, I left. This place, I hate it but I love it, and it always bloody calls me back. I guess I'm trying to find where I belong, lay some ghosts. All very clichéd, I know."

"No, it's really not. I know just what you mean," Elin said earnestly. She could have said his every single word herself.

A silence, as if they were both sensing that something was happening, something that mattered. Out beyond the lake, an animal screeched and they turned towards the sound in unison.

"Someone's on the hunt out there. It's still an untamed place, isn't it? Wildness is always there, like an artery running through it. So different to anywhere else I've ever been," Dylan murmured. "Part of me likes that, part of me fears it."

Again, Elin hesitated, remembering her dark thoughts before

he had joined her. "I understand. It stirs things up, coming back. Are your family still here?"

"My father's long gone. He just upped and left one day not long after I'd gone off to university, which left my sister Cara caring for my mother until she died of breast cancer."

"That sounds really tough, for both of them."

"It was, but Cara was amazing then. It's as if she has a gift, a way of seeing others' pain and easing it. She certainly supports me one hundred per cent." He sighed. "She should have had a life of her own, but she gave it all up, sacrificed so much. I was no use as I couldn't bear to be around to watch Mum fade away. Cara stayed here, and kept the smallholding on even though she could leave if she wanted to."

"Why won't she go, now that she can?" Elin asked.

Dylan hesitated. "She's not well, not *strong*, but I think it's more than that. She stayed there with some mangy goats and a frost-blasted vegetable patch because she's hoping to redeem Mum and Dad's failed dream, I think. It makes me angry and breaks my heart at the same time, if that makes any sense."

The bitterness in his voice was unmistakable, but Elin was unsure how to respond to it. The repeated, raw conflict he felt about his homeland was obvious, and slightly unnerving. "Perhaps she has a strong bond with this place like you and I do, and the larger part of her wants to stay."

"A bond, or a tether? I'm never quite sure, as I have to come back and check she's OK more than I'd like to, but I care about her. People avoid her, because she's a bit *unusual*, but she's a troubled soul, which troubles me."

Now, Elin heard pain in his voice, but said nothing for a few, long, seconds. The right words eluded her. Eventually, she replied, "I can see how much you care about this place, and your sister. I could feel that in your singing. A kind of wistfulness."

"Thanks. Love it or hate it, Eryri gets into your bones, and I want to try and, well, evoke the feel, the *sound* of this place in my music."

"My friend's cottage is called *Cân y mynyddoedd*/Song of the mountains. Perhaps that's partly what you're trying to sing about, but it must be really hard to capture it, let alone describe it to anyone else," Elin murmured.

"*Cân y mynyddoedd*/Song of the mountains. That's a great phrase for describing all the sounds that mingle here and that can change all the time. I need to use it in a song." A pause, a regrouping, before he went on. "So you live in London now, doing...?"

"Writing articles about things I don't care about. It's not my dream job, but it pays the rent – just."

"What did you want to do, back in the day?"

Elin paused. His question stung a little. "I thought I wanted to be an artist, but now, I really don't know. I travelled for years picking up bits of work, but I always wanted a *calling*, a bit like Julie Andrews in *The Sound of Music*."

"Sorry, but I can't see you twirling on the mountaintops in a dirndl!"

"You never know, jobbing pub-singer," Elin said. "And you can't see me at all, if we're being brutally honest here!"

As they laughed, the pub door suddenly opened, and bright light exposed them like insects wriggling under a rock. Both flinched, embarrassed.

"Hey, Dylan! Come and finish your pint!" a man's voice shouted. "Or rather, your *pints*!"

Dylan turned towards Elin, and she saw his face close-up for the first time – his fine, thinly-boned nose, which reminded her of a bird's beak; large, dark eyes and improbably long, curled eyelashes. He was even more handsome than he had looked onstage.

"Better go greet my fans," he said, grinning. "Really good to meet you, Elin. I'm doing some odd jobs in the pub this week, so might see you before you go."

"Hope so," she replied. "*Hwyl*/Cheers."

He smiled and shook her hand gently once more, before vanishing inside to be enveloped in cheering locals.

NINE

The next morning was a bright, sunny one. Elin had not slept well, as her dreams were troubled, so she needed several cups of coffee before she set off to visit Anwen for the second time. The walk up through the forest to her cottage was quicker when the ground was dry. She stopped several times just to take in her surroundings and truly listen to the sounds around her now that they were not softened by rain. The day was almost windless, the trees were silent, but the air was full of joyous birdsong, loud and insistent, a chorus of unseen witnesses. Moss in every shade of green coated the rocks and fallen branches, and a filigree of lichen laced many of the smaller twigs. Elin closed her eyes and breathed in the cold, clear air and felt the energy of this place flood her body.

"Jeez, I'm actually *doing* mindfulness and forest-bathing, the stuff I used to write about, Sadie," she said aloud. "Perhaps it isn't a load of crap, after all."

Anwen had obviously been waiting for her, as the front door opened before she'd even had knocked on it. Smot, her collie, whipped out and sniffed Elin thoroughly before deciding she was an acceptable return visitor and wagging her tail. Looking down, Elin realised that the small, round marking on her head had obviously inspired the name, as she somehow remembered that the word "*smot*" meant "spot" in Welsh.

"Perhaps you're right, and it is all in there somewhere – my Welsh," she mumbled to herself, following Anwen into the house.

"Course it is. Never doubted it for a minute. Come on, hurry up."

Whatever else she was, Anwen was not going deaf.

This time, instead of going into the kitchen, Anwen led the way through to the back of the house and into a lean-to conservatory that was flooded with light. The sun had been warming it since dawn and Elin noted that the plants in here were thriving. There were orchids of all colours and sizes and a spectacular trumpet plant in full bloom, its horn-like yellow flowers filling the space with colour and a faintly sweet scent. Merlin the cat was curled up on a very saggy sofa in the corner today and ignored their entrance completely.

"This is the warmest place in the house at this time of year. I paint here these days, as the cold is agony for my arthritis," Anwen said, rubbing her swollen knuckles together.

"It's gorgeous. And so light. Perfect for painting and drawing. But where do you work in the winter, when it's cold?"

Anwen sighed. "I can't, not anymore."

She led Elin towards a table in the centre of the room. A jug of beech twigs, clothed with crinkled orange leaves, was on one side and a sketch pad, pencils and crayons on the other.

"Time to draw, like you always used to when you came to see me," Anwen said, without the possibility of disagreement. "I'll be busy finishing something over there, but let's see what you can do." She pointed to a canvas on an easel in the corner, a painting of a large blue heron at the edge of the lake, its silhouette of slim elegance perfectly captured. Elin was immediately reminded of Dylan Williams.

For the next hour, both women were so absorbed in what they were doing that they barely exchanged a word. The only sounds were Smot's gentle snores and the occasional skirl of a startled bird as Merlin had decided to go skulking in the garden. Having not drawn anything for so long, Elin's fingers took time to warm to the task, and her first attempts were clumsy and frustrating. She moved the jug nearer to her so she could see the curls and veins of the beech leaves better, and used a softer pencil. As she tried to capture each perfect leaf, she was glad that she had listened to herself and come back here. Whatever came next, today, she had done this.

Over a cup of coffee that was so strong it almost curdled the milk, Anwen began asking her question after question, allowing only the briefest of windows for an answer. She did not want details, only outlines, it was clear, so those were what Elin provided.

What do you do in London? Copywriting.

Do you enjoy it, *copywriting*, whatever it is? No, not at all.

Have you got a partner? Not at the moment. Don't want one either.

Friends. What about them? Yes, some good ones but we are very different.

What are your dreams? I'm not sure I have any anymore.

That's a very sad thing for a young woman to say. What do you mean?

Elin felt increasingly interrogated. As she described her life, she did not need to be told how flimsy it all sounded, and how ineffectual its consolations. Anwen watched her respond incredibly closely, as if she was studying her every feature under a microscope. It made Elin squirm.

"I know it probably sounds pretty rubbish to you, but I have built a life, you know," she blurted. "It may not be my dream life, but I've got a job, and some friends..."

Anwen nodded sadly. "Compromise. Your father did that, you know, with Barbara. Much good did it do him, the stubborn git."

Angry at such rudeness about the person she had loved most in the world, Elin did not trust herself to reply, so she sipped her acrid coffee in silence. The atmosphere in the room crackled with tension but when Anwen spoke again, her voice was softer, gentler.

"I don't mean to be abrasive. I only mean that Llion had such high hopes of life, of seeing the world, of living a creative life, when he was young," Anwen said. "He made sacrifices out of loyalty, yes, but at such a huge cost to himself."

Elin shuffled in her seat. Uncomfortable truths were never easy to listen to, but it was worse if they were only partly told. "Anwen, I know my parents weren't blissfully happy, but you mean more than that, don't you? Dad told me that he hadn't wanted the farm at all, and that if his brother hadn't..."

"Hadn't nothing!" Anwen shouted. Smot jumped up, ears pricked, alert to threat. "Forget I said anything and let's get on with our work."

But Elin persisted. "Did you know my uncle Dafydd? Dad would never talk about him and Mum won't..."

Anwen spun around and stared at her. "Llion kept his silence for good reason, Elin. We must both respect that, even in death. Your mother doesn't want to think about such inconveniences, but for me it has to be as if he never existed, for my life to be bearable. *Wyt t'in dallt?*/Do you understand? Don't ever mention Dafydd again."

Elin, almost frozen with shock, knew she had exposed a deep, deep wound. Anwen had obviously loved this man, as the intensity of her reaction was impossible to fake. What had gone so terribly wrong, to leave him dead and her still living here, but alone? She watched as the old woman left the room with the coffee cups, her head low. Smot followed, her tail between her legs.

The rest of the morning was very subdued. Anwen attempted to repair things by making conversation about Elin's drawing, how she could improve the shading, and what kind of soup she might like for lunch, but Elin was mistrustful of her. She began to find the room claustrophobic as the afternoon sun blazed through the glass, and yearned to be outside, where there was a breeze. When Smot became restless too, she suggested a walk and surprisingly, Anwen jumped at the chance.

"Yes, let's go out. I'll take you to the top of the mountains behind the house, so you can take in the view. It will clear our heads. We need to *dod yn ôl at ein coed*/get back to the trees, as we say up here."

They set off up the wooded mountain slope behind the house at a fair pace, but Anwen was soon breathless and struggling, so Elin slowed to wait for her.

"I should have brought my stick," she mumbled. "In my head, I'm still young and can leap around like a mountain goat. It's my body that won't oblige."

"Take my arm. I don't know where to go without you, remember."

Anwen smiled as she looped her arm through Elin's. "*Wrth gwrs.*/Of course. I'll show you the way."

As the route up through the trees became steeper, and footholds harder to find, the women had to hold on to each other tightly. Smot wove between their legs, as if her movements were knitting them together.

"Her shepherding instincts are still there, even though she's never been a working dog," Anwen said. "She stops me feeling utterly alone, even though I know I am and probably always will be."

Elin heard a hint of weakness, of regret in the old woman's voice. No, Anwen was not as tough as she liked to seem and had suffered deeply, it was clear. She vowed to ensure her old friend never felt that alone again.

It took over an hour to reach the top of the mountain that reared up behind Anwen's home, but the route was a beautiful one. Trees became sparser as they got higher and the sky seemed to widen above them until it felt almost near enough to touch. Whereas the lower slopes had been still and trees unmoving, up here, a flurry of gulls were buffeted by upward drafts. A kestrel hovered unmoving, mastering the strong wind with contemptuous ease. Elin and Anwen sat in the lea of a rocky outcrop and surveyed the view below them with sighs of contentment.

"All that rushing around people do down there all looks pretty insignificant from up here, doesn't it?" Elin said quietly.

"It does. It's good to get a sense of perspective at times," Anwen said. "I spent my younger years rushing about too, until I was forced to stop. Only then, could I hear it clearly."

"Hear what?" Elin asked. Goosebumps rippled her skin. Something important was coming next, she could feel its imminence.

Anwen put a cupped hand to one of her ears. "That," she murmured. "How do you think my cottage got its name? Close your eyes and stay quiet."

So, Elin did. For a minute or so, her senses fooled her into hearing nothing except the wind, but as she sat quite still, and really listened, a myriad of small sounds began to cohere into a subtle symphony. The loudest were the trickle of small mountain streams making their way downwards to the lake, bubbling over rocks and through boggy moss and mud. Then, she heard the "baaaa" of a sheep somewhere out on the *ffriddoedd*/mountain pastures, the sound carried by the breeze. The lonely cry of the kestrel came next, as it cruised the thermals scouring the ground for a meal. Nearby, she heard a thrush banging a snail shell on a rock and nearer still, a willow warbler's insistent song filled the air as the wind caressed her hair and then blew softly across her face.

"Can you hear it, the song of the mountains?" Anwen asked. "You can only hear it if you listen for it. I told you that when you were a little girl."

"I remember, and I hear it," Elin whispered, opening her eyes and blinking, dazed. Yes, they had come here, and they had listened together.

"It will have told you something important, the song you heard today, but you may not understand what it is, not yet."

"Really?" Elin said. "Did it tell you something, the first time you heard it?"

"Yes, the first time and every time. There's always more to see, to hear, to learn in the world... if we are in the *right* world." A pause, while these words settled, like silent snowflakes on the ground. "We should go down now. Once the sun dips below that ridge over there, it gets cold."

Elin saw, then, that this place, these mountains, had forged Anwen, made her the woman she was, which was why she had come back and spent most of her life honouring them in her work. Helping the old woman up, she remembered George Eliot's words:

"*For there is no creature... so strong that is not greatly determined by what lies outside it.*"

"What time shall I come tomorrow?" Elin asked as they began, slowly, to pick their way downwards.

"I'll be tired after today. Tomorrow, go somewhere else, learn something else," the old woman replied, wheezing. Her chest rattled and she coughed so violently she had to stop to catch her breath.

Where exactly she should go, Elin had no firm idea, but she did not ask. Anwen's response would be to do what, where and when felt right.

TEN

Elin slept late the following morning, and woke only when the rapping of a branch of the huge sycamore tree outside her window on the glass became too insistent to ignore. Opening the curtains, the view was as different as it was every morning she had been here. Today, the wind was sending white-tipped wavelets scudding across the surface of the grey lake, and the sky was a dark inky blue. Slivers of sunlight pierced the clouds, but it was hardly the "beach day" she had hoped it would be when she'd gone to sleep last night.

"No hurry to decide what to do anyway," she murmured, sinking back onto her pillows.

Checking her phone for the first time since she'd arrived, there were seventy-five new emails in her inbox, but she resisted the urge to open them. This was her time, it was limited and did not include the outside world; it was sacrosanct.

When she went downstairs, the lobby was dark and the reception desk unmanned, which was unusual. She'd missed breakfast and was hungry, and wanted to order something small before planning her day. Strangely, her appetite had doubled since arriving, for which she blamed fresh mountain air.

"I refuse to ring the bell," she murmured, walking towards the swing door into the kitchen. All heads turned towards her, and the sounds of mixing, blending and chopping stopped. One of the heads belonged to Dylan Williams.

"Oh, gosh, sorry. I just... I was looking for..." she stuttered. Seeing him there, in daylight, in a white chef's apron and in such a different context threw her. He had said he was working at the pub, of course, but she felt herself blushing.

"Need food? Hear you missed breakfast," Dylan asked with a broad grin. "Lunch starts at half twelve. Can you wait another half an hour to eat? Or I'm free at two if you want an afternoon out..."

Innuendo-laden giggles rippled around the other staff in the kitchen.

"I'll wait – for food, I mean," Elin said, quickly leaving the kitchen to more giggles. Dylan's face was a picture of shock. Had she given him the wrong impression the other night? Had he told everyone that she was next on his list of conquests? Anyone that good-looking, who sang about love as he had done, must have a long list of them.

Once outside in the cool air, she decided that a walk would help her calm down. The sky was clearing a little as the rainclouds were moving away from the mountains, so she headed off around the left-hand side of the lake, towards what locals called The Lagoons. Gwenda had told her that this area was very busy in season, but today, only a few hardy kayakers were enjoying the peaceful, meandering inlets around the periphery of the lake. Elin, flustered, was glad to see nobody she needed to speak to.

As she walked, both her breathing and her thoughts slowed as she concentrated on putting one foot in front of the other. She was not here for long and had not come for anything other than to see Anwen and to think about her life. She and Dylan were grown-ups, so obsessing like a teenager about what he might or might not have meant back there, or what she wanted from him, was immature and a waste of energy. She might go back and see if he wanted to spend the afternoon together, or she might not. Right now, she was walking, mindfully, here, in this beautiful place, on her own. End of story.

An egret was fishing at the water's edge, its snowy plumage vivid against the murky mud and weeds. Elin stopped, stood quite still and watched as it lifted one slim, black leg out of the mud and then the other, until it was nearer whatever it was watching in the water. Suddenly, it pounced, and she saw a tiny silver fish wriggling in its beak and then disappear, swallowed, its small life ending as quickly and quietly as it had been lived. A breeze had sprung up and the crisped autumn trees rustled happily, as if this rather murky day had not started well for them either. Elin had been disappointed not to be seeing Anwen today, but when she was back in London, she would only be able to recall this beauty, this stillness if she focused on it now, she told herself. Thoughts of Dylan Williams would not leave her, however, and it was his face she saw in the rippled surface of the lake and his voice she heard in the breeze.

She ate a rather watery tomato soup and a cheese sandwich in a café in the village instead of going back to the pub for lunch. Avoiding Dylan would be childish, however, and she was determined not to be that. When she walked through reception almost two hours later, ready to explain her seeming-rudeness, and saw him buttoning his coat ready to leave, her tummy did a somersault. He spoke first.

"Hi. Really sorry if I embarrassed you earlier, suggesting a day out," he said, scuffing his toe on the carpet. "I'm off home now anyway. See you around."

Elin hesitated. He looked so awkward, so hurt; his suggestion of spending a little time together was hardly lecherous or threatening. In fact, it was very kind and could even have been fun. When was the last time she had any of *that*?

"Don't worry. It doesn't take much to embarrass me, so sorry I overreacted," she said.

He smiled, a slightly crooked smile which revealed an endearing gap between his two top front teeth. "Oh, great. It's just that I'm free this afternoon, and I thought you might like a trip down Memory Lane, revisit some of your old haunts, you know, but absolutely *dim strach o gwbwl*/no stress at all."

Elin smiled. What other plans did she have? "Sounds good."

"I've got a motorbike, by the way... but I don't go too fast," Dylan added quickly, as if she might think he did. "I'm a positive snail. My father was South Welsh, and fatally risk-averse. Should have followed his example in my younger days."

Elin nodded to show she'd understood, but a slew of memories hit her like a thump in the belly. Hadn't she and Antoine begun with just such an innocent offer, to show her the sights of Paris? She had been standing outside a metro station wondering which way to go when he had pulled up next to her on his vintage blue Vespa, lifted his helmet... and she had been lost.

And why had Dylan felt it necessary to reassure her that he no longer drove fast? There was obviously backstory here, but over-thinking was a habit she was desperate to break. Being on the back of a motorbike through the mountains with the wind in her hair was tempting, but she was still very wary. Barbara had taught her that spontaneity usually entailed risk. As Dylan shifted coyly from foot to foot, she finally made a decision.

"OK, I'll come, but it's 'no' to the motorbike, however slowly you go. I've got a pretty crappy hire car, so I'll meet you back here in fifteen minutes."

"Yes, sir!" Dylan replied, saluting her with a smile. "I'll bring supplies."

Back in her room, Elin was disappointed in her inability to be daring, to *trust* Dylan, but as she stuffed a mac, hat, gloves, water bottle and her phone into a backpack, she told herself it was easier to keep yourself at a safe distance from a man you hardly knew in a car than with your arms wrapped around their waist on the back of a motorbike. They had chatted easily enough in the dark, so surely this little outing would be fine, and what did she have to lose by spending an empty afternoon remembering the past with another

Welsh exile? The words sounded logical, but they still did not convince her. Trusting any man still did not come easy.

Dylan had packed a few choice leftovers from the pub lunch in a brown paper bag and brought a bottle of fresh lemonade. Elin, who was already starving after her meagre lunch, felt relief flood through her. Such simple, kind gestures spoke volumes.

"So, my choice of destination first as it's my car," she said.

"Have Nissan Micra, will travel, eh? You're the boss today."

"So, I'd like to drive the little track that goes through Nant Ffrancon first, please. That's where our farm was, well still is of course, but it's not ours anymore... if that's OK with you, that is."

"Of course it is, Elin. This is *your* day, remember? I love that track, and it's got the best 360-degree views in the world. You don't need me to navigate, I'm sure," he said, fastening his seatbelt. "Let's hit the road!"

Elin revved the Micra a few times, reducing both of them to helpless giggles and triggering a tweak of net curtains from a bungalow across the road. Setting off, she realised she was already more relaxed in this man's company than she had been with anyone for a very long time.

ELEVEN

They drove towards the tiny turn-off that led to the road running along the bottom of the valley, and as they got near it, Elin's hands trembled on the steering wheel. She had not been back to *Wern Farm* since her father's death, when the funeral tea in the downstairs parlour had only postponed the dreadful finality that lay only months ahead – its sale. Driving slowly, almost reverentially, towards her childhood home, green-felted mountains reared up on either side, ribboned with drystone walls and looped with stone sheep pens in which the flocks were kept for counting or for the winter gathering. They met no other cars and saw no other people; winding the windows down, they heard only the wind and the occasional *preep* of a cruising bird of prey.

The farm itself was set back from the track slightly, and the sheer height of the mountain behind it made its stone walls look almost toy-like in comparison. Today, the stream that ran down over the rocks and gave the house its water supply was gentle, nothing like Elin had seen it in a winter storm, when its crashing sound filled every room of the house and flecks of foam clouded the windows so that it was almost dark inside in the daytime.

When they reached the house, Elin gasped. The front door was battered and the paint peeling, and both the barn and the *beudy*/cow house, Llion's pride and joy, were missing some roof slates. The swallows who flew in and out every minute or so were probably descendants of birds who had lived and bred here long before she was born. Llion had worked so very hard to maintain the farm as his father had before him, but now, it looked uncared for, as if his life had been wasted, which almost broke Elin's heart. She couldn't remember much about who had bought it in the hurried auction after her father's death other than that they were English; she had not wanted to know details. Barbara would have sold it to anyone, however, Elin remembered that.

Up on the *ffriddoedd*/mountain pastures, a few sheep still dotted the slopes. The farm's fields were steep and mined with rugged boulders, so only the hardiest Welsh ewes could thrive in the harsh conditions each winter brought. Elin hoped they were still being cared for, unlike the farmhouse. She tried not to brood upon the fact that she might have helped their ancestors come into this world, when out lambing with her father. Life here followed its own, relentless cycle, she had always known, but how could so much history unravel so quickly?

"Do you want to stop, have a look around? Doesn't look like there's anyone around to object," Dylan said. She could hear his concern without seeing his face. Shaking her head, they drove on in silence.

"Would you mind if we went to Tryfan next?" Elin said, when she felt less upset.

"I'd love to revisit good old Tryfan. Climbed that beast many a time with my mates," Dylan said cheerily. "We always used to jump..."

"...between the two rocks at the top, as a dare?" Elin cut in. "That's a stupid macho 'thing' up here, isn't it?"

"Er, yes, it is. But how do you know that?" Dylan asked, surprised at her tone.

"My uncle died up there, doing just that. My dad was with him, they argued and he fell. Dad never got over it."

When she saw Dylan's face crumple, she added, "Sorry, a bit of ancient history, that's all."

"Ah, the worst kind, and we all have plenty of it," Dylan replied softly. "Sometimes, we have to revisit the past, to get to a future that's free of it."

"I sure hope you're right, because right now the past feels much more real than either the present or the future," Elin said miserably.

The A5, the road that leads through the heart of Eryri and out, past Tryfan, continues on through flatter, gentler scenery and eventually, to England. It has always been the road everyone who leaves North Wales grows to love, for all its slowness and infuriating caravan-towers. Many still prefer to use it rather than take the coastal dual carriageway crammed with jet-skis and campervans heading to Anglesey, and Elin and Dylan were amongst them. Today, the mountains looked resplendent against the blue sky and the sunlight played across *Llyn Ogwen*/Ogwen Lake as they passed it like a million tiny jewels. When the full majesty of Tryfan came into view, both Elin and Dylan gasped aloud. It was, quite literally, breathtaking. Looking up, they could glimpse the edge of the summit, but clouds obscured the two topmost boulders, Adam and Eve, that stood above the valley as they had for around 500 million years, as if defying anyone to risk challenging their supremacy.

"Think of all these rocks have witnessed," Elin said. "We're like ants, scuttling along down here, crushed in a nanosecond, but they are constant, whatever we or the weather throw at them. They have been there every single day of our lives and that of everyone we've ever known."

Dylan nodded. "And they're in our hearts, and always will be, I think," he said. "I read about the bushmen in the Kalahari once. They have such a close connection with nature that they believe that they can *hear* the stars – isn't that an amazing thought? I wish we could hear them too, as well as look at them if we're lost, like ancient mariners. Perhaps we just need to listen harder, like those bushmen."

"Hear, hear!" Elin said, smiling at him.

This man's openness amazed her, but he intrigued her too, because things he said chimed with things she had felt her whole life but never dared say in case they sounded, well, *weird*. It felt so good not to have to worry about such things today, but to be as much her true self as he was.

"Let's park, get out and see if we can hear that song of the mountains you mentioned," Dylan said. "If we can hear it anywhere, it'll be here, but I might need to eat something first!"

They pulled up beside the road at the bottom of the mountain, climbed over a stile and walked towards the base. Half an hour of clambering over rocks, through swathes of dried heather and over squelching bogland mantled with mosses and cotton plants led them to a good place to stop. Sitting on a flat slab of rock, they both turned towards the weak October sun as it lowered in the sky and felt its fading warmth on their faces. A few minutes later, Dylan pulled what he called their "pilfered picnic" out of his backpack – half a quiche, a tub of potato salad, two bread rolls and a mango.

"Good luck peeling a mango out here," Elin said.

But when Dylan produced a penknife and began doing exactly that before handing her perfect cubes of ripe, juicy fruit, she laughed.

"Is there anything you can't do?"

"Too many things to list now. Let's just eat, and listen, shall we?" Dylan said.

And so they did.

They listened as the breeze from the icy mountaintop high above them rustled through the grass. They heard the stream next to them ripple endlessly over, around and between the rocks. There were a few cars on the road, but those that passed made only a distant, muffled hum. A V-tailed kite circled above them, its haunting cry piercing the sky as it cruised above the crags. Finally, a mountain sheep bleated as it trotted along one of the countless sheep tracks that criss-cross the land, and the song was complete. Finally, they both opened their eyes, and smiled at each other.

Dylan tentatively reached for her hand, but Elin could not take it. This was too much, too soon and she pretended not to notice as he quietly withdrew it. They sat and watched as the sun began to set over the mountains before both closing their eyes again to listen, and to remember.

TWELVE

Elin could not help but wonder if the delicious dinner she ate that evening had been chopped, cooked and served especially for her by Dylan, in the kitchen. She had chosen Welsh lamb, which her father had been so proud to produce, and locally grown vegetables smothered with a gravy that tasted heavenly. Farming here was tough, but each bite of this homegrown food restored her pride in her family's history, and her father's lifetime of hard work.

Full, contented and in her pyjamas in her room after dinner, Elin could not remember when she had enjoyed herself as much as she had that afternoon. Dylan was so unlike the men she had spent a fortune having dinner with on dating apps in London. He did not try to be liked, did not talk endlessly about himself, what he wanted to do or where he wanted to see next. Instead, he was himself and he wanted to know as much about her as she wanted to tell him, but no more. They had a lot in common, after all. He dreamt of success in music as much as she yearned to find the right path in life, but he had returned to North Wales to reconnect with a part of himself first and see his sister, just as she had, to see Anwen Jones. He had no intention of staying forever and neither had she. He would stay for as long as it felt right to stay, and then he would leave, as she would, in a few days' time.

A few days' time.

Elin was surprised at the mix of emotions this bald fact provoked: sadness was in there, and regret, but so was relief. If she stayed longer, she was not sure what would happen between them, or whether she wanted it to. In the past, her trust in a man had been so viciously betrayed, her need for love roundly rebuffed. Why would this quirky wannabe musician be any different?

She told herself that Dylan Williams certainly wouldn't be thinking about *her* right now, however pleasant the day had been, so when she saw a text from him ping into her inbox at 10.35 p.m., she was taken aback – they had not even exchanged numbers, so how had he got hers? Her heart sank. Was he going to suggest she go downstairs for a nightcap, that they repeat their stargazing experience, or tell her that the moon was full that night and they should go for a midnight swim? Surely, he would not be that corny...

"Please don't spoil today, Dylan," she whispered, opening the text:

> Hi, got your number from Emlyn. I hope you don't mind that, or me messaging this late. Just want to say I had a great afternoon. Until we meet again, which I hope we do, let's hold onto our hiraeth and keep in touch. Kindred spirits are few and far between. D.

For the next ten minutes, Elin analysed each word, his tone, the subtext and his possible intentions. It got her nowhere, but was a learnt, self-preservatory habit she could not leave behind. Making herself vulnerable right now was not going to help her sort her life out, however easy she had felt with him, but the thought of never seeing him again was strangely painful. In the end, she replied quickly, pressing send before even re-reading her message:

> I enjoyed today as well and do keep in touch. I'll let you know when I'm next back. Hwyl/cheers. E.

The moment she had sent it, she regretted it.

· · ·

The next day was Thursday, so Elin had very little time to see Anwen before going back to London. She would spend Sunday in Tooting, bracing herself for work and Sadie's inevitable wrath on Monday morning. Until then, it was vital to make the most of every single minute.

It was drizzling lightly, and moisture hung in the air, misting the treetops, rising off the lake and giving the slates on all the town's rooves a soft sheen. Again, Anwen was waiting for Elin when she arrived, and Smot did not need to sniff her at all today before wagging her tail in welcome. Her owner's welcome was less kindly, however and her face, steely with determination.

"Today, you're doing some painting, to show me what you remember," Anwen said. "You'll do better with watercolours. You always did, but even then, you were never what I would call *good*."

Elin was hurt. She wanted to say that she had last used watercolour paints almost twenty years ago, when she had come to visit her as a sulky teenager before she and her father had stopped coming at all, but knew it was pointless. A faint smell of boiled cabbage and burning hung in the air as they went through the kitchen and into the conservatory. Without sunshine, it was a far darker space today and Elin noticed new condensation sliming many of the windows. It felt such a different place from the day before yesterday. It was clear, today, that Anwen's time in this room was limited, as it would soon be too cold. How much worse would her arthritis be after another long Welsh winter?

On the easel in the corner was a blank canvas, with a palette of watercolours, brushes and a glass jar of water. Propped up against the jar was a large photograph of the lake, the surrounding woodland, the mountains and the slate slopes with the colourful town of Llanberis nestled on one side.

"There's your inspiration. See what you can do with it," Anwen said, sitting down and pulling a blanket over her knees. She looked tired and old, older than her years. In fact, she was probably only a few years older than Barbara, but that morning, looked several decades senior. Her harsh, lonely life had taken its toll.

"Are you not going to join me?" Elin said, glimpsing the painting of the heron propped against the wall, still unfinished.

"My hands. I can't, on a day like this," Anwen replied. "Fingers won't work. I'll just sit here and watch you. Help me light this cigarette before you start, though, will you?"

Elin did so, but the old woman's hands still shook as she tried to hold the cigarette steady.

Feeling as if she was ascending the gallows, Elin began to cover the paper with a light watery wash. At first, Anwen's eyes seemed to bore into her once again as ash dropped silently onto her clothes. Soon, however, Elin forgot about this scrutiny, about where she was, and even why she had come back to Wales. The photo, and trying to capture even a tiny part of its perfection, absorbed her total attention. It was only when Anwen emitted a guttural snore instead of her usual cough that Elin realised she was asleep, and dared to relax. The old woman did not look at all well, though, which was worrying. She moved the packet of cigarettes out of sight, in the vain hope Anwen might forget to want them when she woke up.

The looseness with which Elin's hands and arms moved as she worked was uncanny, as if a long-lost muscle memory was guiding her in a task she'd thought she stood no chance of ever completing. Having spent the last few days looking, really looking, at her surroundings, she knew almost instinctively how the shade fell on the trees and how the slopes of rocky scree glittered when the sun hit them. The water of the lake was more difficult to convey, as it was both dark and iridescent at the same time, its depths and dangers concealed beneath a surface of shimmering particles of light.

"Like silver pennies," Elin murmured. "Who was it that told me that it looks like that?" And yet she knew it could only have been one person: Anwen.

By the time the old woman stirred, yawned and opened her eyes, Elin was fairly pleased with what she had done, but how would a professional, a master of conveying the essence of what she saw, of conjuring magic with a few strokes of her brush, judge her? Elin found herself feeling a yearning for kind words and reassurance, just as she had as a child.

She watched as the old woman got up with a groan, cough and shuffle over to squint at her canvas, scratching her bristly chin with one hand for a minute. A long, silent, minute followed in which Elin felt her heartbeat quicken.

"For the time you had, and the experience you have, this is not too bad. It shows promise. More than anything, it shows that you are *seeing* things now."

"Thank you. I think that's good news," Elin said, unsure whether it was or not.

"I don't think you should give up your day job, but I've seen worse."

Elin gulped, feeling put back in her place once more.

"And you never told me what you did yesterday. It seems to have helped the way you look at things, whatever it was," Anwen said.

"I went back to *Wern Farm*, with a man called Dylan..."

"Dylan Williams?" Anwen asked, with an expression on her face that Elin found impossible to read.

"Yes. He works at the pub. He's a cook, but also a singer. He's very good, and he's from here too. Do you know each other?" When Anwen did not reply, she gabbled on, feeling strangely wrong-footed. "We went back to the farm, and then to Tryfan. He used to climb it too, and do that stupid game, jumping between the two rocks."

Almost as the words were said, Elin realised her mistake. That "game" had cost her uncle his life and Anwen had told her very clearly never to refer to him again. All the blood vanished from the older woman's face in an instant and she looked as if she had been struck by lightning.

"I'm sorry, Anwen. I forgot..."

"I know you did. People do. Perhaps it's time for you to go. You can try again tomorrow, with oils or gouache. You might do better with them. Less subtle."

Elin was angry now. She was not a child, and this woman was not her mother.

"No, I can't come here again either unless you explain why you are being like this, so *mean*. Am I undergoing some kind of test?" she snapped.

"Of course not. But you hardly know that man, and I *worry* about you."

Elin, slightly alarmed, chose her words carefully. Something was going on here that she could not read, and did not understand, a rippling beneath the surface. Was Anwen *jealous*?

"Look, I went out for the day with a nice man whom I'll probably never see again, end of. I don't need to be judged by you or anyone else." She paused, and seeing Anwen's face, went on in a calmer voice. "I didn't come back for anything other than to see you again, and perhaps find a bit of the person I used to be before life obliterated any dreams I ever had."

"You need *new* dreams, the right ones," Anwen said urgently. "And I genuinely didn't mean to criticise, but some men can be *dangerous* and love even more so."

"I know that. I really do."

"Oh, I'm sorry, *cariad*/dear. I know you do. Antoine, of course." She paused, looking upset. "I've always pushed anyone I care about away, hurt them, you see, but I don't mean to. I have more regrets about doing so than you can begin to imagine."

"My mother does the same thing, so I'm used to it."

"I suppose we both have our reasons, different reasons," Anwen said, dabbing her eyes with the corner of her cardigan. "But I'm very sorry."

"Me too," Elin said. "And you don't need to worry about me falling in love with a random Welsh musician, honestly."

"Thank goodness for that," Anwen said, sniffing. "Welshmen are the worst!"

Both women moved together in a clumsy, shuffling movement and hugged each other, a hug that both welcomed. Smot wrapped herself around their legs, just to make sure they were friends again.

Half an hour later, they were sitting down in the kitchen eating a lunch of potato and leek soup and some sourdough bread that was more "sour" than "bread" and things between them felt calmer, as after a storm. They chatted more easily than they ever had, and Elin felt able to ask something she had not been sure she could, before their argument.

"There is something I need to do before I go back to London, and I was wondering if you would come with me."

Anwen raised an eyebrow. "Apart from our walk the other day, I haven't been out of this cottage for months, so that will depend how vital it is that I come anywhere."

"I haven't got enough time to go up Yr Wyddfa this time, but want to drive up to Pen-y-Pass to see it, and then down to Nant Peris, to visit Dad's grave."

A silence followed, in which Anwen absent-mindedly stroked Smot's soft ears.

"I haven't been there since I had to stop driving last year. Why do you need me there, to visit your own father?" she said eventually.

"I think it's because I remember us three together, being happy, being *at ease* with each other... and I have never felt that since."

"Neither have I," Anwen replied, "but we cannot go back, cannot recreate something that has gone forever. Llion and his brother are both... dead, Elin. You know that." She wiped her eyes once more.

Elin nodded. Again, the emotional mention of the uncle she had never met, but she did not react to it. "I do, of course, but it's something I need to do before I go back to..."

"... to a life you hate. That's the knub of all this, isn't it, not a romantic yearning for the Welsh hillsides?" Anwen said, pausing. "But do you have to go back?"

Elin sighed. Yes, she had to go back. Sadie was expecting her, she had a flat, friends, plans, a cat called Mouse... and what was here for her once Barbara had sold her house? London life was the only life she had, however much she hated it.

"Yes, I do, but if you care about me at all, please come with me to visit Dad," she said, looking into Anwen's eyes.

"Well, I can see more soul in those eyes now than when you arrived, so there is hope for you yet, *Elin fach*/Little Elin. Yes, I'll come."

THIRTEEN

The road through Nant Peris and up towards Pen-y-Pass and the base of Yr Wyddfa makes for beautiful, but not easy driving. In winter, its narrow loops threading between mountains can be treacherously icy, and in summer, gawping drivers looking for the perfect Insta shot make the drive slow and frustrating. By the time Elin had gone back to the pub, driven as far as she could up Anwen's hill and then guided her down to the car, the weak October sunlight was fading and the air already chilled. There could be hard frosts this high even at this time of year, Elin knew. As they wound their way upwards, Anwen said nothing, but she leant forward to look up at the landscape they were passing through, with the occasional fond "ahhh" as she recognised a familiar crag, boulder or wooden stile at the beginning of a foot-path. This was a place she had lived in, and loved, all her life, until age and arthritis had deprived her of its glories; Elin shared her joy at this long overdue reunion. The view from the top, where walkers park to begin the ascent of Yr Wyddfa, had some rare spaces, so they stopped for a while to take in the spectacular panorama laid out before them. The peace on Anwen's face erased all tiredness, pain and age: she breathed it in without her usual cough, like oxygen for the soul, and Elin knew that she was glad she'd come.

They drove on to the church at Nant Peris, and she took the older woman's arm as they walked through the gatehouse and then towards the low-rooved stone building. Around them, on all sides, were the towering mountains of Eryri, as if protecting this place where people had worshipped for many hundreds of years. The sun was now completely hidden by the hills, and long shadows from the slate gravestones fell across their path.

"He's over here, your father, in case you've forgotten," Anwen said. "I think I'm the only person who's visited him for years."

Elin flinched at this undeniable truth, but she had not forgotten where her father's grave lay. Her memories of the cold, drizzly day they had buried Llion in this place were undimmed. She could still see the rectangular trench two local men had dug, and her mother, thin-lipped and composed, throwing the first handful of earth on top of the coffin that Llion's four old school friends had gingerly lowered into the ground. Elin heard the church bell tolling as it had done before the funeral tea where she had drunk too much and said too much to the old woman now standing next to her. Anwen looked on as Elin knelt on the damp grass and read the inscription she had helped Barbara compose – mainly in English, as she had insisted, with some Welsh, on which Elin had insisted:

HERE LIES LLION PUGH. A GOOD HUSBAND, A GOOD FATHER
AND A GOOD MAN.
BYDDWCH MEWN HEDDWCH./BE AT PEACE.

She hoped her father was, indeed, at peace. He deserved to be. She picked up one of the small, white pebbles from Penmon, their favourite fishing spot, that she had placed on his grave on the day they had buried him, put it in her pocket and closed her eyes. His face swam in front of her: his blue eyes surrounded by deep wrinkles and his skin almost leather-like after years of facing blasting wind and rain out on the hills. When she opened them, and he was gone again, she turned to find Anwen. She wanted to ask her exactly where the uncle she had never met was buried, as she had said only "in a corner, under an ancient yew tree", but the old woman had gone into the church without her. Elin followed slowly, shuddering at having to leave her strong, gentle father in the ground under a slab of slate.

Anwen was standing in front of the altar in the church, a shaft of light illuminating her white hair with an almost angelic evanescence.

"Your parents got married in this church. I don't think they were happy together, but they stayed together," Anwen said, adding, in a lower tone, "And they did a good, kind thing."

Before Elin could ask the inevitable question this raised, the old woman had walked off towards a table where a bowl of water and a plate of small pebbles were placed on an embroidered cloth. A sign suggested that visitors pick a pebble, place it in the water and "think of all the things in your past you need to leave behind".

"If only it was so easy to leave our regrets behind," Anwen whispered, but she did slowly put a pebble in the water and then turned to Elin with a girl-like smile on her face. "Go on. Your turn."

Reluctantly, without thinking too much about what she might need to leave behind her, Elin placed a round, white pebble in the water. However little she believed in such things, she convinced herself that she felt more at peace as she threaded her arm through her old friend's and they walked outside.

"*Diolch am ddod efo fi*/Thank you for coming with me," she said quickly, as she helped Anwen back into the car.

"See, your *Cymraeg*/Welsh is flooding back now!" the old woman exclaimed. "Told you it would. You just need to trust yourself."

Elin smiled, but a voice inside her head told her that was the hardest thing she could ever be asked to do. She had given herself, body and soul, to a young Frenchman on a Vespa who had showed her how life could be lived away from the dourness of her child-hood home and her parents' loveless marriage. Then he had betrayed her. She could never, ever trust herself to risk that again.

The afternoon was beginning to drift quickly towards dusk as they drove back towards Llanberis. Bats flittered in a caramel-coloured sky and rabbits' eyes shone like little metal discs in the headlights before they scuttled away. By the time Anwen was safely back in her house, it was pitch black and the cold air was full of the scratchings and hootings of the night.

"Today was very tiring, but it was a good day, for us both. It was an *important* day, in fact," Anwen said firmly.

Buoyed by this, Elin wondered if her friend would come out with her tomorrow as well. It was a risk, but the chance might never come again.

"Do you remember us going to a beach together, you, me and Dad?" she asked, as casually as she could.

The old woman smiled and her face softened. "We did, yes. Many times, in fact, when you were little. Your mother didn't like the beach, too *messy* for her, but Llion loved it, and so did you."

Fiddling with the buttons on her coat, Elin asked the question that she knew could either be answered with calmness, or with the explosion that follows the lighting of a fuse.

"Will you come with me to the beach tomorrow? To one partic-ular beach, actually, one I remember, one I painted as a child. It had dunes behind it and sand that went on and on."

Anwen sighed. "More memory hunting? Not sure all this revis-iting of the past is a good thing, as I keep telling you. I remember we went to Penmon, and sat by the lighthouse once while your father fished, but I can't remember the sandy beach at all."

Elin waited, and for a minute or two the only sound was the ticking of the ancient carriage clock on the mantelpiece above the range. With each second that passed, it seemed less likely that Anwen would agree to come as her face was stony and unmoving.

"I took a photo of my painting of the place, if it jogs your memory," Elin said. She handed her phone to the old woman. "It's not that good, I know. I remember it being so windy there that I crunched on sand when I ate my sandwich, but it was beautiful, like one of these white-sanded Caribbean beaches in the glossy adverts. Strange, that I can't remember where it was, though. Can you?"

More ticking of the clock. More waiting.

"Aberffraw, it was, but the sand was like molten gold, not white," Anwen said softly, as if it was an outward breath. "We swam, you and I painted and Llion fished at the water's edge as the tide came in and swallowed the beach up."

"You remember now? So, will you come there with me tomorrow? It's my last day here, before I go back to London."

Anwen sighed. "*Ydw*/Yes, I will. It's been such a long time since I saw the sea. But be prepared for the sea to speak to you, just as the mountains did."

FOURTEEN

For October, the weather was kind the following morning when Elin collected Anwen for their second day out together. Although there was a chill in the air, the mountains glowed in autumnal sunshine and the lake was mirror-calm, reflecting the blue sky in pure, unrippled perfection.

Anwen said little during the drive over the Britannia Bridge and onto the island of Anglesey, and then on the fast road across it, towards Aberffraw. It was only when they turned off the dual carriageway onto the back roads that meandered through tiny hamlets and past rows of windblown trees that she seemed alert to the passing landscape, and the imminence of the coast.

Winding her window right down, she inhaled deeply. "Ah, it's good to smell the sea again," she said, turning to Elin. "Now that I can't drive, my world has shrunk so much. The mountains give me space to breathe, but the *sea*... that's a taste of infinity itself."

Walking along the sloping banks of the estuary that led to the beach at Aberffraw was a challenge for Anwen. There was a strong wind, just as Elin had remembered, blasting off the sea they could not yet see. The old woman clutched Elin's arm as tightly as a vulture does its prey, pinching her flesh in her concern not to lose her footing. When Elin winced, Anwen explained:

"When you get older, one of the many things that changes is the meaning of the word 'fall'," she said. "Suddenly, the phrase 'having a fall' replaces 'falling over', as you did as a child. A fall can be life-threatening, a broken hip, a presager of death instead of a grazed knee, wounded pride and a kiss from your mam. I hate it."

But once they rounded the corner of the dunes and the crashing sea was revealed, her arm, and indeed her whole body, relaxed into Elin's. She closed her eyes, and took another huge, deep breath, followed by a raw cough.

"Now that is life-*affirming* in the truest sense of the word," she said, when she could speak. "Take it in before you go back to London and breathing fills you with pollutants and smog."

Elin did as she was told, and felt almost dizzy with the purity of the cold, salt-infused air as it hit her bloodstream, like a shot of good alcohol. This was bliss.

They walked onwards, towards the sea, which the wind was whipping into a lace-edged cauldron of waves that coated their faces with spray. There was not a single other person on the beach. Surrounded by rocky headland on two sides and dunes at their back, the open ocean ahead seemed to Elin to promise a limitless freedom that stretched beyond the horizon. Day and night, through all four seasons, its metronomic rhythm continued, whatever she was doing, wherever she was living, that unseen constancy was its message, its song to her that day. As Anwen had told her, she was in the wrong life; she knew it now without a modicum of doubt.

"What am I doing sitting at a desk in an office when all this is here, unwitnessed? Why am I wasting my life writing about rubbish?" she cried into the wind.

Anwen tutted in irritation and ignored her outburst, more focused on finding somewhere sheltered to sit, where the wind would not assail them quite so violently. When they had done so, she said:

"I understand why you do it. We all have to earn a living, and our choices lead us to where we find ourselves at any one moment in our lives – me in my draughty cottage up a bloody mountain and you, in Tooting, surrounded by shops and people and excitement and culture that this place could never match, remember." She patted Elin's hand lightly, comfortingly. "Both have their time, and their purpose. The trick is to decide which one feeds your soul at which time in your life."

Elin nodded shyly, before replying, "I know. And I was never here full time, was I? I was away at school and my mother, who *was* here, still hates the place and can't wait to leave it. Let's be realistic. What would I do up here, and where would I live?"

"These things tend to become clear with time," Anwen said. "You could start by listening to the sea, as you did to the mountains. They've both been guiding people for centuries."

"Like the stars," Elin murmured.

"Yes, them too."

But when the two women parted that evening, she could only hope her old friend was right and she would be granted some guidance as to what to do.

Elin got the only direct train back to London the following lunchtime. Leaving North Wales was difficult, but she had promised Anwen that she would return at Christmas, which made it bearable. She fought the urge to contact Dylan again after her last lukewarm message. In reality, the chances of their paths ever crossing at home again were slim and the phrase "keep in touch" meant nothing. He would go wherever his career needed him to be, and following in the slipstream of a man had never proved wise in the past. No, she would forge her own path this time and try as hard as she could to forget about him completely. It was better, safer, that way.

When she arrived at Euston station, a biting wind blasted through the bleak concourse crammed with commuters rushing for their evening trains. Pulling up her collar, she bought a large bar of chocolate and began to walk to the Tube station to make the trek across this vast city to the one, tiny corner she called home. Shoving her hands into her pocket, she felt the smooth white pebble she had taken from her father's grave, and it brought a lump to her throat. Wales already seemed so far away, and her time there so long ago. London is not an easy place to call home, and Elin had landed here after her travels, her heartbreak and her father's death, but she had never intended to stay long. That day, whether she could be brave enough to leave it was a question she could not bear to ask herself. Instead, she ate all the chocolate.

Her flat had smelt of damp when she'd opened the door, and the worktop was peppered with tiny pellets that looked suspiciously like mouse droppings. Mouse, despite his name, had always been a haphazard mouser. A crust of toothpaste had formed in the bathroom sink as she'd left in such a hurry, and her answerphone was flashing frantically. Elin pressed "delete all messages" without listening to any of them. Lying in bed, she scrolled through last week's WhatsApps from her small group of old school friends, none of which she had opened. Sighing, she messaged *"Back now. Let's meet soon"* before deleting them too. As she tried to sleep, a car alarm went off in the street, ignored for so long that its pulsing whine became a shriek. She could not help but remember the birds over the lake in the small hours, their liquid cries gradually filling the darkness with hope of the approaching dawn.

Sunday passed slowly, punctuated by chores and overshadowed by dread of returning to work the following morning. After a sleepless night, Elin decided to follow the affirmation that appeared on her phone, one generated by a free app she'd downloaded a few months earlier: "Feel positive, be positive". Yes, she would commit to feeling positive, as the alternative was too dark to contemplate. If this was her life right now, she had better make the best of it if she was too scared to change it: she could almost hear

Anwen telling her so. She washed her hair, chose her clothes with care and applied more make-up than normal before setting off for the broiling purgatory of the Northern Line. It felt important to look *focused* and to fend off the temptation to wallow in self-pity and regret. Anwen would have no time for that either. She needed to be strong, sensible, if she was to see the right path forward and make decisions that were more than whims. By the time she arrived at the office, she was hot and exhausted but at least braced.

Her positivity was blown out of the water the moment Sadie greeted her with an unconvincing "hope you're feeling better now", followed by a glacial smile. Elin managed to respond with a "Great, and thanks so much for understanding, Sadie," but felt like a walk-on comic character in a very serious play who had come onstage in the wrong scene. Opening her inbox made things worse. More than two hundred emails about deadlines, team meetings and an article about scatter cushions which she was instructed to write by lunchtime.

"Well, at least I dodged non-slip rugs," she muttered as she worked her way through all the emails as fast as she could. The only one that produced a fillip of interest was the one proposing a campaign on "bringing nature indoors for Christmas". This was solely because, at Christmas, she would be back in Wales, surrounded by far more nature than overpriced "swags of fresh-cut ivy" or "bracts of aromatic fir" than Borough Market could ever compete with. Any positivity about her London life had vanished by 11 a.m.

When she checked her phone at lunchtime, her friends had besieged her with requests to "debrief" that evening in a wine bar they all loved. Elin was tired, and unsure, as she needed more time for all she had seen and done in North Wales to settle in her own head before she could bear the arc-light interrogation of her friends. How could she describe Anwen so they wouldn't imagine a stereotypical bewhiskered eccentric? And if she even hinted at how much she had liked Dylan, her mates would be on the trail like a pack of hungry bloodhounds. They cared about her, but how much did they *know* her, she wondered. To give herself breathing space, she eventually replied:

> Can't do tonight, sorry. Tomorrow, 6 p.m.?

Within minutes, a rash of thumbs-up icons confirmed their date.

FIFTEEN

Elin had made almost no friends since those she had made at boarding school. She had analysed this situation and deduced that there were two reasons for this. First, the forced emotional dependency forged in the loneliness of Parkdean School could never be replicated in any other context and secondly, all the other students she'd met at art school were unbearably pretentious. Her schoolfriends Abigail, Florence and Saskia, the three girls who'd been in her room at school, had shared the pain of first periods, the agonies of acne and a shared obsession with dieting. Even though Elin had refused to join them in salivating over boy bands and French kisses, theirs was a bond forged in the sadness of being despatched far from family and home, however inadequate both these things had been. At eleven years old, the four girls had zipped themselves into their own tiny world as tightly as a banana in its skin.

Decades had passed, and Florence and Abigail were now both married, and parents. Saskia's wife was undergoing IVF so they could become them, but their bond remained as strong as ever. Nobody else, not even partners, was allowed into this inner circle. This bond had held fast through all that life had thrown at them... until now.

As Elin approached the wine bar to meet them two days after

her return from Wales, she was incredibly nervous. In herself, she felt different, as if already set on a different trajectory in life to the more mainstream ones her friends had chosen, but exactly how much of that change they would see or sense, she could not be sure. She arrived slightly late, so they'd be at least a large glass ahead of her, which she had hoped would soften their questions. In fact, it emboldened them to make them even more direct.

"Right, get your bum on this seat and spill all!" Abigail carolled as soon as Elin came through the door. The mother of year-old twins, Abigail's chronic exhaustion was slightly masked by the flush of fast-drunk wine, but she blinked long and slow as she waited for an answer as if opening her eyes quickly was too hard.

"What the hell did you go back to North Wales for?" Saskia added. "You *hate* that place."

"Perhaps we should be asking *who* you went back for?" Florence said. "A long-lost sweetheart, rambling across the hills pining for you, perhaps?"

"Ooh yes. The lonely goatherd himself. Did you tumble in the bracken?" Abigail added with a slightly hysterical laugh that hung in the air like a bad smell.

Elin sighed. She really was not up for yet another evening of her friends bewailing her persistent singleness before listing their own partners' many, many shortcomings. It was time, gently, to head all this off at the pass.

"Look, I went back because my mother announced she's getting married and selling up and I wanted to revisit some old haunts for the last time," Elin said firmly. "Sorry to disappoint you on the goatherd, girls."

A short silence followed, before Abigail's uncontrollable hiccups made them all dissolve into giggles.

"Barbara's getting married again? Bloody hell," Saskia said. "Found another saint, has she?"

Elin smiled, but she preferred not to think about what her father had put up with in his marriage, or her mother's new life in Bath that would not, could not, ever include her. "Yup. A total crapfest. But she says he is very *respectable,* girls, so that's good. Right, next round's on me, but I refuse to go up to get it and risk getting hit on by that weirdo sat at the bar," she said. Abigail and Saskia turned to look, exchanged weary looks and got up to get the drinks together.

"So, how do you feel about it all really?" Florence said quietly as the others ordered wine and nibbles. She was the quietest of the group and the one to whom Elin felt closest. Both women shared the knowledge that they had not come to Parkdean from a wealthy background and private school, but on a scholarship from a state school, which had made their bond all the stronger.

"Sad for me, but kind of glad for Mum. Why shouldn't she be happy... I mean... just because...?"

"... just because you're not," Florence said, filling Elin's glass to the brim.

Elin looked down at her knees. "Oh, I don't even know what would make me happy, Flo. I'm so bloody confused about it all. Perhaps I've just got to try and make the best of my life and stop yearning for someone perfect to rescue me."

Grinning wryly, Florence said, "Even Lizzie Bennet took a while to realise that the wrong man was actually the right one. Perhaps you need to compromise a bit too."

Elin baulked at this. Hadn't Anwen warned her that compromising in a relationship was a worse fate than loneliness? Her father had made that mistake, and paid heavily for it.

"Do we? When does compromise become selling yourself short, or expecting another person to come on as a substitute because you can't score a goal yourself?" she said. "No, I refuse to do that, sorry."

"All I'm saying is that sometimes we can't see what's best for us, who's best for us," Florence said, hiding her hurt. "I just don't want you to be sad, that's all."

"You just don't want me to be an embarrassment in all your lives as the sad old spinster, you mean," Elin replied, taking a large glug of wine.

"You are very far from that," Florence murmured. "And that was really harsh, El."

A pause. Elin felt guilt wash over her in hot waves.

"Sorry. Yes, it was," she mumbled.

"Forget it. We're having a party gathering thing on Saturday and I'd love you to come. Nothing formal. It will do you good to get out, talk to people," Florence said.

"Why? Are you short on numbers?" Elin snapped back instinctively.

"Please let's pause the 'singleness obsession'. I get why you feel like that, and it's tough, but why not just come and have a pleasant evening? That's all. No pressure, honestly. 7.30 p.m. Nice food, nice people."

"All generally *nice*, in fact," Elin said, adding, after a deep sigh, "Well, I can't say I have any plans for Saturday..."

"Then come. Great. And actually, there is a man I think you might like – Theo, an old friend of Marcus's from school."

"School being Eton, Flo. I hear alarm bells already."

"Yes, Eton, but to be honest, he's OK. I reckon you'd probably match with him on a dating app and he's very easy on the eye."

Elin groaned. "I'm bloody well done with those apps too. Why can't people meet people as they used to, in a pub, on a park bench, or a pottery class?"

"Or over a relaxed dinner at a friend's house...?"

Elin grinned sheepishly. "Point taken."

Taking one of Elin's hands in hers, Florence smiled at her. "Look, we love you, you stupid woman. We worry that you're, well, a bit lost."

"I think I am, Flo. It feels as if I'm always the spanner in the works, you know – someone the algorithms don't know what to do with and people skirt around because I don't fit the mould." Elin's voice began to wobble. "I mean, is there something the *matter* with me?"

Florence squeezed her hand very tightly indeed. "You've been through so much, remember. The whole terrible Antoine rejection, your dad dying and now your mum getting married to someone you've never met and upping sticks forever. It's a lot, Elin. We see that."

Elin sniffed. "I know, but your lives seem so *sorted*. Partners, jobs you can actually stand, mortgages, babies, Labradors, home deliveries from Waitrose – I mean, you've all 'made it', and I haven't even got a foothold yet and life's racing away from me like a bus I can't seem to catch. I bet even Theo will take one look at me and head for the hills."

"Oh, stop it! For all his money, Theo's had his heart broken too. Who hasn't at our age?" Florence replied, a very slight edge of irritation in her voice. She had young kids. She was tired.

Both women silently sipped their wine, until eventually Elin said, "Remember my favourite writer, George Eliot?"

"Of course! You were obsessed with her. You were the only person in school who read *Middlemarch* for pleasure, aged sixteen!"

"I still love her, but I think she summed me up when she had Philip Wakem describe himself as a bit of a dilettante, someone who never quite gets to grips with life, if that makes sense. *I flutter all ways, and fly in none.* That's me, Flo. I *flutter*, but can never seem to *fly*."

Elin looked over at her other friends who were coming back to the table and guffawing at a joke that only wine could make funny.

"I felt I could in Wales, though," she said quickly. "I felt connected with a part of me that I thought had been shut down after Dad died. And I *did* meet a man there, called Dylan Williams. A musician – well, an aspiring musician. We spent a day together and it was so, well, *easy*."

"Sounds good. Will you ever see him again, do you think?"

"I doubt it. But I guess I have to think that it was good to meet him at all," Elin replied, raising her glass. "Here's to ships that pass in the night!"

SIXTEEN

"Christ, I knew I shouldn't have had that second glass," Elin muttered, when she opened a message from Flo the following morning.

> PLEASE come on Saturday. You promised, remember? You don't have to exchange a word with Theo, Marcus's mate. I want to hear more about the mysterious man in Wales. ;) F. x

Gobbling a bowl of cereal, she decided to apply cold logic to a spark of gossip that could become a wildfire if it went any further. Dylan was a pub singer with a poetic turn of phrase who had no intention of putting down roots anywhere anytime soon. She really did not need someone like that in her life and the sooner everyone, including herself, accepted that, the better.

She replied:

> Flo, it was a day out, nothing more. Honestly. See you at 7 p.m. on Saturday. E. x

The rest of that week was clouded by a malaise that refused to lift, however hard Elin struggled to "stay strong" and "face the fear" as the morning affirmations told her to do. One evening, she made a list of what she could do to make her life more fun, more *affirming*, but as there was no chance of her affording gym membership, organic food and uplifting weekly trips to the theatre in the West End, this only made her feel worse. Her mother messaged from Tuscany rather than call her, as promised, which hurt. Barbara's tone-deaf text was full of plans to put her house on the market before Christmas and genuine-sounding hope that her daughter could find a man "as kind as my George", which didn't help, so Elin responded with the only thing she could think of that might deflect her; saying exactly what she wanted to hear.

> I'm going to dinner at Florence's on Saturday, and she's going to introduce me to her successful, handsome friend Theo. He's very rich and he went to Eton. x

She did not have to wait long for Barbara to add an "oooooh" emoji.

As the weekend crawled into view, Elin began to look forward to Saturday night at Florence's house in Clapham more and more. Despite her huge reservations, she decided to "go with the flow" (that morning's affirmation). It was, after all, the only event on her social calendar for several weeks. She decided to dismiss any preconceptions about Theo too. Hadn't she always striven to follow her father's example in taking people as you found them? She did indulge in some online shopping, however, telling herself that she needed to feel confident when she walked into the room. As soon as she'd pressed "buy now" for a very expensive, perhaps-too-revealing dress, she felt a bit sick, but when it arrived, her worries evaporated when she saw how it skimmed her slim hips and hinted at a full cleavage she was quite proud of.

She could not quite resist googling Theo Rowley, however. This confirmed that he was indeed a very handsome ex-Etonian and the co-founder of a hedge-fund company in Canary Wharf. Despite her reservations about "City types", as she dubbed them, a slight buzz of anticipation, of possibility, began to grow in her belly. Flo had said he was *an old friend,* and she was a discerning woman, so that counted for something. People *do* meet at dinner parties, and miracles do happen, so why not to her? By Friday morning, however hard Elin tried to shut down the fantasy life that filled her head whenever she thought about him, it popped up like a stubborn weed, complete with a house in Twickenham, two kids, a dog and a cream Aga.

"You came! And look at you! Amazing dress. Come on in."

Following her friend down the hall, Elin glimpsed the cheeky faces of Flo's kids, Archie and Lily, crouched at the top of the stairs with Marta, their Spanish au pair, watching people arrive. She winked conspiratorially to let them know their secret was safe with her. The hall led straight into the large kitchen extension at the back, and Elin heard laughter billowing towards her like a warm cloud. It lacked the saccharine top notes of some of the London "do's" she had been to where everyone was looking over your shoulder to check if someone more important was there. The room was full of trendily well-dressed people standing around holding glasses of bubbly. At least a dozen faces turned towards her as she was introduced, and, as usual, she blushed like a schoolgirl.

"This is Elin, one of my bestest friends ever," Florence announced. "And she needs a drink!"

"On it!" said Marcus, Florence's kindly solicitor-husband, sloshing champagne into a huge flute. "*Yakky da*, as you Welshies say."

"Isn't it *iechyd da*/good health?" a deep male voice said from across the room. "Though how I managed to remember that, I have no idea."

Lukewarm laughter rippled around the room before other conversations were resumed, but the speaker moved towards Elin, his hand already outstretched.

"Hi. Theo Rowley. I think I actually learnt that phrase on a team-building course in Llangollen years ago, in case you think I'm fluent or anything. So you're Welsh through and through, are you?"

Elin blushed again as her hand was taken and shaken by one much surer of that everyday gesture than she was. Her initial impression was of a good-looking, confident man in the prime of male life (i.e. anything under fifty-five) and a quick scan of his clothes, haircut and clearly barbered shave confirmed it. Too groomed for her liking, but it had to be said that success was almost oozing out of his pores. She wondered, briefly, what that must feel like.

"I grew up in North Wales, if that counts, but I've forgotten nearly all the Welsh I knew as a kid," she said nervously. "You were right, though; it's *iechyd da*."

He smiled with more warmth than she'd expected. "Great country," he said. "Been to Snowdonia a few times. Stunning place."

His speech was so succinct, so *military*, that Elin felt as if she was being peppered with airgun pellets.

"*Eryri*, you mean? It's not known as Snowdonia anymore."

Theo sipped his wine in reply. "Go back much?"

"Yes, I was there recently. Probably for the last time actually, because..."

"Right. But you're based in London now. Like it?"

"Er, there are more opportunities here, but, well, I..."

"Known Florence and Marcus long?"

"Flo, years and years, but..."

"So, what do you do?"

Elin hesitated before answering this time. She had never met anyone like this before. Why did he ask her questions but not want to hear her answers? Talking to him felt like trying to pin jelly to a wall. She was relieved when Marcus called everyone to the table, and when she felt Theo take her arm and steer her firmly towards the chair next to his, she almost laughed at the contrast between his surety and Dylan's fingers shyly inching towards hers. And yet she found herself sitting down next to him, nonetheless.

By the end of the evening, she knew all about Theo's childhood, schooling, exploits whilst at university in Exeter and stratospherically successful career whereas he knew only that she was a copywriter and liked being out in the countryside. She had also agreed to be Theo's plus-one at the showing of an avant-garde film his friend had directed. Quite how this had come about, she had no clear idea, but her main reason for agreeing was her visualising Anwen puffing on a cigarette and saying, "Why *not*, you silly girl?".

SEVENTEEN

Every one of the seven Novembers Elin had spent in London had been a time of shared excitement as the city whipped itself into a frenzy of festive overwhelm. She could not resist going to Oxford and Regent Street to ooh and ahh at the glittering lights, or buying impulsive gifts for people who would appreciate neither their cost nor her thoughtfulness. For instance, her father had always been as happy with a bar of his favourite chocolate or a box of nutty toffee as with the artisan fisherman's sweater she had carefully chosen for him, so she made sure she always gave him both. Overall, Elin felt that, when it came to Christmas, the anticipation was much better than the event.

That November, however, things were very, very different, because they were almost totally dominated by Theo Rowley. Looking back, Elin visualised that first evening at Florence and Marcus's as the one of the seductive leaves of a Venus flytrap. She was oblivious to their teeth or the fact that, once you ventured too near, you were doomed. At the time, however, each day with Theo seemed pure, frothy indulgence, as he deftly organised her life, which meant she didn't even have to think about it. Soon, she found herself basking in the attentions of a man who had chosen her to be by his side for one glamorous freebie after another and, despite herself, she loved it. It was a bubble bound to burst, a small voice reminded herself in the small hours, but for now, she chose to ignore said voice. This was *fun*, wasn't it? A good thing? Perhaps this was what life could be like if she let herself live a little... since Antoine, she had never dared find out. Once bitten, forever shy.

In fact, for the first few weeks, life was more than "good". Work become much more endurable when a lovely evening awaited, perhaps at the theatre or the opening of an exhibition in parts of London she would never have dared venture to without the new clothes Theo bought for her. Even if the film/exhibition/play/drinks party was rubbish, it was great to be living the London life she had always fantasised about. A weekend in the Cotswolds, snuggled around a blazing fire in a country pub, was infinitely preferable to deciding which series to binge-watch or whether to dye her hair pink or purple to leaven her boredom. The spa he paid for her to join made her glow before she headed to his flat in Barnes in time for him to finish work at 8 p.m. and then head out to a Japanese or Korean restaurant for a late supper. She almost didn't mind cleaning for him every Saturday morning, or doing his washing while he went to the gym; surely it was a small price to pay? Yes, it was tiring, as everything was fast, almost relentless in fact, and Mouse was a bit miserable left alone in the flat in Tooting too often, but Elin decided it would be petty to complain, or to refuse one of Theo's glossy options for a quiet evening in with her cat. Paying her neighbour Yan a fiver to fill the cat bowl once a day was an absolute bargain, but she missed her cat's pawing, purring sessions.

Elin chose not to acknowledge that Theo's interest in her was, well, limited, and there was almost no emotional connection whatsoever. She decided to see this as a plus, as it meant she was unlikely to get hurt. The enthusiasm for Wales he'd expressed at the party was never seen again, which was disquieting, but *nobody can have everything*, Elin chanted like a mantra, and for now this situationship was more than passable. Her friends' enquiries as to how she was and whether they could see her before the next millennium were largely ignored; she was too busy, she told herself as yet another beautiful dress arrived by courier with a card from Theo saying "for tonight".

But by the time December arrived, she was exhausted with the sheer effort of it all. The canapés (which did nothing to head off a terrible hangover the next day) and small talk (usually very small indeed, and about nothing worth hearing) had begun to pall. When Elin realised that she was very much a convenient add-on at events, the possibility of being seen as his "arm candy" made her feel nauseous. She began to feel a pressure to perform, and wondered why he had selected her, before finally realising that it had been almost totally opportunistic: she was *available*. This "fun" was fading fast.

There was no talk of love or commitment, and the sex, which had, at first, excited her after so long without any, had become a cursory exercise, as routine for Theo as reading the Sunday newspapers or checking the stock market. Elin's occasional suggestions of going for a walk in Kew Gardens, or wrapping up and taking a boat trip down the Thames, were always shut down in favour of meeting his friends for sushi, or for brunch on the King's Road. What had felt like a stroke of luck in her life soon felt like an unpayable debt.

One night, as Theo snored lightly beside her, her shallow dreams took her back to Llanberis, to the *Noson Lawen* in the pub, and the sting of raindrops on her face as she clambered up to Anwen's cottage. The intensity of her longing to get out of bed that minute, get a train and go back to Wales was so strong that she had to get up and splash her face with cold water to resist actually acting upon it.

When Theo told her that Simon, another old friend, had bought a small art gallery in Dulwich and was hosting an opening "do", Elin felt her spirits lift a little. She read online that this gallery prided itself on its eclectic collection: minor, more traditional works nestled amongst modernist, pricier ones. She scanned the list of paintings on show and her heart leapt when she read:

Dawn over Llyn Padarn – Anwen Jones – October 1990

Getting ready for the evening was more enjoyable than usual, as she was buzzing with anticipation of seeing one of her old friend's works in all its glory and in such a celebrated setting. Theo could network away; she'd be just fine.

When they arrived, he was immediately surrounded by besuited men that Elin found it impossible to differentiate. She had concluded that most of these men were, like him, experts in "boomerasking", a newly identified social habit that saw people asking you a question (such as "Where did you spend the summer?") only to reply to their answer with a monosyllable ("Right"), followed by a long and detailed exposition about themselves ("We were on Corsica, fabulous snorkelling... blahblahblah"). Once she had spotted this habit, Elin could not unspot it.

When, with a slight nod, Theo gave her permission to browse the paintings on her own, she grabbed a glass of wine and walked quickly around the perimeter of the main room, scouring the paintings for Anwen's. Finally, in a rather gloomy corner, she found it, badly lit and badly framed, but still resplendent amidst the other, rather affected, artworks that surrounded it. Elin went within inches of the canvas and gasped at the visible brushstrokes, the gentle dappling of clouds and the iridescence of the water that Anwen had somehow managed to capture and convey. She felt herself drawn into it, breathing deeply as her eyes drank in the unfettered peace of the scene: the woods in which only she knew that *Cân y mynyddoedd* was hidden; the lake, glittering in the early sunlight and the grey-black, looming mountains that surrounded it. Painted in the same year she'd been born, Elin, when she closed her eyes, could almost feel the breeze on her face, see the queue of noisy gulls gathered on the wooden jetty. But however hard she tried, however much she longed to, she could not hear the soft medley of sounds that made up the song of the mountains. You had to be there, to experience that, and she was not.

"What on earth are you doing?"

Theo was behind her. When Elin opened her eyes and turned around, his annoyance was clear.

"Sorry. It's just that my friend, the old lady at home I told you about, painted this. Isn't it brilliant?" she said excitedly. Surely, he would remember someone so important to her, and something she had told him about at some length? If he had forgotten, it would be a huge red flag.

"The old lady you once said you wanted to spend Christmas with, you mean?" he said. Theo had been pushing their going to a villa in Capri over Christmas with a group of friends, but Elin had not committed yet.

"I did promise her I would go back, yes." A pause, in which tension hummed. "For now, just tell me what you think of her painting – I really want to know."

Theo sniffed. "It's nice, yes. Suitably dark and moody." He looked at his watch.

When it seemed that was all he was likely to say, Elin persisted:

"Yes, it is, but when the sun shines, it's so..."

"Yes, yes. Come over here and join me. There's a chap I need to meet."

A hesitation. An intake of breath, before Elin said, "I'll be there in a minute."

He nodded briskly, and walked away, his hands linked behind his back.

She really needed that minute to think.

EIGHTEEN

Things did not improve between them as Christmas drew ever nearer and by the middle of December, where to spend those crucial few days had become an issue. Everything came to a head one Thursday morning a week before Christmas. They were both at work, but Sadie had taken the day off to go shopping – which was fortuitous, because Elin could do no work whatsoever once the barrage of messages from Theo about Sicily began. She replied calmly that she had to do what felt best, and that was going home to see Anwen, as she'd promised, but she hoped he would have a lovely time with his friends on Capri. She wanted to say that surely theirs was far from a relationship, but more of a mutually beneficial partnership, but didn't dare.

An hour or so later, she received his reply:

> I really think, after everything I've done for you,
> you ought to come with me. Your old lady won't
> even remember your promise. I need a decision as
> flight prices are ROCKETING.

Immediately, one of George Eliot's gem-like phrases popped into her head:

"I am not magnanimous enough to like people who speak to me without seeming to see me."

Theo was one such person; he did not see her, the real her, and neither did he want to. She fulfilled a purpose in his life, but she had no real place in it. Anger began to stir in her belly; anger with herself for being so easily drawn in, and with Theo, who clearly saw her as something he had bought and paid for. He had used her as much as she had used him, but she would have no more of it.

Looking back, Elin always said that moment had been what her favourite literary heroines seemed to have on a regular basis: an epiphany. What had been *fun* had now become three stark *facts*:

1. She had to agree with whatever Theo said.
2. She had to do what Theo wanted to do.
3. She had to wear, eat and say whatever Theo decreed.

How on earth had she allowed herself to be boxed-in like this?

Messages from Theo stopped until just after 4.30 p.m., when the markets closed in London. Then, another one pinged into her inbox as she was struggling to finish a piece about non-alcoholic festive fizz and vegan entremets:

Elin, I need to know NOW.

She faltered. Googling Capri quickly, it looked gorgeous. And would Anwen remember her promise to go back? She hadn't heard a word from her since her return to London, though Elin knew she despised using mobiles. And true to form, Dylan had not been in touch, nor she with him. When her phone rang, she was trembling as she answered, expecting a furious Theo.

"Hello, is that Elin Pugh? It's one of the district nurses in Gwynedd here. Anwen Jones has given your name as her next of kin. Is that correct?"

Shocked, Elin said nothing. *Next of kin?* In seconds, she understood. Anwen had no real "next of kin", so perhaps had had no choice but to nominate her. Elin felt a tingle of pride that she had done so, nevertheless.

"Yes, er, well, I suppose so. Is she OK?"

"No, I'm afraid she's had a fall. A hill-walker found her, in her garden, apparently and she was very lucky as it's such a remote spot. No broken bones, but plenty of wounded pride to be honest with you. She's in *Ysbyty Gwynedd*/Gwynedd Hospital and her dog's with the people at the hotel."

Elin recalled Anwen warning her about the fear elderly people had of having a fall. Nobody, not even Anwen Jones, was invincible.

"Hello, are you still there?" the nurse continued. "She's stable and could go home in day or two if there was someone at home to keep an eye until she's steady on her feet again. I don't suppose there's any way you could help, is there? She said you work in London, but had planned to come back to Wales for Christmas, and she's so... *fed up* in here."

"Oh, I can imagine," Elin replied, laughing. "I'll try and be there the day after tomorrow, Saturday. And I'll pick her dog up too."

"*Mae'n fendegedig.*/That's fantastic. *Diolch*/Thanks."

Elin hung up, and sagged back in her chair with a huge sigh of relief. Anwen *had* remembered her promise, and she'd expected her to keep it. Looking after an immobile and irascible old woman would not be easy, but it would be infinitely preferable to Christmas in Capri with Theo and his boomerasking mates. She would have to take Mouse to Wales this time, as Yan would be going home to Poland, but her cat would probably love basking by Anwen's fireplace with Merlin and Smot. It would be idyllic. The only flies in the ointment were telling Theo and Sadie.

The moment she was home, she got into her dressing gown, poured herself a large glass of wine. Then, she texted Theo:

Anwen is in hospital after a fall. I have to go and
look after her as she has nobody else. Sorry about
Capri. E.

A very long ten minutes later, his reply arrived:

Understood, but bad form imo. She's not your
mother.

Feeling her courage rise, she wondered what her father would
have replied to this shoddiness. She knew that he would tell her to
be "dignified but decisive", so she tried, very hard, to be both:

I'm sorry you feel like that. I think whatever we had
together is over, Theo. I'll collect my stuff and
leave the key tomorrow. I'm leaving on Saturday.

Then, she blocked his number.

As Mouse circled on her lap, purring and kneading her legs
with his paws, Elin succumbed to a minute or two of self-pity, but
she had no real doubts and no regrets; this was for the best, and she
was free to carry on seeking her own future, her way, even if that
meant doing so alone. She was used to that.

The only niggling doubt she had was whether she should
message Dylan, in case he was going to be at home, just on the off
chance that they could meet up, go for a walk, a drink, a chat. She
agonised about whether she was only doing so because things were
over with Theo, and whether he had, in fact, forgotten all about her
anyway. At 11 p.m., she finally sent:

Hi. Hope you're well. Going to be back in Wales
for Christmas, so perhaps we could meet up. E.

When his reply appeared within five minutes, she smiled.

Yes, great. I'll be home as well but got lots on tbh.
Wela di yn fuan./See you soon. D.

The tone was friendly, casual, which was just what she'd

expected, and matched her own message. And yet Elin could not suppress a flicker of sadness at her inability to convey what she really felt, hiding, instead, behind a barricade of bland informality that few people would spot, let alone bother to break through. She could not risk exposing how often she had thought about him, and their time together. Everyone was busy with their own lives, their own needs. How could she expect Dylan to trust her, when she could not trust him?

NINETEEN

Sadie was not at all happy at the prospect of Elin going off to North Wales before the official agency Christmas break. When she summoned her into her office, her face made a phrase Barbara often used spring to Elin's mind: Sadie looked "as if she was sucking a lemon".

"Sit down, Elin. We need to have a chat," she said, shutting down her PC and swivelling her chair to face Elin head-on. "This is not on, I'm afraid. We need total commitment here at Green Olive, to the agency and to our reputation for excellence, and I'm not feeling either of those things from you."

The only reply Elin could muster was, "Right."

"I understood your need for a break in the autumn, as you said yourself your work wasn't up to scratch, but I can't agree to this request. We all have pressures in our lives, but the work still needs to be done and you're being paid to do it."

"I know," Elin said.

Sadie sat back in her chair, warming to her theme. "We have just landed a big contract with one of the biggest biscuit producers in Europe, and I need copy that sparkles in the campaign – words that jump off the page, break the mould." She paused for effect. "Do you think you can produce that, Elin? Your piece about

Christmas nibbles was dull, dull, dull. This agency aims high, and we need the whole team to be…"

As she talked, Elin watched, mesmerised, as a huge crane outside the window swung around 180 degrees, causing the steel girder at the end of some cables to lurch precariously. In its cab, a tiny man in a tiny yellow hat was gesticulating wildly as the girder was slowly lowered to the ground and out of view. Elin found herself picturing Sadie in a yellow hard hat, waving instructions at her for an endless cycle of utterly pointless tasks for the rest of her thirties, and beyond. It simply could not happen, whatever the cost.

"I have to go back to Wales and look after my friend. I'm sorry, but she needs me," she said, her voice low and calm. "I know it's not ideal, but…"

"No, and it's not *possible* either," Sadie said. "You've had all your leave this year and I can't let people have days off willy-nilly."

After a slow in-breath, Elin said, "I will make the time up next year, but I really do have to go."

A crimson flush spread up from Sadie's chest to her neck and into her face. "I do not give you permission to do so."

Several thoughts rushed through Elin's mind like a mini-tsunami. She needed this job to pay her rent, and she would soon owe £850 for January. Copywriting was not her dream, but it was a career, and her mother had said she was good at it. Sadie was scary, spiteful, and could probably jeopardise her getting another job in another agency. And everyone had to compromise in life, didn't they? Hmm, that one always jarred.

"If I don't go, I'll never forgive myself. Anwen is more important than biscuits," she said, eventually, with a boldness that almost shocked her.

Sadie spluttered in astonishment. "Really? You think so? Then go – but you won't be coming back if you do. We are not a charity."

Ten minutes later, Elin was jobless, standing in the street with a cardboard box of the few things that had been on her desk. The agency operated a "clean desk" policy in case their trade secrets were shared, an affectation Elin had always laughed at, but now made her *feel* like a character in a movie she'd once seen as she looked up at the soulless glass and metal office building for the last time.

An hour later, as she closed the door of Theo's flat and posted his spare key through the letter box, she recognised a slight swell of panic, but when it had passed, she felt strong and sure. She would give in her notice at the flat, pack up and leave London before another month's rent was due. But before any of that could happen, there were three messages she had to send.

First, she messaged Barbara whom she knew was spending Christmas with George:

> Mum, Anwen's had a fall, so I'm spending Christmas there to look after her. Decided to leave London, so I might need to stay at home (Bethesda) once she's on her feet again. Could you possibly leave the spare key in the cupboard in the shed this one time? Have a good time in Bath. E. x

Feeling she had to remind her mother where she thought of as "home" was painful, but she appreciated Barbara's swift thumbs-up emoji reply. She was obviously too busy to split hairs this time.

Second, a message to her friends informing them that she was moving back home for a while but would keep in touch, followed by muting the group as a defensive tactic.

Finally, she messaged her landlord to give in her notice, hoping he would be lenient with the month he had asked for when she'd moved in seven years earlier. He was, telling her it was fine as he could put the flat on Airbnb next week and make much more money anyway.

"Win-win," Elin muttered. "It's so easy to leave your life behind. Who knew?"

It was dark by the time she got home, and the air was crisp. Frost was already stiffening the grass in Tooting Common, and when Elin glanced up to the orange-tinged blackness blanketing the city, a few pale stars dotted the sky. She was drifting now, a ship without a course, but then she remembered what Dylan had told her: the stars have guided the lost for hundreds of years – all we need to do is trust them. Theo had been a distraction, and one she had willingly followed, but the knowledge that she would never see him again only distilled her certainty that it was better to be a lone traveller than to be on the wrong road, or not to be travelling at all. Again, some of George Eliot's words floated into her mind, as apt now as when she had first read them at school.

"I would not creep along the coast but steer
Out in mid-sea, by guidance of the stars."

Wherever the stars led, her future would be hers, and hers alone.

TWENTY

Anwen was a pitiful sight when Elin brought her home from hospital. Her face was badly grazed all down the right side and she had a spectacularly black right eye. Her right arm was in a sling and although no bones were broken, everything was so bruised and sore that she could not move it without crying out in pain. She was angry and difficult, pushing Elin away if she tried to help her get up, or offered to cut her food up to make one-handed eating easier. Smoking with her left hand proved especially tricky as she couldn't quite reach the ashtray, so a thin layer of ash soon coated the entire cottage floor. Smot seemed to know not to go too near her and lay, miserably, on the floor beneath Anwen's chair.

Things were far from comfortable for Elin as well. She slept on the saggy horsehair sofa, and it was so cold in the cottage once the fire had gone out that she could see her breath. She often found that Mouse had snuck under her thick woollen blankets both for warmth during the night, and to hide from Merlin and Smot, both of whom were obsessed with her. Elin was not sure which one of them was more stressed, her, or her beleaguered cat.

She tried to encourage Anwen to eat some homemade soup or listen as she read out interesting articles from the newspaper, but her friend was resolutely maudlin and ate very little. When Elin asked her how she had fallen, the old woman snarled that she had tripped over something when outside feeding the chickens, and had just been unlucky, but it was obvious that things would never be the same again, and she knew it.

"I will never drive again. I'm trapped, marooned," she wailed, and Elin had not the heart to tell her that everyone in the area had already been giving her ancient Renault 4 a very wide berth for years. Harder to hear was her cry of, "I will never paint again. What will I *do* with myself if I can't paint?"

When things got too gloomy, Elin made an exhausted Anwen a warm drink laced with brandy and took Smot out for a walk as soon as she was safely asleep. The cold air made her gasp, and she often slipped on the slew of frosted mulch under all the trees that never thawed as the day was never warm enough, but she needed those hours of chilly solitude. It gave her time to think, as she had to make a plan, decide on something, but however hard she tried, the future stretched ahead with no landmarks in its long, blank vista. Seeing this as something exciting was incredibly difficult at times, and she pushed the fact that she was nearly thirty-two, single, childless, jobless and homeless into touch time and time again. Yes, what lay ahead was a *tabula rasa*, which was not ideal, but as the dust started to settle on her decision, she decided it was cathartic to have cast off from the anchors of her past – her mother, her friends, Sadie, Theo, even Dylan, whatever he represented. Right now, the only things linking her to the universe were Anwen, Mouse, Merlin and Smot; in most ways, that felt good.

On a day cold enough to freeze the water in the chickens' bowl, the sky was a stunning blue – a stark juxtaposition that Elin had only ever experienced here, in North Wales. She remembered her father cracking the ice for the cows in the barn whilst the wintry sun made the mossy roof steam. Here, seasons could nestle alongside each other, warning against assumptions that winter was always cold, and summer always hot. The sea could feel at its warmest in October, but the weather might be absolutely appalling.

Whilst the district nurse checked Anwen's progress and changed dressings, Elin drove the old Renault 4 down into Llanberis, and steeled herself to drive the lovely, lonely road through Nant Ffrancon again, and past *Wern Farm*, her childhood home. It would be painful, but she was drawn to it as one of the few immutable things in her life, a constant that had always been there, and always would be even if she would never live in it again. The farmhouse looked even bleaker than when she and Dylan had seen it. The front door had now been padlocked, more tiles on the roof had slipped and one of the windows had a large, jagged hole in it. It had been abandoned.

As she drove away, she glimpsed an elderly man, head down, leaning on his gnarled wooden walking stick and walking very slowly towards her with two beautiful collies trotting alongside him. When he lifted his head, Elin stopped and got out of the car to greet him. Ifor Llewellyn had always been their postman, and she had looked forward to his smiles and occasional rides to the end of the road in his red van.

"*Ifor! Sut dach chi?*/How are you?" she said.

As she watched, his expression changed like quicksilver from initially startled, to wariness and finally, into a hesitant smile.

"*Sori, pwy wyt ti?*/Sorry, who are you?"

"It's me, Elin Pugh, Llion's daughter, from *Wern Farm*," she said gently, moving closer to him so that he could see her more clearly. His glasses were as thick as bottle-bottoms.

He stepped back, and stood staring at her with his mouth wide open.

"*Elin fach*/Little Elin," he replied after a very long silence. Gingerly, he put his hands on her shoulders and stared some more. "You look... *hyfryd*/ beautiful, yes, that's what you look."

"*Diolch*/Thanks," Elin said, and Ifor looked at her, clearly expecting more. It had been so long since she had used her Welsh that her mouth could not produce more of the words she had once known well. She resorted to English:

"Have they gone, the people that bought it? I never knew who they were, but the old farm looks empty."

The old man shook his head. "Back to the Home Counties, and with their tail between their legs. Couldn't cope with the weather, the sheep or the damp, I heard. Silly idea, to come here if you're not born to it, and aren't used to hard work, *a dweud y gwir*/to tell the truth." His accent was so broad, the consonants so thickly spoken, that Elin had to concentrate hard to understand him at all.

"That's a bit harsh, Ifor. I'm sure they wanted it all to work out."

The old man snorted. "Wanting won't help you if you can't farm, however keen you are. The farm's for sale, but it'll be a fool that buys it, in the state it's in now. Beyond rescue, I'd say. Probably be sold for a song, done up by some property developer and rented out, with hot tubs in your mother's vegetable patch," Ifor said bitterly. "Still, someone needs to take care of it again, like your father did, and his father before him, come rain or shine."

When Elin did not respond, as a huge lump in her throat prevented her from speaking, Ifor took his cap off and scratched his head. He saw he had upset her.

"Aren't you living in London these days? Where are you staying? With your mother in '*Pesda*/Bethesda?"

"Er, no," Elin said. How much should she say? Perhaps Barbara's engagement and her plans to sell and leave Wales had not yet reached the active local gossip network yet. Any doubts on this score were soon quashed when Ifor answered for her.

"Hear she's getting married again, and moving back down South," he said. "She never settled here, poor woman. Square peg, round hole, see?"

Suppressing the urge to giggle at his phraseology, Elin chose to be honest. "I'm staying with Anwen Jones, actually. I've left London. She had a bad fall and needs some help, you see."

Ifor's face paled. "Bloody hell. Anwen Jones. Still up in that cottage, is she? We all used to say it was haunted, and she was a witch, you know."

"I thought that, too, when I was little, but she's just a... very strong character," Elin said, slightly unnerved. Did *anyone* have a good opinion of Anwen? "I like it up there, actually. I used to visit her cottage as a child, in fact, with Dad. Do you know her well?"

The old man looked up, and his expression was odd, so veiled that Elin did not know how to react. This was getting weird.

"Well, I knew her in as much as I delivered her mail from the first year she came back to live in that cottage, until they changed my round to this one. Everyone knows about Anwen, *cariad*/love, but nobody really *knows* her, if you get my drift. She got up to plenty of mischief back in the day, some things everyone's heard about, and a lot more they haven't," he said.

Elin was *very* curious now. Barbara had been similarly oblique when talking about Anwen's shady history.

"I know she had a colourful past, as my mother put it, but is there more I should know? I'm the one that's living with her now, remember."

"*Duw*/God no. Well, nothing you need to worry yourself about right now anyway," Ifor said. "Water under the bridge." He shifted from foot to foot uneasily.

Puzzled, Elin decided it would be best to change the subject, so she asked a question that had been buzzing around inside her head like an irritating fly for weeks.

"Ifor, as you know everyone around here, did you know Dylan Williams' family? The parents are both dead now, but I think his sister is still on their smallholding."

The old man cleared his throat. "I knew the father back in the day. A fool and a rascal, leaving his poor wife, and her so ill. The girl's a strange one, but nice enough. Dylan was always the best of the bunch I recall, and he had a really hard time a few years back, but he's headed for fame and fortune, I hear. Probably a *poen yn y pen-ôl*/pain in the bum by now."

Elin could not help but laugh at this.

"Well, if he's not already, he probably will be soon," she said.

"But you're sure there's no dark secret about Anwen that I should know about, Ifor?"

Ifor hesitated, then shook his head firmly. "She's a tricky old bag, always was, but her heart's in the right place. *Reit, rhaid i mi fynd*/Right, got to go."

As he walked away at a much faster pace than he had approached her, he did not look back at her once to see her waving at him.

Driving home, surrounded by the mountains now lightly iced with snow, Elin's thoughts were free to roam. She decided to try to dismiss any more vicarious curiosity about Anwen. It would make living under the same roof very difficult if she asked awkward questions about her and received similarly awkward answers, and who was she to judge what the old woman had done decades earlier? She had enough to think about.

She thought about the English people who had bought the farm, trying to do something brave and different. The beauty of this place had obviously seduced them, but they had clearly rivalled Dylan's parents in their understanding of the terrain, and the hardships involved in trying to work the land, but at least they had *tried* to follow a dream, which she admired. Mingling with her sympathy for them was relief, however, that nobody else was now warming themselves by the fire after a cold, wet day on the hills, as her father had always done. Whatever lay ahead for *Wern Farm*, it would always hold a special place in her heart; despite everything, it was the only home she had ever known.

TWENTY-ONE

Elin was thankful not to be in London, amidst all the frantic list-checking, queuing, buying and overriding air of panic everywhere you went in the run-up to the grotesque festival of consumerism Christmas seemed to have become. Her friends left breathless voicemails asking how she was, but she could tell that their thoughts were centred either on how to survive three days with their in-laws, what to eat for The Main Meal or whether they had bought enough gifts to be perceived "fair" by their children. She thought of Theo, bound for Capri, and wondered if he had found another plus-one to go with him yet. She had no doubt he would have tried to.

In *Cân y mynyddoedd*, the days inched past, but they followed a comfortingly predictable routine. Conversation began to replace the sullen silence as Anwen's bruises faded, her arm began to heal and her frostiness thawed. When the sling came off, she could resume chain-smoking, and Elin knew that things were looking up when she saw the blissful expression on her face with every cigarette she lit. Still reserved, still reluctant, the old woman eventually allowed Elin to wash her, and even shampoo her wispy hair. When she needed help to go to the bathroom, she called Elin and held her hand when it was difficult to get on and off the commode, but her jaw was tight at the indignity of this. Having always been fiercely selfish and totally independent, the old woman now had to rely on others; it was not easy, but it was happening, whether she wanted it to or not. For Elin, it was a full-time job.

On Christmas Eve, Anwen consented to join her in listening to the carol service from King's College Cambridge on the radio as Elin prepared food for tomorrow, and even expressed some luke-warm interest at the smells emanating from the saucepans.

"Is that mulled wine?"

"Mmm, I can smell minced pies."

"I suppose I might try a bit of that stuffing tomorrow."

Having not cooked much beyond pasta and pesto or poached eggs on toast in her flat in London, Elin relished doing so in the cottage, and had even managed to organise a large supermarket delivery with crates full of ingredients and treats that would, she hoped, lift their spirits as they both faced a Christmas like no other. Awash with memories of Barbara's dry, stringy turkey, she spent hours looking online for recipes which offered new twists on the traditional fare at Christmas, such as stuffing (add chicken broth and celery), bread sauce (stud the onion with cloves) and even Brussel sprouts (roasted, drizzled with olive oil). When she and Anwen sat down to eat at about 2 p.m. on Christmas Day, there was no sound to be heard except their soft murmurs of pleasure. Within ten minutes, both had cleared their plates.

"That was the best Christmas dinner I have ever tasted," Anwen said, emptying her wine glass with a slurp. "I can almost *feel* it helping my poor body heal."

Elin glowed with pride. Praise had always been such a scarce commodity in her home that to be given some so wholeheartedly made her almost tearful.

"Wait until you taste the pudding," she said. "Mum would be proud of me. She was always good at puddings."

"I'm sure she already is – proud, I mean," Anwen said, look-ing up.

"Ha! She's never praised me in her life! Not her style at all."

"Then she's even more of a fool than I thought," Anwen replied, with such a look of sadness on her face that Elin refilled her wine glass to cheer her up.

Two helpings of pudding later, Anwen was fast asleep in her armchair by the fire, mouth open, knobbly hands folded over her rounded *bol*/belly. Mouse squeezed alongside her right hip, equally replete with turkey scraps. Smot clearly needed a walk after the rich leftovers, so Elin tugged on her coat and boots and headed outside before the light began to fade on the day in which so much was, literally, invested by so many millions of people around the world. The sky looked brighter on top of the hill behind the cottage, so they headed up rather than down, towards the lake.

Elin picked her way carefully through the rocks and scatterings of smaller stones around them. At the top, she pulled off her woolly hat and used it as a basic cushion so she could sit on a rocky ledge and survey the scene rolled out before her like a dappled canvas. As she watched, tiny lights started to come on in the village below, specks of light in the darkening gloom. They formed a chain of pearlescent gems down either side of the main street, and looped up into the smaller streets that headed up into the hills. Elin could see garish Christmas lights throbbing in gardens, street lamps with their cold orange glow and strings of jewel-like fairy lights strung between shops. For the first time, she allowed herself to feel sad that she had not heard from Dylan. Had something happened that had prevented him getting in touch? Had he somehow heard about Theo, perhaps? Dylan had a far from straightforward relationship with his sister so perhaps things had been difficult on the small-holding. Despite all her avowals of not really caring, and well aware that she had not contacted *him*, and couldn't bring herself to do so, she wondered how his Christmas was going. Had he thought of her at all on this uniquely intense day, as she was thinking of him?

When a cold breeze rushed through the trees making the leaves shiver and sending a blackbird skittering into the undergrowth, Elin closed her eyes to listen more closely to this, different, variation of the song of the mountains. Whether she saw him or not, even on this short, dark winter's day, there was so much *life* to be relished here if she simply allowed herself to feel it and absorb its energy.

Just as she was starting to get so cold she was considering going back, something altered in the air – a tightening, a tension that made the hairs on her arms stand up. She had not expected to see anyone and was genuinely alarmed when she heard the crunch of boots on the ground, and the breath of a fellow climber. Who on earth would trudge up here today, when family obligations, boxes of chocolates and endless Christmas viewing beckoned? This was not the place for a stroll – it was so hidden away, a well-kept, woodland secret. Calling Smot to her side, she held on to her collar as a low growl made the dog's body hum.

Fixing her eyes on a small opening in the dense tree cover around their rocky platform, a shape began to come into view – a long, large body and a head which had what looked like branches on either side of it. It was not a person, but a stag, magnificent in its perfection, very slowly edging towards her, placing each hoof with silent surety. This was his world, and she was safe in it only with his consent. She watched, breath held, as the stag sniffed the ground, nibbling some succulent greenery only a few metres in front of her – so close that she could smell its muskiness, see the white lining of its ears and see into its large brown eyes. Smot was really trembling now, as if in awe of this creature, this ruler of this mountainside who would stand strong against all comers. Elin gasped as the stag lifted its head once more, its eyes met hers and held her gaze for several seconds before snorting a pale cloud of breath into the air, turning and vanishing into the forested gloom it had emerged from.

She stayed quite still, and could take only small, quick breaths for a minute or two; her limbs felt as if they were paralysed. Sightings of red deer in these mountains were very rare and to see a stag in all its glory was a real gift. When she and Smot carefully walked down to the cottage in near-darkness, she brooded on what it could have meant, to have witnessed something this unique. There must be a folkloric interpretation of something so utterly magical. Anwen would know it, if there was.

She burst into the cottage just as the old woman was waking up, her face still suffused with comfort and warmth from the fire.

"I saw a stag – a huge one. He came right up to me. I could almost feel his breath on my face," she blurted. "It was... it was astonishing!"

The old woman smiled, as if to herself. Elin went and sat on the flagstones near her chair, and looked up into her face as if searching it.

"So, what does it mean, to see a stag like that – to look into its eyes and for it to look into mine?" she whispered. "It must mean something, surely."

"I don't know for sure, but I would say it means you are blessed, *cariad*/love," Anwen said. "And perhaps that you are meant to be here right now, with me."

But Elin was unconvinced that was all her experience had meant. Part of her felt that the stag was telling her more, of possibilities beyond this place, and of a world in which extraordinary things could happen if she was brave enough to let them. If she trusted herself enough.

TWENTY-TWO

By December 30th, Anwen's bruises were a very pale yellow, and she was almost as mobile as she had been before her fall. Her confidence was returning more slowly, however, and she relied on her walking stick to move around the cottage, coughing vigorously as she tapped her way from room to room. Elin felt a little easier leaving her alone to pop into Llanberis or for slightly longer walks, but she was beginning to feel cabin fever setting in. When she had a text from Gwenda in the pub inviting her to come to a New Year's Eve party, she wanted to go so much that she knew it was time to get out, and, perhaps, get away from Anwen for an evening. The two women had been cooped-up together for what felt like an age, and Elin was bridling at how this curtailed her freedom. The old woman's response to her request to go out was totally unlike the sulky disappointment she'd expected, however. Anwen was furious.

"For goodness' sake, do you think I need babysitting?" she'd yelled, dropping her bread roll into the bowl of soup Elin had just given her. "I have lived here on my own for a very long time. I just slipped! I am not decrepit yet."

Mortified, Elin struggled to reply. "I know that. I just wanted to check you weren't worried about being alone all evening." She saw Anwen's eyelid twitch slightly; she *was* worried, but she had no intention of saying so. "I won't leave until about 8 p.m., and I'll be back by half twelve," she added.

The old woman urgently rubbed the splodges of soup on her jumper. "I've always hated New Year's Eve, so I'll probably be in bed by 8 p.m. anyway," she growled, refusing to look up, and at Elin.

"Good. I don't need to worry then," Elin said, before slowly reaching over and laying a hand over Anwen's. "I care about you. I just wanted to tell you."

When the old woman lifted her face, Elin saw that she was grateful.

On the following evening, New Year's Eve, Anwen said she was exhausted, and wanted to go to bed even earlier than usual, at 7.30 p.m. She would "read her book and drink her tea in peace for once", but her downcast expression showed that reality had finally hit, and hit hard. She had begun to realise that she could no longer live alone without more help and Elin had realised that she was not sure how much longer she could spend each day with someone whose life was drawing to a close just as hers was, hopefully, starting anew. This was a painful process for both of them, but a necessary one. Things could not stand still.

Having unmuted her friends' WhatsApp group, Elin found herself laughing at their witty takes on Christmas with tantrums, arguments and elderly relations who discussed their grisly ailments over dinner. How long could she avoid real life here with Anwen without finding she had run aground with no incoming tide to free her? There was no future in hiding here with an ill, old woman.

The whole situation was a tangled web of needs and wishes and difficult decisions, but as she got ready to go out, Elin had a slightly lighter heart, knowing that both of them had at least begun to face the truth and to look to the future.

· · ·

On her way down to the pub, her phone lit up the path, but the darkness around the silvery strip it cast was all-enveloping. Whilst Elin's eyes concentrated on where to place her feet, her thoughts wandered off track. Would Dylan be there this evening? She had tried not to care, but as she walked into the pub reception, she scanned every face for his.

The party was well underway, with most people already flushed and talking loudly at anyone within range. The place was festooned with tinsel, paper chains and fake candles. A log fire burnt at either end of the room and the luridly bright lights on a massive Christmas tree throbbed in one corner, an unignorable pulse. As a wave of intense heat hit her, Elin peeled off her coat, her cardigan and her scarf as she felt her entire body begin to expand. Her dress soon felt too tight and within ten minutes, so she took off her tights in the ladies' and splashed her face with cold water. The contrast between this and Anwen's freezing cottage was almost unbearable.

Gwenda was behind the bar, and greeted her with a wave and a smile, but she was far too busy to chat once Elin had bought her drink – lemonade, as she could not risk walking back through the woods alone after a drink or two. As she looked around, she realised with a creeping unease that she knew nobody else in the room at all. Having felt so welcomed at the *Noson Lawen* last time, she did not feel so now. All around her, groups of lifelong friends and acquaintances were drinking, chatting – almost entirely in Welsh – but she stood alone just inside the door. Nobody greeted her, as nobody knew her, and she had never felt so alone as when she eventually found a small table in a corner and sat down. This had been a terrible mistake.

For the next hour or so, she tried to express interest in the grandchildren of an elderly Welsh couple near her and to look animated when a rotund, middle-aged sheep farmer several pints ahead of her described the temperaments of different breeds to her in incredibly-accented English, but it was hard work and lemonade failed to soften the edges. When messages from her friends began to come in, with accompanying videos of their bijou gatherings and close-ups of bottles of Prosecco in a baby-bath full of ice, Elin felt even worse. She could have been there, with them – or even in Capri with Theo, in a luxury villa overlooking the glittering Tyrrhenian Sea. Had leaving her life in London and coming home to look after Anwen been another stupid decision to add to her collection? Right now, it felt as if it had been. But if this place *wasn't* in fact home, where on earth *was*?

When tears pricked, she stood up to leave – and saw Dylan on the other side of the room, laughing, his cheeks puce and half-empty pint in hand. He had his arm draped around a young woman's shoulder and she was holding his limp hand with both of hers, as if fearful he would let go. Elin took in the woman's basic details in a nanosecond: pretty, dark straight hair, very slim, with angular cheekbones and a slightly otherworldly look about her. Elin watched, unable to look away, as Dylan kissed the girl's cheek fondly and smiled.

"Now, I know why you told me you had 'lots on'," she muttered bitterly.

For the first time, she realised that, despite all her efforts not to risk being hurt, she had allowed a germ of hope to remain, hope that this gentle, unusual man felt the same way about her as she did about him. They had spent so little time together, and yet she had felt something she could not explain, an ease, an acceptance of who she was and who he was too. Obviously, she had been fooled again, and she had merely been a convenient way for him to fill a few empty hours between shifts. Fury coursed through her, she cursed her own weakness. Shoving her way to the bar to say goodbye to Gwenda, who was sitting down for a breather, she found herself asking:

"Do you know who that woman is, with Dylan Williams?"

"Can't see any woman, *cariad*/love, but he's been alone too long, so I'm glad if he's courting again," Gwenda replied, and when Elin looked over to check, both Dylan and the young woman had vanished into the night. Her imagination running riot and her curiosity piqued, she asked:

"Didn't he have much luck with girls in the past?"

"Oh, he did. Lovely girl she was, Alys, but she died in a motorbike crash they had with a drunk driver. It's taken him years to get over losing her. I'm delighted if he has now, and she's a lucky lady, I tell you," Gwenda said, her cheerfulness rising as quickly as Elin's heart sank. "He's doing really well – doing gigs, touring the country at the moment and hoping for a recording contract. We're so happy for him, Emlyn and I."

Elin smiled a smile that hurt her face, grabbed her stuff and sprinted outside, where she took in huge gulps of the icy air as if it were the elixir of life. A familiar voice in her head began to rant, insistent, impossible to silence. What had she expected, when she had made him relive painful memories with her on his afternoon off? His messages had been polite, kind even, but nothing more. In fact, he must have thought her very high maintenance and certainly not worth getting to know any better. Hadn't every man she had ever spent time with come to the same conclusion? They had, so they must be right.

The walk home felt long, and her phone was almost out of charge, so the light it gave was feeble, but with each step Elin felt less scared and isolated. There was nobody else around and it seemed as if the world had somehow paused before it began the endless activity another year would bring. Above her, owls hooted and hunted, their soft wings whooshing as they cruised through the trees. Other noises rang out: a vixen, her primeval yowl echoing off the hills in the stillness; small animals sniffed and scurried away through the leaf mulch once they heard her nearing. They were far more frightened than she was, so she trod with care through their secret world. It was pitch black, and there were no comforting stars pinpricking the sky that night. She was quite alone in the world – in more ways than one – so she was more than grateful to have this night-time song of the mountains around her as the new year began. It surpassed any drunken "Auld Lang Syne" in the pub; it offered her peace rather than regrets for the year that had ended or unattainable goals for the one that had just begun.

No, she did not know where her life path led, and every one she tried to follow seemed to be a dead end, but George Eliot had expressed how reluctant she felt to force things, or second-guess the future:

"Among all forms of mistake, prophecy is the most gratuitous."

TWENTY-THREE

For the following few days, both Anwen and Elin were more subdued versions of themselves. A heavy snowfall on January 3rd deadened any noise outside the cottage, and this uncanny quietening seemed to seep inside too. No voices were raised, no doors were slammed and a weary-seeming Smot hardly bothered to explore this new white world. Both women ate, slept and talked only when they needed to and the days passed slowly. They knew that the cause of this shifting mood in the cottage was that change was coming. Elin told Anwen that she needed to organise more care for her, and that she would be moving out to live in Barbara's house in Bethesda. The old woman was a little frightened, but she understood.

"I want you to feel *free* here, not tethered to me. I am only going one way, and that's down. You need to live your best life, as they say these days!"

Elin saw once more that her friend was perhaps less selfish than her reputation.

Once offices had reopened after the winter break, Elin contacted several local private care agencies to organise help for Anwen and within a few days, a new routine was in place for carers to call twice a day, to help her get up and dressed and ensure she was safely in bed at night. It was hugely expensive, but waiting for a social services assessment would take months, and Anwen said she had plenty of money to pay for care. Elin would still call each day. What else she would do with her time? she asked herself constantly. And on her last night in *Cân y mynyddoedd*, that question arose as they both sat by the fire after supper – fish and chips from Llanberis that Anwen had craved for weeks.

"I don't mind paying for help, you know. Amazingly, I seem to have amassed a sizeable fortune over the years, and your father gave me the name of a financial adviser who invested it well, Gareth Powell," Anwen began.

Surprised, Elin asked, "I didn't know Dad knew any financial advisers. He left things in a right mess for Mum when he died."

"I know. But Llion wouldn't have wanted Gareth, an old school friend, to know the ins and outs of his finances. Your father was always envious of him, as he'd refused to take over his family farm, as he wished he'd done. Llion always said he was a free man, unlike him, 'shackled to the sheep' as he put it."

"Poor Dad. He never wanted to inherit the farm, he told me."

"No. Dafydd wanted it, ironically. Life can be cruel," Anwen murmured.

Elin had learnt not to seem curious, or to ask questions about this man, but in the long silence that followed she could almost feel the old woman ranging over her memories. Whatever had happened between her and Dafydd, Elin could only hope Anwen would one day be able to tell her.

"Do you actually know how many paintings you have sold in your career? Have you kept a list anywhere, a sort of summary of your life's work?"

The old woman shook her head. "No, and that's been on my mind actually. I have no real idea, and I ought to, how shall I put it, get my... *legacy* into shape just in case I slip feeding the chickens again, shall we say." She grinned a whiskery grin.

"You do need to be more careful, yes, and to take the help offered you."

"Yes, yes, stop nagging. I will, if only because it's costing a small fortune," Anwen snapped with such vigour that it made her cough violently. "But there is something important I want to talk to you about, actually, and it *doesn't* involve commodes for once!"

Elin laughed, and the slight tension in the room vanished. She was ready for her own space, and a comfortable bed, but she would miss spending her days with Anwen, and seeing her mercurial moods change in seconds.

"Go on. I'm all ears," she said with mock gravity.

"I know you have no plans other than to be a caretaker for your mother until her house sells, but that's just treading water and won't make you any money or teach you anything new. You need something useful to do, something that will stretch you a little."

Elin felt slight irritation rising, but suppressed it. This was just Anwen being Anwen.

"I'd wondered, well I'd hoped, that you might do something important for me if I paid you enough." She started rubbing her hands together purposefully. "You see, I'm worried about what record of my life and work I'll leave behind me, my *legacy*, as I said. That word makes it sound important, doesn't it? and it is."

"I understand that, but what do you want me to do?" Elin asked.

Lighting another cigarette and inhaling deeply, Anwen continued.

"I need you to help me catalogue my work and then write a book about my working life, an autobiographical biography if you like. We need to list things in order, add dates, places, and delineate my themes and inspiration – draw everything together. I think you'd be good at seeing the bigger picture, bringing out the good stuff hidden amongst all the dross," Anwen said, warming to her theme. "Yes, bringing the best and brightest to the fore so that they can shine, if you like. Yes, that's what I think you'd do well."

Slightly stung at this prosaic-sounding summing-up of her abilities, Elin said nothing, but Anwen went on without noticing.

"I'll help you, of course, but you're a writer by trade, a wordsmith with a fresh eye and a good appreciation of art, and I don't want anyone writing my story or interpreting my work who isn't all those things."

"I don't think I am actually... I mean, organisation is not my..." Elin stuttered.

"Hush! You know me, girl, and you can put what I think and feel into the *right* words, not just any words. There's nobody else I trust to do that."

Elin went to make a pot of tea, and took a few deep breaths as the kettle boiled. This was a huge project. Her father had told her years ago that Anwen's output was prolific, with paintings exhibited and sold all over the world. How could she be the right person to undertake this task, given what Sadie had dubbed her "failure to make her copy sing"? When she came back into the living room, her face said it all.

"I know what you're thinking, that you can't do it, that you're not good enough," Anwen said, wagging her burning cigarette so that it sprayed them both with ash. "But let me tell you, I knew you as a baby, and as a girl, and I see a talent in you that I have not seen in anyone else. You were born with it, it runs through your veins, despite your... limited upbringing."

"Hey, Mum and Dad did their best," Elin snapped. There was an odd undercurrent to this conversation that she could not put her finger on, and it disturbed her. "But all I have ever been in life is mediocre, an also-ran, and what you're asking of me sounds way beyond my abilities. Honestly."

The old woman sat back in her chair, looking annoyed. "I disagree, but I see I need to prove it to you before my time runs out."

"I'm not saying I won't do it. I'm just saying that I *can't*," Elin said. The mention of Anwen's life possibly ending made the task even more terrifying.

"It's nothing we can't overcome, this fatal lack of confidence you carry around like stigmata on your chest. It's silly and I won't hear any more of it!"

Deeply hurt, Elin began to cry.

"Believe me when I say that I can draw and paint, but not well *enough*. I can write, but not well *enough*. I've always been the *almost-there* artist. My tutors are art school saw that, so it must be true!"

Her face riven with guilt, Anwen said, "I can see that you believed them, and perhaps they were right, that you may not be a painter, or a writer, but you are *creative* in so many ways – I know it, I see it in you. You just need to find the right path, the right métier, your vocation, I suppose."

"And how will I find that out? I'm a bit old for careers advice!" Elin exclaimed.

The old woman's expression softened, and her voice, too, was gentle now. "You need to watch and learn from those who *have* found their path, and found it after a great deal of hard work and knockbacks, in most cases. I can help you do that. I know so many artists, so many craftsmen and women, so many makers, potters, sculptors, weavers up here. I think you need to steep yourself in these people, and what they do. Then you will understand what it takes to feel good at something creative, whatever that turns out to be – and there are many permutations, believe me."

"I think I'm more like Barbara, and she wants me to wear peach tulle at her wedding. That's the extent of her artistic flair!"

Anwen threw her head back and laughed. "Peach tulle? *Iesu!*/Jesus! No, you are not like her, and never could be. Trust me, trust yourself, and do what I ask. I think you will feel more alive than you ever have, if you do."

Elin said nothing, but within thirty-six hours, Anwen had contacted at least ten of her old friends who worked in many different media, in many different ways. She asked them to show Elin what they did, tell her how long they had been doing it and how big a role sheer hard work had played in their daily life as a creator. Meanwhile, Anwen promised to begin collating her chaotic records so that, if Elin felt confident enough to join her in writing her life story, they could begin the task together in earnest in the spring, after Barbara's wedding in Bath.

When the old woman presented this plan, they shook hands and Elin agreed to it with what she dubbed "considerable reservations". But when she was alone, she allowed herself to feel glad about the sense of purpose this task could give her, and she remembered perhaps her favourite quotation from George Eliot:

"It's never too late to be what you might have been."

TWENTY-FOUR

Barbara's two-bedroomed terraced house in Bethesda had been on the market for over a month, but there had been no interest or viewings at all. The house had a distinctly musty air when Elin opened the door on the day she left Anwen's cottage and moved in. It was January, but the day was still trying to be one of watery, wintry sunshine, none of which ever penetrated into these dark rooms. Barbara's dated furnishings did nothing to lift the mood. She had always favoured brocade, chintz and sensibly patterned carpets that "didn't show the dirt", taste inherited from her childhood home in Shrewsbury, but they all contributed to the feel of entering into a museum, a place in which there was no life.

All the walls were painted with bespoke crimsons and greens that Barbara had hoped would look *heritage*, but in fact looked *funereal*. Her old-fashioned taste had suited the farmhouse more, with its low beams and rugged stone walls, but *Wern Farm* had still been a cheerless home. As she walked around the dingy rooms, Elin saw that her mother's lack of imagination had seeped into all the houses she had lived in, condemning them and their inhabitants to a lack of energy and colour that dragged everyone down. To counter this, Elin opened every window in the little house wide, shivering as chilly blasts immediately dispelled the smell of damp and with it, the deeper, subtler taint of loneliness.

Barbara had given Elin free rein to change things, and even get rid of things, as she never intended to live in the house again, and so within a few hours, all the dark cushions and patterned draperies were in a black bag, ready for the charity shop. Next, Elin lifted all the hideous carpets, rolling them up and lugging them outside before a trip to the dump in the Renault 4. The house had once had a pretty garden, but Barbara had paved over the lawn and filled the well-established flower beds of the previous owner with slate chippings for "easy maintenance", so the overwhelming impression was now one of a civic car park.

As she stood coughing up all the dust the carpets had produced, and beginning to wish she hadn't taken on house clearance with no experience, Elin glimpsed a small head above the wall separating her house from the one on the right. The face beneath a shock of blonde hair was half-smiling.

"Hi," she said. "Nice to meet you."

The smile broadened into a whole one. "*Haia*/Hi. Are you English, like the other lady with the blue hair?" the boy said, in a thick North Welsh accent.

Elin laughed. Barbara's efforts not to have grey hair had indeed taken her through a wide spectrum of purples and blues over the years.

"Well, I was born here in Wales actually, but I've been away, so..." she braced herself, "*dw'in meddwl dwi'in eto Cymraes.*/I think I'm still a Welshwoman."

Now, it was the boy's turn to laugh. "Your Welsh is *ofnadwy*/terrible!"

"It's very rusty, I know," Elin replied. "I left years ago, but this is my mum's house, Mrs Pugh. She's getting married and selling it, but I'm going to look after it until then," Elin said.

"Getting *married? Ond mae hi'n hen iawn.*/But she's really old."

From inside the boy's house, a woman's voice screeched:

"*Gwilym, dos 'ma*/Come here!"

The blonde head vanished straight away, and a small, grubby hand waved farewell before that too disappeared.

"Meet the neighbours: tick," Elin said with a grin.

For the next few days, her lunchtime visits to Anwen, trips to various charity shops and to Bangor to buy paint and brushes ready to start redecorating were the only things Elin allowed to interrupt her mission to transform Barbara's house into a) a house she could call a home for the next few months and b) a house that stood any chance of selling. She loved every minute of it.

January drifted past, but its short days and long nights did not lower Elin's spirits as they had always done in London. The peaks of the mountains were thickly carpeted with snow, and seemed to bequeath a fresh, magical light to all the slopes, lakes and valleys below them. Inspired by the very first green shoots of wild daffodils in the hedgerows, she chose a vivid yellow for the kitchen cupboards, and they filled the room with warmth and hopefulness. The lounge, she painted a light-reflecting pale blue that made it seem as if she had brought a summery sky inside. Colourful throws and cushions rescued Barbara's drab furniture as, day by day, the house came back to life and Elin revelled in its transformation from a house to a home.

She bought some pots of daffodils and tulip bulbs to break up the dullness of "the garden that wasn't a garden" as she took to calling it. They would explode into life and colour when spring finally arrived. On some days, she chatted with Gwilym over the wall, or threw his football back and laughed when he yelped as it had hit his head, but on others, she saw nobody except Anwen. She was not lonely, however. Both she and Mouse were contented in their surrogate home-making bubble, with the only intrusion in their peace being messages and calls from Barbara, who was whipping herself into a frenzy about The Wedding.

In *Cân y mynyddoedd*, Anwen was always surrounded by the

teetering piles of box files and reams of dusty paperwork when Elin called each day with soup or some bread and cheese. The old lady also seemed contented enough in their new routine, and very happy to be having regular visitors; Elin made her feel alive and her carers made her laugh, she said, almost every day.

"Until you came back, I can honestly say I hadn't laughed for years. I'd even stopped talking to myself, as I never answered."

"But you had a sign on your gate saying *Artist at work. Go away*, remember?" Elin replied drily. "Are you surprised few people visited?"

"You did, though," Anwen said grumpily. "The others were just wimps, too easily deterred."

"I suppose I knew I had to see you again. I couldn't resist this feeling that if I got to talk to you, I would get to know myself better, if that makes any sense," Elin said, understanding her feelings only as she articulated them. "I know that most people would..."

"...I don't care about most people. Never did and never will," Anwen cut in. "I care about *you*, though. Very much. I always hoped you would come back, but I am very grateful, every single day, that you were brave enough to do so."

"Brave? Some would say it was more like cowardice, running away from my job, my friends, my *life*," Elin said, feeling the same knot in her belly she felt in the small hours when she recalled the particularly bleak circumstances of her coming home just before Christmas to care for Anwen.

"Well, it was the wrong life, but you were strong enough to leave it, even though it was the only one you knew. Now, we're going to build you a new one, and a better one!" the old woman said gleefully, clapping her hands like a child.

And so, day by day, week by week, their friendship deepened, sown in the past, and nurtured in the present by their undeclared interdependence into one of mutual respect and deep affection. Their conversations became less brittle and more sincere, and they ranged over subjects Elin had never discussed with anyone before as Barbara had never been interested in her politics, her aspirations or her emotional well-being. To feel truly *heard* for the first time in her life was a revelation and she began to realise that she saw Anwen as far more of a mother than her biological one had ever been.

And so, even before she had begun the programme of visits to artists and makers Anwen had organised, Elin decided that she would at least *try* to help her write her book. She was less sure about taking payment for it, however. Above all, anything she learnt from the other artists would be interesting, if not necessarily useful career-wise. She would go with an open mind, because Anwen had organised it, and Anwen *cared* about her; she had said so, and it had felt wonderful.

TWENTY-FIVE

The first visit Anwen had arranged for Elin was to go to her old
friend Jac Evans' studio in Rachub, a small village nestling in the
lea of three hills called Moel Faban, Moel Gwyrn and Moel
Wnion. His studio was in his house, a small sanctuary in the midst
of the hugger-mugger of slate-rooved buildings that formed the
heart of the village. At first, Elin walked right past it. Only when
she retraced her steps and glimpsed an old man through a smeary
window, bent low to examine a row of beautifully identical bowls
with his tongue between his lips in concentration did she realise it
was there. Anwen had warned her that Jac could be grumpy, but
that he was "no worse than me when you get to know him", so Elin
knocked and then waited several minutes for him to open the door.
When he did, her first impression was of a character from a fairy
story, as his white mane, slightly squashed face and prominent nose
reminded her of an image of Rumpelstiltskin in a book she had
loved as a child.

"Ha, Anwen's girl?" he blurted. "Been waiting for you.
Come in."

Elin started at being called "Anwen's girl", but managed to
hide it.

Inside the little house, she could tell at a glance that Jac was much more ordered in his creativity than Anwen, who seemed to thrive on chaos. Wooden shelves lined the walls, some stacked with mugs, some with bowls but all meticulously placed the same distance apart as if to be able to breathe. Some pieces were finished, delicately decorated and glazed, but most were fresh from the kiln: all were unique, and yet so perfectly formed that Elin was full of mute admiration. She took them all in for several minutes, before saying:

"These are lovely, Jac. How do you get each one to be so smooth, so *natural* in shape, as if the clay had no choice but to be shaped exactly like that?"

"I take my inspiration from nature," the old man said. "More than enough perfection there for me to reflect in my work."

"Is each one slightly different?"

"Of course. Have you ever seen two leaves exactly the same? Look closely, girl – none of them are."

Elin nodded, and then watched Jac bustle around the studio in silence. Chat seemed inappropriate as he gently lifted a pot to check the base, or rubbed the surface of a bowl to remove a film of dust only he could see.

After an hour or so, it became clear that Jac was uncomfortable being watched for any longer, so she left, but as she walked down to her car parked in the lower part of the village, Elin quite understood why Anwen had sent her here: this man truly loved his craft and no effort was too great to try and produce the very best he could. It mattered enormously to him that each piece was exactly right.

The following week, Elin was glad of a break from decorating to drive to Criccieth, a picturesque coastal town she remembered visiting once as a small child. She had come with her father and a woman, but again, it could not have been Barbara, as she complained of nausea on bendy roads. When she remembered being bought a *double* cornet from Cadwaladers, the famous ice-cream shop, the likelihood that it had been Anwen seemed proven. Elin realised how many of the special days in her childhood, the ones that shone brightest in her memory, had included that woman, and understood a little more about why she had yearned to return and talk to her again.

"She was there for the best times, the happiest times, when Dad and I were ourselves. Anwen was the catalyst for joy in our lives," she murmured as she parked on the seafront. "And I need her to work her magic again now."

She was in Criccieth to meet Olwen Rees, another of Anwen's artist friends, who lived in a small house facing the town's romantically ruined castle at the top of a pretty street in the town. Elin had misjudged the journey and arrived early, so she walked along the prom and into a wind so cold that she was reluctant to inhale too deeply. She had remembered blue sky and sunshine in Criccieth, but today, it was end of January weather, and bleak with it. The sea was ribbed with choppy waves, and sky a relentlessly drab grey as it reflected the sky above it. She sat over a coffee in a spectacular art deco-styled restaurant designed by Clough Williams-Ellis, the whimsical mind behind the nearby Italianate village, Portmeirion. She googled him and images of his unique vision popped up on her phone, filling the screen with colour and light. He, like Jac, had been so inspired by the landscape around him in North Wales that his home, Plas Brondanw, was designed to showcase its surroundings rather than impinge on them. It seemed impossible for any creative mind up here to ignore such natural beauty, Elin concluded; it was everywhere, and everything.

Olwen was considerably easier to talk to than Jac had been and her artistic style was poles apart both from his, and from Anwen's. Her house was immaculate, with antimacassars on the chair arms and displays of silk flowers, and there was an air of precision in her home, as in her work. Olwen favoured a realistic technique, which aimed to reproduce her subject in mirrored detail, each rock, each ripple in a stream, almost photographically accurate. Whereas Anwen used bold slashes of paint, and Jac organic shapes, both inspired but not limited by their subjects, Olwen's palette was far narrower and her vision, less broad. Elin *admired* her paintings of the castle, of the undulating countryside around her hometown, but she did not *love* them.

"Do you want to paint, dear? Is that why Anwen's sent you to see my work?" Olwen said, her cheeks flushed and her blue eyes agleam. She was at least seventy, Elin decided, but she had the curious manner of a young pup.

"I don't know, to be honest," Elin replied. "I painted a lot as a child, and Anwen encouraged me then, but lately... I don't know how to begin again, how to express what I want to either in art, or in my life. Does that sound odd?"

"Not at all," Olwen said. "That's why Anwen is sending you around North Wales seeing her old friends, I suppose. We all live and work in radically different ways, I think you'll find, but they are all as valid as each other."

"Have you known Anwen for long?"

"Oh, for years and years. And old Jac too – I hear you went to visit him as well. Amazing how differently we all developed."

"Your work is so precise, so careful," Elin said, almost reverentially.

"That's how I express myself, but it may not be what you do or how you do it," the old woman replied thoughtfully. "Anwen doesn't want to clone you into versions of us, I'm sure; she wants to free you, to be yourself, whoever that may turn out to be."

Elin left Olwen feeling calmer, wiser, and deeply grateful for an insight into how she saw the world.

February saw snowdrops sheltering beneath drystone walls up in the hills, early snow-white lambs on the *ffriddoedd*/mountain pastures and a little more daylight each day. Barbara's dark terraced house was now a bright, welcoming place, and felt surprisingly spacious. Viewings began, but the housing market was slow, estate agents told her. Barbara was in no rush to sell, and for Elin, as Anwen grew stronger and more independent, there was the possibility of being able to think about her own future rather than whether her friend had mobilised enough today, as the physiotherapist put it. The only place she wanted to be was here, where she had been born and raised. She remembered discussing *hiraeth*, the strange longing for their homeland that many Welsh people feel, with Dylan on their day out together. She knew, now, that it was very real.

Elin visited several more of Anwen's friends. Maggie, a brilliant textile artist who used all kinds of fabrics, buttons and beads to recreate the beauty of North Wales and rhapsodised about the painstaking process involved in each creation; Budi, a batik artist inspired by traditional designs from Java, a land he had left four decades earlier, and who put hours and hours, and all of himself, into everything he created, and Megan, a sculptress who aimed to bring out the hidden soul of every piece of wood or stone she carved. In her hands, a piece of sea-battered driftwood became a mercurial fish and a hunk of discarded slate a spiralling seashell. Elin adored all their work in different ways and for different reasons, but above all, she was astonished at the sheer variety of creativity in the area. Her visits had been, as Anwen had intended, an experience that had filled her with understanding both of the process of being an artist, and the dedication and, often, disappointment involved. None of these artists had made anything like the money her friend had. A couple had even lived hand-to-mouth, doing what they loved best because they simply had no choice but to do so.

These visits had achieved another of Anwen's aim as well. It was becoming more and more clear to Elin that she was not destined to be a creator. She lacked original ideas, the ability to take risks with her process or her materials, but she recognised these gifts in others. Hadn't Anwen said that those who value artists and who sensitively curate and promote art also need skills that not everyone possesses? She tried very hard to believe her as she began to wonder where these unusual but useful skills might take her.

Any embryonic plans were curtailed by Barbara, who called one rainy morning bewailing the fact that her wedding plans were not going well *at all*. Caterers were proving fickle, her dress fitted badly and George was getting bad-tempered about the whole thing. Reluctantly, Elin decided to go to Bath to help her mother and soothe some ruffled feathers. She had to ask her to reimburse her rail fare as she had done as a teenager, as her meagre savings were all but gone. Very soon, earning some money was going to be essential. Could she really accept a wage from Anwen for helping her? It still did not sit easy with her to even consider doing so.

Her heart was heavy as she packed to go to Bath a full fortnight before the wedding. Anwen had enough care in place and Gwilym promised to feed Mouse, but having to leave Wales and postpone the last of her visits to Anwen's fellow artists was especially hard as they were helping her clarify her thoughts as never before. She desperately needed to have some idea what lay ahead to forget about the loss and disappointment that lay behind her.

But helping her stressed mother felt more urgent than finding her life's calling right now, as she struggled to explain to Anwen. Amazingly, she agreed with her:

"She needs you. Go and help her, even if you feel she was never there when you needed her. She did her best, which is more than many."

<h1 style="text-align:center">TWENTY-SIX</h1>

The first thing Elin noticed when she stepped off the train in Bath after an endless-seeming journey was that it was several degrees warmer, and the air was different – less clear, thicker, somehow. Barbara was having a dress fitting, so had said that George would meet her, but Elin realised as she stood waiting that she had no idea what her stepfather-to-be looked like. All the men she could see within his age range were clearly well-fed and well-dressed, but which of these affluent middle-class white males was George? When she felt a hefty slap on her shoulder and turned to see a moustachioed man in a green wax jacket with a sweep of grey hair and large, blue-rimmed glasses, she knew.

"Ellen!" he cried. "Lovely to meet you at last. Shall we?" he said, holding out an arm for her to take and picking up her bag. She resisted correcting his slight mispronunciation of her name, but it had stung. Had her mother never actually *said* her name out loud in all these weeks and months?

George did most of the talking at first, mostly about Barbara and what a "fine woman" she was, but soon he was preoccupied that one of the windows on his vintage Daimler was not functioning properly and conversation dwindled. As they passed through the beautifully proportioned streets of a city she had never visited, Elin felt as if she had landed on another planet from the one she had left that morning. There were shops with attractive window displays, coffee shops and bustling, smiling shoppers. Everything was softer, less angular and the honey-coloured stone of many of the buildings even made the light feel different. There were no dark slate rooves or rain-slicked stone walls here, but barley-sugar pillars made of the famous Bath limestone and pristine sash windows. Most people wore long, warm winter coats, stylish hats and boots instead of the walking boots and well-worn outdoorwear most people in North Wales lived in during the long winter. She began to run through the meagre selection of clothes she had brought in her head and decided they were all totally unsuitable, but she had no money for a shopping spree.

Fifteen minutes later, they pulled into a gravelled drive and stopped in front of a handsome Georgian villa on the outskirts of the city. Two manicured bay trees stood to attention either side of the glossy front door. A climbing rose had been surgically pruned to trail above it in the summer, Elin noted. When Barbara appeared in the doorway, she hardly recognised her. Her hair had been elegantly coiffed and subtly coloured, she was wearing a neat, tailored skirt, pale pink cashmere sweater and brown leather boots that positively gleamed. She also looked about a decade younger than when she had seen her last.

"Darling!" she said, coming towards her daughter with her arms open. When her lipsticked mouth kissed her on first one cheek, then the other, Elin stood rooted to the spot. Her brain simply could not match this sweet-scented woman with her mother, Barbara Pugh, the rather drab and miserable widow of farmer Llion Pugh from *Wern Farm*.

Leading her inside, Barbara continued talking nervously, pointing out the sweeping staircase, the tasteful blue-and-cream-striped stair carpet and asking Elin to take her shoes off before going upstairs because it was new. "Your room is the first on the right. Go on up and settle in, dear. George will bring your bag up once he's changed into house clothes."

Elin dismissed a sudden vision of George reappearing in a smoking jacket and cravat, and pulled off her grubby trainers before going up the stairs. She stood for a few moments, taking in the luxurious décor and delicate lavender bag on her pillow. What on earth was going on here? Her mother had metamorphosed into a woman she barely recognised: she looked different, she smelt different, she sounded different – even her voice, which had always retained the twang of Shropshire, had risen several semitones. Confused and disorientated, there was only one person she wanted to talk to about it – Anwen. She called her, pacing up and down, hoping the old woman had remembered how to answer her mobile and read the caller's name on the tiny screen. It rang for at least a minute, and Elin pictured Anwen scrabbling for her glasses and squinting at the "alien box" as she often called it.

"What's wrong?" she barked eventually. "Is Barbara dead?"

Luckily, Elin's response was to laugh. "Bloody hell, Anwen! No, she's not... but yes, she sort of *is*, actually? She's, well, reinvented herself as Margaret Thatcher!"

"Ah, she's found her niche, and she's changed her plumage to suit her new nest," Anwen said. "No surprises there."

"Really? I know she always wanted all this, but I don't know how to *be* with her," Elin replied, feeling a niggle of panic. "I'm know I'm supposed to stay here until the wedding and support her, but..."

"Then stay and support her! It's all she's ever wanted, to be safe, and comfortable. She's had a lot of sadness in her life, you know."

"Has she?" Elin said, full of sudden dread. "What do you mean?"

"Well, for a start, your mother lost two babies before you came along. One, a girl, died at six months, a sickly little mite she was, and another, a little boy, was stillborn."

"What?" Elin managed to croak. She closed her eyes and allowed this new knowledge to seep in. Outside, a dog yapped, punctuating a silence that seemed to last for hours.

"I didn't know that," she whispered eventually.

"O *Duw*/Oh *God*, didn't she ever tell you? You must never let her know that I have – she'll throttle me."

"She had two babies before she had me?" Elin said, deeply shocked. "She must have thought she was being punished, or that there was something terribly wrong with her body. That must have been *unbearable*."

"Yes, I think it was, but please don't fret that you've inherited something that means *you* can't have children yourself," Anwen said, with a brusqueness that would have offended Elin a few months earlier, but not now. She had learnt that the old woman rarely responded to anything in a predictable way.

"Of course I won't, because she had me afterwards," Elin said, mainly to reassure herself. "And no, I won't tell her you told me." Feeling slightly dazed, she sat down on the chaise-longue behind her.

"It was an awful time, and it had consequences of its own."

Elin felt all the hairs on her arms stand on end. She waited for Anwen to go on.

"It hit her very hard, and your father too. I think it drove a wedge between them, as they blamed each other. The marriage never mended after that, and neither did she, despite... having you," she said, a rare softness in her tone. "Losing a child is a pain that never eases. It hardens you, however it happens."

"I'm sure it does. And poor Dad actually had the son he would have passed the farm onto – he was born, perfect, but he was dead. All he was left with was me. He must have felt cursed!"

"Stop that! He loved you, and you know it. You were perhaps the only person he truly loved with his whole, true self. He only allowed me to see glimpses of that until, eventually, he shut me out of his life completely."

Elin desperately wanted to ask *why*, but didn't. She wondered again if Llion had loved Anwen too, which would explain their closeness when she was a girl, but she knew better than to quiz her. This was not the time.

"Listen, this is Barbara's last chance at happiness, Elin," the old woman went on urgently. "She's a selfish woman, and a shallow one, but she has suffered, and she deserves this, so let her have it, and don't fret too much about the past. You can't change it, so let it go."

"I understand. See you again soon," Elin said, and hung up. Then she sat in her room looking out of the window and seeing nothing for a long while, letting what she had just heard find its place among the many ways she saw her mother and father. There was still something missing, a chapter that made her parents' sad story cohere into a whole, she was sure. The sound of Barbara calling her prevented her brooding on it further.

When she went downstairs to join her mother and George for an aperitif in the conservatory (a phrase she could never have imagined her mother saying), she felt as if a different filter had been laid over them all, one that removed the trivial, even the annoying and gave the scene a new warmth. She saw Barbara gently touch George's hand, and tried as hard as she could to sound enthusiastic about the wedding plans, even agreeing to a fitting of the dreaded peach tulle dress in the morning. They seemed so *happy* and it was so far from the unendurable tragedy of lost babies, or the lonely years in the farm, when her mother and father had rarely exchanged a kind word. Yes, Barbara had suffered indeed.

This was very far from her idea of happiness, but it was her mother's, and Anwen had been right: she deserved it.

TWENTY-SEVEN

On the morning of Barbara and George's wedding, the weather was relentlessly wet. Luckily, Barbara had been firmly steered away from a marquee by George's taciturn son Rufus, who reminded her that it was, in fact, March and not high summer. Instead, they had selected a luxurious hotel in Bath's Royal Crescent, where the ceremony would also be performed. Barbara wanted the photographs taken in the acre of stunning gardens.

Elin had not found meeting either of George's children easy, but did her absolute best to ensure this did not show. Rufus, who seemed to have decided in seconds that neither Barbara nor her daughter were worthy of more than minimal attention, was a property developer in Richmond and always seemed to be reading a very important message or taking a very important call. Harriet, George's daughter and a PA in London to someone *very high-up,* was the other bridesmaid and her face told Elin that she shared her low opinion of peach tulle. In fact, Elin very quickly got the message that, though they were soon to be stepsiblings, the relationship would be in name only. There was a toxic cocktail of snobbery, money and jealousy at play here.

As Barbara was getting dressed into the painfully elaborate ivory silk dress she had chosen to get married in (and in which she could not comfortably sit down as it was so tight) Elin and Harriet, who were sharing a dressing room in the hotel, were forced to chat.

"Why on earth did your mother choose this ghastly colour for our dresses, and tulle as the fabric?" Harriet said, pulling up her zip with a vigour that threatened to break it. "We're both in our thirties, but we look like silly flower girls and we're going to freeze."

Elin took a breath, and replied as calmly as she could. "I know. It's not to my taste either, but Mum chose it, and it means such a lot to her, all this."

Harriet grunted. "When my parents got married, it was all so understated, so... classy. You can tell, even in the black and white photos."

Elin stopped herself. She had seen the snaps of Barbara and Llion's wedding: the bride, more resigned than blushing, had been wearing acres of white netting and carrying a plastic silver horseshoe, but there was no way she was sharing that with Harriet.

"Is your mother coming today?" she said. "I'm sorry, I don't know the circumstances of..." She stopped, aware that she was venturing into a potential minefield, but she had long since entered the danger zone.

Harriet wheeled around, her face livid. "No, she is not, because she *died* ten years ago! Didn't she tell you, for Christ's sake?" she hissed.

Elin was mortified. Barbara had told her that George was a widower in their very first conversation about him, but she had forgotten, to her shame. She had been too preoccupied with her own minor miseries. An apology would not stop Harriet now: she was in full furious flow.

"My father was coping well on his own, Rufus and I felt, and we were coming up to see him pretty regularly until he went up to North Wales on that bloody walking holiday and met... *Barbara*." She said the name with such distaste that Elin felt a very strong urge to hit her. She resisted – just – but hurt and anger boiled not far beneath the surface.

"My father died too, in case you didn't know, and I think my mother was very lonely, but I didn't see it at the time as I was too busy thinking about myself." Elin waited for her words to strike home before adding, "I'm just glad they've found each other, and I hope they'll be really happy together."

"Let's hope so, given the amount of his money she's blown on this wedding, and all the changes she's made to the house," Harriet muttered, adding, "all of them knocking thousands off its value, no doubt."

"Well, I think your father looks pretty contented. Perhaps he wanted a few changes around the place, freshen things up a bit." There was no fellow feeling from Harriet, but Elin was glad to have got to the source of the ill-feeling and proved her hunch correct: snobbery, money and jealousy.

When Harriet had swished out of the room, Elin gulped a glass of lukewarm Prosecco, shoved the silk flower head-dress on her head and marched downstairs, flushed with the triumph of mostly good over decidedly evil.

By nine o'clock that evening, Barbara and George were married, and the first, mainly very elderly, guests were beginning to leave. Amongst them, however, were Rufus and Harriet who "had to get back to town". Elin was glad to see that the happy couple barely noticed this slight. The ceremony had gone smoothly, the food was delicious and the sun had appeared in the afternoon to enable the photos in the garden, as Barbara had wanted. Exhausted after hours of small talk with people she would never see again, Elin slipped upstairs as her mother, slightly tipsy, was regaling the remaining guests with their honeymoon plans. She looked happier than Elin had ever seen her, and she was genuinely glad to see that.

Squeezing herself out of her sweaty, crumpled dress and into some jeans and trainers, she headed out into the night, desperate for fresh air and some quiet. The streets were not empty, as they would have been in Llanberis, but neither were they busy, as Tooting's litter-strewn streets would have been. A few well-heeled couples were walking back from the theatre, a meal out or a quiet drink in a cosy pub and Elin once again felt the contrast between her life and theirs. Part of her envied their moneyed ease, but most of her preferred where she lived, in all its spectacular wildness. She looked up at the sky hopefully, but clouds obscured any shy stars and within minutes, a heavy shower hid them entirely. Pulling her coat around her, she dived into a pub and ordered a pint. After a day of Prosecco, champagne and elaborate food, her palate craved cold beer and peanuts. From one end of the pub, she heard music drifting through from an adjoining room – a singer and a guitar, with minimal accompaniment from a violinist. She could hear little above the babble of drinkers surrounding her, so took her pint through to listen; there was something about the sound, the voice, that stirred a memory.

Up on the small stage, Dylan Williams was sitting on a high stool, his head bent over his guitar, as she had first seen him in the pub in Llanberis. His hair was again tied up, his curls confined to a few loose tendrils around his face. The notes of the song drifted between him and the fiddle, and it was a few moments before he sang – long enough for Elin to spot the slight, dark girl she had seen him with in Llanberis sitting in the middle of the front row, right in front of him. The girl looked completely focused on Dylan, as if hardly aware of the music at all. Too in awe of her man, Elin concluded, with a spark of jealousy she struggled to dispel.

Keeping in the shadows, Elin remembered Gwenda telling her that Dylan was touring the country, and assumed that this was one of the small music venues on the circuit of aspiring musicians. The incredible coincidence of him being here, tonight of all nights, struck her as one nobody would ever believe if she told them – which, of course, she never would.

As she turned to leave, Dylan's voice suddenly soared above the small crowd, piercing the air and making goosebumps appear on Elin's arms. No wonder his reputation was spreading and he was hoping for a record deal; his voice spoke to the soul. Each word was clear, sung with a purity and surety of tone that astonished her. She listened carefully, and heard:

> "And we sat, she and I, and we listened
> As the mountains watched and waited
> 'Til the moment came and they sang to us
> And our longing was abated."

As the crowd applauded, Elin watched as the girl stood up and hugged Dylan, their smiles synchronised, their fondness for each other obvious.

Again, Elin wondered what might have been with this man. As she walked back through the quiet, wet streets of the city, she realised that the words of that song had been sung to her, by a man who would never say them, and who now loved someone else. She would never see him again, as the trajectory of his life was a million miles from hers, but they had shared something once and both of them knew it. She had lost her chance, and such chances rarely came twice. As ever, George Eliot's words described how she felt perfectly:

"Only in the agony of parting do we look into the depths of love."

TWENTY-EIGHT

Elin had agreed to stay in Bath for a few more days after the wedding, ostensibly to help Barbara calm down from the manic high she had inhabited for the last month or so. This proved almost impossible however, because her mother was now obsessed with preparing for her honeymoon in Tobago, and whether the ludicrously expensive going-away outfit she had bought would still fit her after all the rich food she'd eaten at the wedding. Elin tried to remain patient, but went on a *lot* of long walks. She was ready to go home.

Anwen had coped without her daily visits, but Eva, one of the Polish carers, had called Elin the day after the wedding to say that the old woman seemed fed up and was not sleeping well.

"And the cigarettes, and the coughing – *ojej*/oh dear."

"I know. I wish she'd give up, especially when you're there, and obviously pregnant," Elin said, resigned to the fact that it would never happen.

"I ask her to stop it, but she says everyone pregnant used to smoke and their babies were fine," Eva said.

"Typical! She must be the most maddening person I know."

"I know, she is... *difficult*, but I think she needs you, Elin. You have work to do together, and not much time, she says to me."

Elin sighed. "We do, and I'll be back as soon as I possibly can, and we'll begin. Can you tell her that, and don't try lifting her on your own anymore, OK?"

Eva assured her that she wouldn't, but Elin could hear that she was troubled. It was a huge responsibility to care for someone so elderly, frail and difficult to manage when your schedule allows you so short a time to do so. In the second trimester of her pregnancy, this was taking its toll.

Elin, too, felt time pressing. She was wasting time trying to soothe Barbara into behaving less like a child and more like an adult when she had a lot of work to do in Wales. Getting everything that had happened in Anwen's life, all her many achievements, awards, exhibitions and experiences into any kind of order was a massive undertaking, and the old woman had not been well since her fall. She seemed to be deteriorating generally, however well her bruises were fading and Elin felt deeply uneasy, coupled with a strong sense that she was in the wrong place at the wrong time. One afternoon, she went to find her mother, who was packing and unpacking her suitcase again and again.

"Mum, would you mind if I went back to Wales this afternoon?" she began. "Anwen's not doing too well, and I think you're fine here until you go away."

Barbara sighed and put down the vividly coloured dress she had been folding, and sat down. Her face, as yet without the expensive make-up she usually now wore, looked much more like the one Elin knew so well. It was tired, had wrinkles and was the grey-pale colour of most British faces in March, before the spring sunshine has lifted their pallor.

"Elin, I've wanted to talk to you, love, about, well, what happens next," she said. "I'm grateful that you've been here to support me – I really am. I saw all the little things you did, you know, and I also know it's not easy for you to accept a new dad, and new siblings."

Elin looked down. Did Barbara suspect what she thought of George, let alone Rufus and Harriet? Yes, she thought George was probably OK under all the bluff and bluster, but she would never, ever call him "Dad". Instead, she murmured, "Any time, Mum. I'm glad to see you happy at last."

"I was never happy in Wales, and I couldn't hide it from you as perhaps I should have done. I was always sad there, about lots of things, and I can't tell you how good I feel about never having to go there again unless I want to."

"I understand, Mum," Elin said. And for the first time, she did. She had no idea how her mother had borne losing two babies, the harshness and isolation of her life, her husband's monosyllabic company when her ideal was what she had here, in this gorgeous house with her wealthy, respectable and predictable new husband. Llion Pugh had been none of those things, and living with him, whatever had bound them together, must have been incredibly hard. As to whether she had stayed for *her*, as many mothers did, Elin was not so sure.

Barbara folded her hands on her lap, which Elin had learnt in childhood meant that *something important was about to be said*. Was her mother going to suggest she move down to Bath? Had George found a little job for her, or, even worse, had Rufus? She held her breath.

"I know you aren't sure what to do right now, or how you'll make your way in the world, but if there is a way I can help you, tell me. Your father and I could never offer that, because the farm took every penny we ever had, but perhaps I can put some things right now."

A stillness descended on the room, a thick, soupy silence that Elin recognised as similar to the quiet that had preceded her mother telling her that Llion had cancer, and that it was terminal. Quietly, calmly, Barbara went on:

"I want you to feel that you can stay in the house in Bethesda for as long as you want to. I don't want to set foot in it again, and I trust you to do what's best with it. If you want to leave and rent it out, keep that money and enjoy yourself. If you want to sell it, do so. *Wern Farm* was never the home you deserved, but perhaps you can make that little place your own. You were born up in those hills, grew up there, and it's in your blood, so perhaps you will want to live there. I am always thankful that you love the place as I never could; it meant so much to your father that you did."

Elin was speechless. This went against everything she had ever thought about her mother; that she didn't care about her happiness, that she thought her decisions foolish and her choices unwise. When she could respond coherently, she said:

"Thank you, Mum, but it's always *your* house, if you need it for any reason."

Barbara stood up, opened her arms and hugged her tightly. This shocked Elin even more and so she stood, rigid, in her mother's embrace until they both stepped back.

"I know that, but I think I'll be fine. It's you I'm worried about."

"I'll be fine, too, and you know where I'll be now I have somewhere I can call 'home' for as long as I need to."

"Wales has always been your home, but it was never mine. I'm glad to be able to help you now, when you need it most."

"Thanks," Elin said, almost overwhelmed by this, the most honest conversation she and Barbara had ever had. "I guess I'd better start packing, and let Anwen know I'm on my way home."

"Yes. And tell Anwen... tell her that I'm glad her wish has been granted, and you are back with her at last. She will take good care of you now. She's wanted to for a long, long time."

"OK, I'll tell her," Elin said, but her mother's words sent a ripple of concern through her. They had sounded like a farewell. Was she on her own now, permanently cast adrift from Barbara's new life, as she had suspected would happen? She was not at all sure how she felt, if that was the case.

On the long journey back to Wales, Elin was so exhausted that she slept for the first hour, mouth wide open and probably snoring. When she woke up and watched the patchwork of fields between towns speed past, her feelings began to calm and her anxiety levelled out. What lay ahead of her was an interim period, a stasis before new life truly began. It was not a time of upheaval or great change: those things had happened already, in her leaving London, her job and Barbara's marriage. It was a time of reflection, of letting the dust settle. Above all, it was the time to help Anwen get stronger, look back over her life and put things in order, as old age nudges so many to do. She had a lovely home, lots to do and more to learn. It was a pretty good way of spending a summer, and perhaps longer. Things could be much, much worse despite the fact that Dylan was firmly and finally out of her life.

Her thoughts during these hours of enforced idleness on the train returned to the frantic time before the wedding, the day itself and the strange days that followed it. A few things floated to the surface, some good, and some not so good. Foremost in the latter category was her acute disappointment in her stepsiblings Rufus and Harriet. She would not see them again until one or other of their parents' funerals, she was almost certain. No great loss there. A good, even great, moment had been Barbara's face as she had walked towards George, radiant in her ivory finery and blushing like the carefree bride she had waited so long to be.

But other memories, and some words, lingered longer. Barbara had said "you were born up in those hills", but the hospital in Bangor where she had always assumed she had been born was several miles from the mountains. Why had her mother, who was not usually of poetic bent, said "in the hills"? And why had she made such a point of saying that Anwen's wish had been granted in Elin coming back to her? These things were unsettling, but Elin could only hope that, as she helped knit the threads of Anwen's life together, the snags in the weft of both their stories would be explained.

As the train crawled up the coastline and skirted the edges of Eryri, Elin could not rid herself of the thought that, without any drama, regret or distress, the main responsibility of her care had been quietly transferred to a woman who understood her far better than Barbara ever had, or ever could.

TWENTY-NINE

April had brought spring to Bethesda while Elin had been away, but there was still a chill in the evenings and a few trees remained reluctant to explode into leaf. Whereas the cherry trees in Bath had been in full blossom-mode, in North Wales, the change of seasons was always more careful. Tentative bursts of sunshine warmed the mountains and cloud-shadows moved across them with silent speed, but indigo skies could bring sudden, torrential rain and often did. Wildflowers peppered every hedgerow with banks of celandines, daisies and dandelions, all spread wide to absorb every single ounce of sunshine, but in shadier spots, small clumps of violets celebrated the warming days in their own way, their quiet beauty unacknowledged.

The house felt more welcoming than it had ever done once Elin had opened all the windows and brought in some fresh-cut lilac to scent the air. The crystals she had bought in a health food shop in the village sent rainbows spiralling around the rooms when the sunlight caught them and she felt happier to be in this home than in any other. There had still been no viewings, as the housing market was in the doldrums, flooded by second home-owners desperately trying to sell their bijou retreats in the face of higher tax thresholds. This all meant that Elin was guilt-free when she told the estate agent that the house was no longer on the market.

Her reunion with Anwen was less positive, because the old woman seemed so much frailer than before she had left for Bath. The veins on her forehead now formed a delicate map just beneath her skin, her arms were skeletally thin and she had a constant, racking cough. The cottage was more of a mess than ever, as she had emptied boxes, files and plastic bags crammed with papers onto every surface. Elin's heart sank.

"Have you made any progress with cataloguing your work, ready for us to start?" she asked, braced for a sharp retort.

"Huge progress, yes. It's all in my head now, so I just need to tell you everything and then you need to write it down," Anwen replied, sweeping a hand over one of the shoals of paper on the table near her. "Everything is here, unearthed, ready to be rooted in words, *your* words, don't you see?"

Elin did not, but she decided to trust her friend. "Right. So, where shall we begin?"

"With my childhood, a misfit of a girl who grew up in the mountains, played with two brothers and always yearned to capture what I saw in a picture," Anwen said. "But I do want you to finish all the visits I've lined up for you as well, to all the old friends of mine. I need you to bear witness to their skills, their dedication to their craft. It will help you find your own path, 'grist to the mill' and all that."

"I will, I promise. I've learnt so much about how many ways people can be creative," Elin replied. She did not add "even if I'm probably not one of them", because, although both women knew it, saying it aloud was still difficult.

"And how many ways there can be of feeling fulfilled, and getting your self *expressed*," Anwen replied, her eyes meeting Elin's unflinchingly. "You need to learn those things so you can *use* all this new knowledge in the way that's right for you." She stopped to cough. "And yes, there are many kinds of people and many ways of living, but your most important task in all this is to find the one that matches your gifts, and allows you to share them with the world, if you like. I'm giving you a crash course in *how to live life*. Yes, I like that phrase. Where it leads you, I will never know."

Elin hesitated. Was this more melodrama, or was something behind her comment? She hedged her bets, saying, "Even more reason to get started on writing your life story."

"Yes, before time runs out on me," Anwen said, lighting a cigarette with a phlegmy cackle. "It will, you know, and sooner than you think."

When the old woman saw Elin's face fall, she shook her head.

"Oh dear. Let's not get too maudlin here. We'll start tomorrow, I promise, but I won't find it easy to remember some things. There may be gaps, spaces, where my recollection is hazy or I'm not sure how I want things to be recorded. You'll just have to fill these *lacunae* in... at the end. Will you do that for me?"

Googling "lacunae" without Anwen noticing was tricky, but it revealed that it was a Latin word for "an unfilled space", which left Elin able to reply:

"Of course I will," she said, but she smelt a slight whiff of deception. Anwen knew full well the things she was willing to share, but Elin needed to find out the things she was not; this reluctance to tell her was a worry if she was to write an honest book about this astonishing woman.

Elin was also worried about money. Her savings were gone, and the returned deposit from the flat in Tooting had long since been spent. Her outgoings were minimal, but she still needed some source of income and wondered if getting a part-time job would be a good thing and take her away from Anwen from time to time; her company was enriching, even exhilarating, but equally exhausting. She considered asking Barbara for a loan in the meantime, but was unsure what her new husband would make of that. This worry went round and round in her head at night, and she could not yet see a solution that did not involve taking money from Anwen.

. . .

Elin's final few visits to artists in the area were perhaps the most thought-provoking of all, and helped her impressions of the immense creativity she had witnessed in her homeland cohere into a recognisable whole. Bronwen, a ceramicist, grumbled about the availability of cheap imitations of pieces that had taken her years to develop and weeks to create, and Non, a weaver from generations of Welsh weavers, saddened her with a rant about people's "expectation of perfection" that saw them unwilling to accept the differences in texture or colour that a handmade piece inevitably contained.

"My heart, as well as years and years spent mastering my craft, went into making what I make and sell, and they complain about the pattern not being exactly even, or it being too expensive," Non told her. "If I tell them how long it took to rear the sheep, prepare the wool and then spin and weave it, they don't believe me. When I say it costs a whole lot less than their bloody Range Rover, they're offended! If only they could see the process with their own eyes, feel it all with their own hands, if you like – then they would know what's being passed down here, and how vital it is that we conserve it."

The last of the visits to local artists Anwen had arranged for Elin was to see Geraint Jones, a drystone waller whose family had built many of the walls that laced the slopes of Nant Ffrancon valley. He was waiting at the gate of his small cottage when she pulled up, his thick grey hair only partly contained by a woolly hat and his face bearing evidence of decades spent out on the mountains. His skin looked almost varnished, and both his cheeks had a rosette of boyish pink in them, but the skin of his hand, when Elin shook it, was cracked and hard. She could not help but be reminded of her father, whose face had also borne testament to the harshness of life up here.

"*Duw*/God, it's good to see you again. I remember you as this high." He moved his hand down to just above his knee. "You used to come and find me and we'd *cael sgwrs*/have a chat." He paused, and Elin felt a lump in her throat. This man's voice, his accent, the musical emphases in his speech were also redolent of her father and of her childhood. She could only nod in response. "So, your mother's gone back to England. New husband," he said.

As these were statements rather than questions, Elin simply nodded again.

"She always wanted to do that," Geraint said, adding, his brown eyes narrowed in curiosity, scanning Elin's face. "I remember her saying how much she hated it here, the weather, the people, our language – it was always a wonder to everyone that she stayed with Llion at all, *a dweud y gwir*/tell you the truth! They were ill-matched from the start, in my view."

Elin had wondered about these same things for her entire life, but there was something in Geraint's tone that made her think he knew more.

"She was happy to leave, and I don't know why she stayed so long either. Worried what people would say, perhaps. Perhaps she had other reasons I don't know about..."

"She put you first, remember that, and people do things for many reasons. Let's just leave it at that." He started walking briskly towards a stone outbuilding, so she followed him. "I'll get my tools, and we'll set off."

This slight tension dissipated as they walked up the rock-strewn slopes together, and each step took them higher, giving them a more spectacular view. They both relaxed as a burst of sunshine warmed them and lit up the landscape in all its rich and varied beauty.

"Are you married yet, *cariad*/dear?" Geraint asked.

"No. Not found anyone good enough to risk it, yet," Elin said. "It didn't bring my parents much happiness, from what I could see. Anwen says there are more important things for a woman to do than get married."

The old man looked at her, his face sharp and alert. "Well, she would say that. It was never right for Anwen Jones, but she always did choose herself above anyone else. Your mother did her best, remember that. As for your father, well, he was a man of duty and loyalty and you'd do well to be like *him*, I say. And don't dismiss marriage before you've tried it."

He snorted and picked up his tool bag. "*Reit 'ta.*/Right then. Enough talking. Let's get some work done."

Slightly stunned, Elin followed him on up the slope to the stone-walled sheep pen Geraint was to repair that day. As she took some photos of him at work, he did not speak again and she was thankful for it; he had shaken her. It seemed that there *was* more to know about her parents' marriage, but she needed to proceed with much more caution if she was ever to find out what it was.

For the rest of her life, Elin associated the sounds, the scents, the *feel* of winter gradually metamorphosing into spring and then into summer with the months she spent helping Anwen set her memories down. They sat together, hour after hour, as the old woman tried to tell her story, occasionally flapping a piece of paper – a sketch, or letter – to back up her ramblings. This haphazard method proved so stressful for both women that Elin soon started recording what Anwen said on her phone rather than trying to write it down, as her voice was weak, her speech often unclear and her concentration, sporadic. But the old woman found this difficult and embarrassing, saying she felt like a performing monkey expected to spout on cue. She refused to continue.

Knowing how much Anwen despised her mobile, Elin bought her a simple Dictaphone to use if and when she wanted to, or when she had forgotten something. Recording it herself, in her own time, made her feel under less pressure and enabled her to remember things in incredible detail in a relaxed way, and in private. In the small hours, when she lay awake, she roamed over her memories and highlighted certain events that glowed like embers in the ashes of her past. She loved what she called "the little speaking machine" and recorded what she recalled of a dance held at harvest time at which she had first been kissed by a boy called Iwan and the annual gathering of the sheep off the mountains in which everyone in the community, young and old, took part. She recorded her memory of a game she had played with two young brothers in which each dared the other to jump over a rushing stream. Elin did not have to be told that these brothers were her father Llion and his brother Dafydd because Anwen's voice became a whisper as she spoke about them:

"They were as close as a conker and its case; each depended on the other until… it had to happen, it was inevitable, after…"

Elin listened to the recording, but Anwen did not go on. There was only a long silence until she heard the click of the machine being turned off. This fraternal bond, so strong, irrevocably shattered by an accident on Tryfan, had lain at the heart of her father's terrible distress on their walk that day so many years ago, and had underpinned his life, so Barbara had told her. He had "never got over it". Frustrated, and feeling she had a *right* to know more, Elin dared to ask about the uncle she had never met once more.

"I know Dafydd fell and died on Tryfan, and that Dad was with him on the day of the accident, but I have no idea what actually happened or why they argued, and I think you are the only person who can tell me."

A pause, punctuated only by the low tick of the antique clock over the fireplace. "To use your clever-clever language, I could, but I won't," Anwen said. She was shaking, putting her teacup down with exaggerated care, but her voice was firm. "Your father and I swore we would not tell you about that day, or what led up to it and I will never break that promise."

"But why…?"

"*Because I say so!*" she shouted, making Smot flatten his soft ears to her head in fear. "I have allowed you access to my past, my work, even my *heart*, but my soul remains my own, with its darkest secrets intact. I am not a shell to be prised open to find the pearl inside me! I told you that when we began this task. There will be *lacunae*." She doubled over, coughing uncontrollably.

Now, Elin understood. The accident remained the largest, most significant of the omissions in the story, but there were more. For instance, Anwen had given her no details at all about the early years after art college, her years of travelling the world, after which she'd returned home to North Wales in her late thirties, having decided that "the beauty of her homeland would be her muse". When Elin had pressed her about it, the old woman had snapped:

"I hadn't produced any work of note until I was almost forty. There's nothing to tell, because nothing of interest happened in that fallow time. I was too young and foolish."

But Elin had not entirely believed her.

By the end of May, a first draft of Anwen Jones' life story, travels and ground-breaking career as an artist, was almost complete. Elin spent innumerable hours reading letters, articles and reviews, piecing together which exhibition was triumphant in which gallery in which city in which year, and then slotting in the random thoughts the old woman had recorded herself at the oddest of hours, gems of clarity that made their settings sing. Often, the sequence of events seemed impossible, almost fantastical, as it was so packed with coincidences, strokes of luck and unexpected revelations, but this was the story as Anwen remembered it, so Elin was respectfully faithful to that. She remembered George Eliot's words:

"*No story is the same to us after a lapse of time: or rather, we who read it are no longer the same interpreters.*"

The complex puzzle was almost complete, but Anwen was exhausted. When summer arrived in a blaze of colour and sunshine, both women needed respite from their joint undertaking before the final lap of what felt like a marathon. Elin often found Anwen asleep when she arrived, her breath shallow and her parchment-thin skin stretched over her cheekbones and jawline giving her a haunted, vulpine look. She was happy to make sure Merlin and Smot were looked after, but Eva adopted her four raggedy chickens, who needed considerably more care than they were getting. A true carer, Eva was increasingly reluctant to be responsible for Anwen, however, especially as her baby was due fairly soon and someone else would be taking over Anwen's care.

"I worry. Anwen only eats when you come, and she's a proud lady, but... she's a little *smelly*," Eva confided shyly. "The next person won't know her as we do and treat her right."

"I know," Elin said. She had noticed a ripeness in the cottage of late, a foisty smell that even the constant pall of cigarette smoke could not disguise. "But if you're thinking about residential care, how can we even *go* there?"

Eva shook her head. "It cannot be. She will never leave this place unless she is dragged, but she must rest more. You must tell her."

"I will. I promise," Elin replied, slightly disturbed at the urgency in the young woman's tone. Was there more to know about Anwen's health? If so, Eva was tight-lipped on detail.

And so, the two friends' relationship shifted again, a kaleidoscopic pattern that was ever-changing, tied to their needs and feelings. Anwen needed Elin more than she would ever admit, and it felt good, if unfamiliar, for Elin to *feel* needed. When, one afternoon, having received a final demand for electricity and gas that she had no means of paying, Elin felt she had no choice but to confess to being completely broke, Anwen immediately insisted on paying her for the work she was doing, and told her to "stop fussing".

"You are doing a job only a professional could do. Let's have no more nonsense about not taking my money," she'd said. "It's the least I can do for you – too little, too late."

As the swallows danced each evening above the slate roofs of *Cân y mynyddoedd*, Anwen sat outside and let the sun warm her while Elin cooked her supper and then stayed the night on an ancient double airbed Eva had lent them. The old woman was too ill to be left alone in her remote home anymore. When Anwen was asleep, Elin often sat outside wrapped in a thick, Welsh woollen blanket and looked up at the stars as she sipped a glass of red wine. Despite herself, she thought of Dylan then, and wondered where life had taken him since the brief time they had spent together. Far from here she was certain, and yet she still felt his calm presence as she traced a pattern of stars in the sky with her finger. Some people are easier to forget than others.

When Anwen's life story was written, Elin was relieved, even proud, but she knew that no publisher would accept the manuscript of an autobiography so devoid of any personal element. Anwen had never married or had children, and she had been in love with Dafydd, her uncle, Elin was almost certain, and yet there was no mention of love or lovers in the memories she'd shared with her thus far. Again, it was a risk, but one warm June evening as they sat watching male glow-worms light up the sky for the poor ground-bound females, she dared to ask for more.

"Did you have lots of affairs as you travelled, conquering the art world? You must have done – you were pretty stunning, but you never married."

The old woman did not take the bait. Instead, she said, "I saw no need for all that. I had my work. It would've got in the way." She paused. "We've talked about this before. Do you really still see marriage as the main goal in your life, the thing you were put on this earth for?"

Elin felt uncomfortable, interrogated. "No, I don't think I do, but I do want to be loved," she replied warily. The old woman nodded silently, and Elin dared to add, "Have you ever been truly loved, Anwen?"

The old woman sighed, and closed her eyes for a moment. When she opened them, she snapped. "Yes, I have, but it brought only suffering to all involved. Why must you keep asking me about it? I don't want to answer questions about... that kind of thing. *Stopia!*/stop!"

Elin, shocked, said nothing. There was clearly no point in pushing for more either for herself, or for the book they were writing. Anwen seemed content that the factual outline, the broad sweep of her life, was chronicled, but Elin could not help but long to know the links between events that Anwen would not tell her, the things that had made her the woman she was. The chances of that happening looked impossibly slim.

THIRTY-ONE

Once the schools broke up for Whitsun, Llanberis became much busier almost overnight. Holidaymakers invaded the town and campervans formed a white barricade around the lake, much to the chagrin of locals. Despite this annual invasion, the shift in mood in the town when the sun deigned to shine was almost palpable, as if everything and everyone sparkled again after the grey skies and regular rain of the winter. The slabs of cut slate around the old quarries glittered like glass and pink dog roses spooled through all the hedgerows. It was a time of hope and the promise of warm, long days.

Unlike Elin, Anwen was attuned to every change of weather, having lived in these hills her whole life, and so she greeted the arrival of summer as her own, private holiday, giving her permission to relax. She spoke very little, but when she did, her voice was soft and gentle, as if being angry was too much effort now and ran counter to nature's ease. It also made her cough more.

When she dozed, her legs splayed in front of a rickety deck chair outside the cottage, Elin decided that it was as if her body needed to soak up the sunshine to recharge, as reptiles do. At times, the old woman was so quiet and still that Elin had to put her ear next to her mouth to check she was still breathing. There was huge relief when she was, but there was also something concerning her about this strange softening of mood and growing inactivity. What was Anwen conserving her strength *for*? A final explosion of creativity, a dramatically swift decline or an emotional outpouring? All three options were possible, and so Elin watched her friend with growing concern. Something was wrong here, she knew, without it having to be said. With no work, no friends nearby and no plans, this slow, predictable routine was shot through with the ominous stillness that precedes a thunderstorm.

The storm arrived, but it came in an unexpected form when Florence and her two kids, Archie, a rambunctious three-year-old, and fifteen-month-old Lily, arrived. Elin's first instinct was to fob Florence off when she rang very early one morning asking if they could come, but when she heard her friend's taut voice, she knew she had no real choice. Anwen would still be looked after and perhaps meeting Flo and her adorable, if energetic, kids would lift her?

"I'm so tired, El. I can hardly put one foot in front of the other. Marta is back home in Spain for a month and Marcus is on some big case in the Crown Court, so I get 24/7 childcare for a week as part of my so-called holiday!"

Flo's tone had told her that she would rather have her wisdom teeth extracted with a garlic crusher than stay in London, but Elin was surprised. Her friend had always seemed to have the work/life balance sorted with her lovely home, successful but kind husband, obliging au pair and part-time editorial job in a well-respected publishing house. Elin simply listened as her friend poured her feelings into a safe space – her ear. It took quite a while.

"I know I'm probably the worst mother on the planet, but it's relentless, El. It's 365 days a year without respite and I just want to go for a walk on my own, or watch a daft sitcom without any interruption, or have time to rinse out all the conditioner before someone yells my name or drink a cup of tea before it's cold. I love them, I truly do, but I need... I need..."

"You need to come here for a few days, so pack up and get

here," Elin said. "I've got space, and we can take them out and about."

A sob came down the line. "I think I'm too tired to drive all that way, though. Are there any trains?"

"For goodness' sake, yes – we even have running water here now, you know," she said. "Get a direct train from Euston to Bangor. You'll be here in under four hours, all being well. So how about tomorrow?"

She could hear Flo already tapping frantically on a laptop. "How about today? There's a train arriving in Bangor at 16.45 p.m.... if that's OK with you, of course, El. Do say if not."

Elin smiled to herself. "See you later. And bring macs and bikinis."

Hanging up, she felt good. If anyone deserved a break, it was her friend Flo.

For the following four days, Flo, Archie and Lily invaded Elin's life and home so completely that she could hardly imagine how she'd filled her time before they were there. The weather obliged with a spell of gorgeous sunshine, which meant that they spent most of every day outside. Flo could hardly believe how early, or how willingly her children went to sleep each night, but when Elin told her that the air up here would sell for a fortune if it could be bottled, she got it. Elin still slept up at *Cân y mynyddoedd*, but they all spent the mornings together, either on the beach, in the playground beside Lake Padarn or playing in Elin's "garden that isn't a garden". Drawing a hopscotch grid on the ugly stone slabbed-path Barbara had laid proved a huge and unexpected hit.

After lunch, she went back up to Anwen's, leaving Flo to relax while Lily napped and Archie watched cartoons. Lily, a child who so rarely spoke that Marcus had suggested she might be an elective mute, was besotted with Mouse, Elin's cat, and was often found babbling confidences into the long-suffering feline's ear. She knew that Mouse would never share them.

On the day before they were to leave for London, Eva offered to babysit so that Elin and Flo could go to the sauna next to Lake Padarn, and then for lunch in a wholefood café in town. Anwen had said she definitely wanted to meet Elin's visitors before they left, so it was arranged that Eva would take the children up to Anwen's cottage and they could meet up there.

"Remember not to smoke when the children are in the house," Elin had told her sternly. She had given up telling her that Eva was pregnant, so also should not have to inhale her smoke.

"Then I will take them *out* of the house, so that I can," Anwen replied, winking.

The day was, once more, a warm one, but there was a keen breeze, so the pavements were speckled with a confetti of leaves and petals and the surface of the lake was rippled like molten glass. The sauna was tiny, but had a breathtaking view over the water and both Elin and Flo felt totally reinvigorated after their hour spent either being very hot or very, very cold when they plunged into the ever-freezing lake to cool off. Lunch was both healthy and delicious, and as they began the slow climb up through the woods towards *Cân y mynyddoedd*, Flo rhapsodised about what she'd dubbed her "sanity break".

"I feel almost drunk, El. It's so, so beautiful here, and the air, as you say, fills your entire *body*, not just your lungs. And there's no sense of rush, or wishing for more – everything we've done this week has seemed enough in itself, if that makes any sense. Nothing could have made this experience any better, and I'll never forget it – and neither will Archie and Lily."

Elin blushed with pleasure. This was exactly what she had hoped for, and a small part of her delight was the knowledge that Flo would go back and tell the others in their little group that Elin had made a good decision in coming back here rather than running away from life, as they'd probably suspected. She also hoped that they would not decide to visit as well. Both Abigail and Saskia, wonderful as they were, were best kept at a safe distance for the moment. She did not have the energy they would require, and expect.

"I have to say, I'm curious to meet your eccentric artist friend. I looked her up, and she's really quite famous. She's got pictures in big galleries."

Elin smiled, remembering Llion telling her just the same things about Anwen, in almost the same words, when she was a child. But as they neared the start of the narrow, stony path that led up to the cottage, they stopped dead, as a man and woman stood right in front of them on their way down: Dylan Williams and the young woman Elin had seen him with here in the pub and in Bath. His face exploded into a broad grin when he recognised Elin, but the woman scowled and continued walking quickly downhill without a backward glance.

"*Elin, sut wyt ti?*/How are you?" Dylan cried, almost losing his footing on some rough ground in his eagerness to stop. "Wow, it's amazing to see you again. I wondered if I might. Hey, wait a second! This is that friend of mine I was telling you about!" he shouted after the young woman, but she was already almost out of sight.

Elin sensed Flo prickling with curiosity, but she felt as if she had been shot in the chest; she could hardly breathe. What was Dylan doing here, in these woods, stalking her in a place that meant safety, no, *sanctuary* to her, and with his scrawny new girl-friend too? She had not thought about him for, well, *a few days* at least and she did not need him back in her head, or her life.

"Think you'd better go," she said, her face stony. "Looks like you're needed elsewhere."

"Argh, I'm sorry that she comes across as so rude. She's just shy," Dylan said. "I can see you're busy now, but please, let's meet up, as I'm back for a few days. I know I said that at Christmas, but, well, stuff came up. Sorry."

Elin kicked some small stones on the path, as she simply could not look at him. Eventually, she said, "I get it. I've got a lot on at the moment as well, with Anwen, and my friends from London staying. Perhaps see you around sometime."

Dylan's hurt was obvious, and he struggled to swallow. "OK, sure. Look, I'd better go and catch up with her... but it would be great to see you again, Elin, properly I mean. You've still got my number, haven't you?"

Elin nodded again, feeling Flo's glare almost burning her right cheek as Dylan walked slowly past them, mumbling, "Right, OK then, I'll be off. Hope to, er, see you around... perhaps, if you have time." His stooped shoulders showed just how dejected he felt.

Flo turned to Elin the second he had been swallowed by the trees, saying, "That girl was rude, but so were you, El! And that man seemed really happy to see you. From the way you reacted, I guess that's the one who showed you the stars, and you spent a blissfully wonderful day with?"

Elin put her head in her hands. She had never been so rude to anyone in her entire life, but it was the only reaction she could muster and she had shocked herself. What on earth had prompted such a visceral response? Confused, she decided to cover her shame with anger.

"I know I was rude, and I'm embarrassed, but really, why on earth would I want to spend time with him and his grumpy girlfriend? He completely pied me at Christmas. I'm worth better than that," she snapped, striding off up the hill. "Let's see Anwen, pick up the kids and forget all about it."

"She might not be his partner, you don't know that for sure... and he seemed so *nice*," Flo spluttered, trotting up the hill behind her.

"You said Theo was 'nice' too and look how that turned out! I've seen them together before, OK, so just let it go please," Elin said, before stopping and taking a deep breath. "Sorry, Flo, but I really think I'm better off single. I've accepted it, so why can't everyone else?"

But as they walked on in silence, Elin felt shame creep up through her body from her toes to the top of her head. She had just behaved appallingly, and Dylan's wounded face would be etched on her memory for a long, long time. Yes, that girl had been rude, but she probably felt threatened if he had told her about the time they had spent together which both of them had known was unforgettable. Eventually, shyly, she took one of Flo's hands in hers and mouthed "Sorry" once more and was instantly enveloped in a hug.

As they walked up the last part of the path, Elin remembered words she had said to Anwen: 'I do want to love and be loved.' That, of course, was why she had reacted so vehemently. She had dared to hope she might finally have had that with Dylan.

THIRTY-TWO

The sun had dipped below the peaks opposite the lake by the time they reached *Cân y mynyddoedd,* and the trees were sending long, spidery shadows across the garden. Eva was sitting with Archie, reading him a story and Anwen, in her usual deck chair, was cradling a sleepy-looking Lily on her lap. The scene was so peaceful and perfect that Flo stopped and took a quick photo before they were seen. Elin, still jangling from their encounter with Dylan, hung back and watched.

She noted the soft look on Anwen's face, framed by her hair, her profile as she cradled Lily, humming a familiar melody. The combination of things she knew for certain and memories she could only glimpse crowded in on her, so vivid that they were beyond the brain trickery of *déjà vu.* This woman, this baby girl, this small, domestic tapestry formed an image she recognised. It had happened before, and it had happened here. When Anwen saw her, she looked up and smiled gently before turning to Florence.

"You are the mother of these two darlings, I assume?" she said.

Florence nodded, almost dumbstruck at the sight of an elderly lady with copious whiskers wearing a pink silk kaftan and holding her baby. When she remembered that this was Anwen Jones, the international bestselling artist and renowned eccentric recluse, she was *completely* dumbstruck.

"Oh, we've had such a blissful afternoon. Little Lily's been chatting away and Archie is a delight," she said. "You should be very proud, my dear."

"*Chatting?* Really? But Lily's always so quiet. She never speaks, in fact. We've been worried about her, wondering if we need to get a specialist opinion. Marcus thinks we should, you see," Florence gabbled. "I mean, that's absolutely amazing. I'm Florence, by the way. I know you're Anwen, because Elin's told me all about you."

Lily opened her eyes and said, "Mummy!" before scrambling off Anwen's lap and running towards her. "I like dis house here."

"Now, you're a bloody miracle-worker as well as all your other talents," Elin muttered to Anwen as she pulled the kaftan over the bare, knobbly knees Lily had exposed. "But you'd better put these away, for everyone's sake."

The evening started wonderfully. Florence, initially awestruck by Anwen, relaxed after a large glass of wine drunk too fast, and it was soon clear that they would all be staying overnight. Both children, exhausted after their afternoon, fell asleep on a mound of cushions in the conservatory with Smot at their feet, keeping guard. Anwen sat giving orders from her armchair with Merlin in her lap as the others cooked a simple pasta, demanding her glass be refilled at regular intervals. Seeing her old friend's cheeks alight with the happiness of company quietened Elin's growing worries about her health for a while; such lovely moments should be savoured, she had learnt.

They ate by candlelight, which seemed to reconfigure their features into shapes and shadows Elin had not seen before. Her and Flo's skin glowed with fresh air and youth, as both were still only in their early thirties, but Anwen's face, criss-crossed with deep lines and the tracks of past struggles and a long life, told her own, rich story. Elin began to wonder if the world actually needed a book about her work, her success. The woman she had been, and the woman she was, were both writ large on her cheeks and in her hollowed eye sockets. If it was not even truly complete, truly *honest*, was it worth anything at all? Having told Flo that she felt Anwen was holding a lot back to safeguard both her privacy and her legacy, she was taken off guard when her friend began firing questions at the old woman after her third glass of red.

"Anwen, I'm just amazed at how you got Lily to talk to you so easily," Flo slurred, her eyelids drooping with the bone-weary tiredness only people with small children know. "She won't sit on anyone's lap, not even my husband's, but she was happy as Larry in yours. How did you know what to *do* as you haven't got any kids yourself?"

"I may not strike you as the maternal type, Florence, but I spent a great deal of time with Elin when she was small, and also when she was *not* so small, as she will tell you," Anwen said briskly, adding, even more briskly, "Lily is a gorgeous child. Perhaps you should speak to her more, so that she learns the skill herself."

Elin touched her friend's arm, and when she turned, her face warned: "carry on like this and you will get hurt".

Luckily, Flo brushed the slight off with a fake laugh. The storm clouds that had been gathering above Anwen's head began to dissipate, but in Flo's attempt to move the conversation on, they gathered above Elin's.

"We met a friend of El's on the way up, a young man," Florence said with slightly forced cheerfulness. "Perhaps you saw him, as you were all out in the garden?"

Anwen's posture stiffened slightly. "Yes, I did. Him and a young woman who looked rather like a greyhound, all legs and a thin face. We greeted each other, but I know him anyway, or should I say I know *of* him."

Elin blurted, "I told you about him, Anwen. He's called Dylan and we spent a day together last year. He's a musician... and a cook, sometimes."

"I remember. You went to Tryfan together," Anwen said. "Dylan Williams, his name is. It was splashed all over the local paper when he had that motorbike accident that killed his girlfriend," she said, her eyes fixed on Elin's face.

There was an immediate chill in the room. Elin had the sense of being in the midst of a game of tactical manoeuvres, one she did not like at all.

"Yes, Gwenda at the pub told me about it. Awful, for everyone, and not his fault, either, the police investigation concluded," she said, almost robotically. Why was Anwen being so *brutal*?

"I heard he was going too fast, even though he was absolved of blame on that occasion," Anwen said, ignoring Elin's stricken face. "His parents were oddballs, and his sister Cara is a bit of a problem, I gather. Someone once told me she was a witch, in fact, mixing potions and all kinds of weirdness. All nonsense, I'm sure, and I can't judge what I haven't seen. He's very loyal to her, which says a lot about him in my view. I like loyalty in a person. But getting too close to him can prove dangerous, it seems."

Elin stared at Anwen. The old woman had just veered from condemning Dylan to almost praising him before issuing an ominous warning. What was going on here? Why was Anwen trying to steer her away from him? Did he present a possible rival for her attention? She had wondered this before. This cold insensitivity mirrored the way she had greeted her when she'd first returned, as if she was constantly testing her. Elin hated it.

"Please stop being so nasty, Anwen. There's no likelihood of me ever seeing him again anyway. He's got a new partner, is very successful and has long since forgotten all about me, I'm sure," Elin said firmly.

"I don't think so," Anwen said, equally firmly. "And I *do* think he came past here to look for you."

Another long pause, in which there was so much tension it felt like a field of active static in the room. Flo got up and went into the conservatory, mouthing, "I think I'll check on the kids."

"What on earth do you mean?" Elin asked, her heart beginning to pound. "Did he say something to make you think he came this way deliberately?"

"Well, he asked if you were home at the moment, so I told him you were and that you were on your way up to see me," Anwen said, in a slow, measured tone. "He looked so hopeful, poor lad, and I remembered that last year, when you told me about him, you said he had stirred something in you."

Elin snorted. "That's absolute nonsense and you know it. I never said anything of the kind. I actually had a full-on relationship in London with a man called Theo after that one day Dylan and I spent together, and neither of us got in touch again," Elin said, too quickly. She could feel Anwen's eyes watching her very closely indeed.

"Then I beg your pardon, but you shared something in that short time, didn't you? Sometimes, people make a mark on our souls, and that stays with us," the old woman said, trying not to cough. "I do think you need to know what baggage he comes with before you meet again – the burdens he carries with him, the dangers he could pose to a vulnerable person like you. We all carry the past with us, some more than others, but I always advise caution when it comes to affairs of the heart. And I may be wrong, but I think the unusual-looking young woman he was with today was Cara, his sister, not a new partner."

Elin gasped and felt goosebumps prickling her arms. The girl had the same high cheekbones and thick hair as Dylan, but her thin face, unlike his kind and open one, was shadowed with sadness. Yes, it did seem at least possible that she was his mysterious sister, not his lover and that her perceived rudeness was, as he had said, a deep shyness.

"Oh my goodness, you could be right," she murmured. "He

said he often came home to check on her, and she didn't look either well, or happy, poor girl."

"No. I hear she is neither. Eva is my only source of local gossip these days so it may not be correct, but apparently, she sees nobody and only ever wears black. A lost cause, on all fronts."

"I hope not. That's a truly terrible thing to be," Elin murmured. She had often considered herself one of those, and it was not good.

A log hissed on the fire, and Merlin the cat moved to sit on the rug in front of it, stretching her long body out to absorb as much heat as possible.

Elin stretched her legs out too, and exhaled slowly. "Oh, it's all so strange, Anwen. I spent so little time with Dylan, and yet I've never met anyone who made me feel like he did. I'm not sure whether that's good or bad, but I suppose I need to find out. I hate taking risks. They always backfire."

"Yes, they can, but in my experience, risks can sometimes be opportunities," Anwen said. "It was a risk, your coming back to see me after all these years, for instance. Such chances don't come twice."

Elin smiled at her. "I thought just the same myself a while back."

After she had helped Anwen into bed, Elin went outside to clear up the detritus of the day. The sky was ink-black, the stars were obscured by a thin veil of cloud and it was bitterly cold. Dylan was only a few miles away right now, in his family smallholding, perhaps looking up at the same starless sky. The fact that he had probably come up here to see her was flattering, but still, she was not sure what to do about it. Anwen was right – he carried wounds, scars from the past, as she did, and they both had other hopes, other dreams. Elin was determined not to let herself be distracted from them by the vague possibility of a relationship. She had done that before, and paid dearly.

And yet, as she drifted into sleep next to Flo on the airbed, she felt a quiet contentment she had not felt for a long time. Dylan felt drawn to her, as she did to him: perhaps that was as good a foundation as any for whatever was to come next. Some of George Eliot's words came to her, as they so often did when she was troubled:

"A woman may get to love by degrees – the best fire does not flare up the soonest."

THIRTY-THREE

When Flo, Archie and Lily left, everyone, including all the pets, were very upset to see them go. Flo had spent hours talking to Anwen about what inspired her creativity as her own had evaporated since having kids. She was tearfully grateful when the old woman gave her a rough sketch she had done of her children, heads bent low over a caterpillar they had discovered in the garden.

"I shall treasure it always," Flo said.

"Treasure them, because each day you have with them is sacred," the old woman replied, her thin hand round Flo's arm. "They will soon be gone, and you'll regret seeing them more as burdens than as gifts, believe me."

Lily had formed an incredibly close bond with Anwen and had to be almost prised out of her arms when it was time to say goodbye. Archie wept bitterly when he had to bid farewell to Smot, whom he had grown to love.

Flo had not dared to mention Dylan to Elin since the tense evening at Anwen's. When she got their cases out of the car at Bangor station, she could contain herself no longer.

"What do you think you'll do about Dylan? I mean, I'm not going to insist on your seeing him again, but I am going to very strongly recommend it. He's much more than 'nice' – he's *unique*, like you. Even Anwen felt it – you heard what she said about him: 'I liked him'. Now, she can't say that very often."

Turning to her friend, Elin said, "I know, and she doesn't, but I'm not sure I want a relationship right now, let alone one with a man who's probably just passing through. And I don't think Anwen's well, so I need to focus on supporting her and getting her book finished."

"OK, but a message to say you're sorry about that weird encounter the other day wouldn't do any harm. Poor guy."

"It was toe-curlingly awful, wasn't it? I will apologise, but I won't make a promise to him that I can't keep."

Flo hugged her. "I know, but I can't bear to think of you being on your own, especially if Anwen's health is deteriorating and there's a sad time ahead. I think she's very ill – that cough of hers is awful."

"I know. I'll talk to her, get her to see a doctor. But I have plans for the future, don't worry – ones that Anwen has helped me initiate, and ideas that will keep me busy if things get tough."

"But..."

"But nothing. Let's get you to the train, because you'll have to pay a king's ransom for more tickets if you miss it," Elin said, opening the passenger door. "I'll keep in touch, but promise me not to waste time fretting about me. Enjoy those kids instead!"

Flo nodded. "I promise. For what it's worth, I think you did the right thing, being here for a while. It suits you, all this space, all this *wildness*, but don't let it bury you alive, as it did Barbara. People need people, you know, and love – we all need that."

"Yes, but I'm done with compromising with men like Antoine and Theo. Surely there are many ways of being useful and happy that don't have to involve marriage and kids?" Elin said, wanting Flo to go now, and leave her in peace.

"Look, I can testify to the fact that both those options for happiness have more holes than a Swiss cheese, but don't let yourself be *lonely*, El. Anwen has spent a lot of her life steeped in regret, for all her success as an artist. I feel that, when I'm with her, don't you?"

"Yes, of course I do, but she won't tell me *what* she regrets, and the book's not finished until she does. I need to know, as much as she needs to tell me."

"She will, I'm sure..."

"...when the time is right, I know," Elin added impatiently.

On the drive back to Llanberis, the sun was setting the sky alight with a subtle wash of pinks and creams. The outline of the mountains was the same as it had been for millennia, both smooth and rugged, each peak taking its allotted place in the range and forming an indelible part of the perfect whole. In the warmth of the evening sunlight, the spectrum of greens that each tree, each hedge, each field created formed a stunning tapestry that Elin had never seen anywhere else. In comparison to this constancy, this permanence, her needs, her doubts, felt so small and insignificant. She had a comfortable home; she was fit and healthy; she was free of the ties that fettered so many women her age and she was no longer shackled to a job she despised. Instead, she had a worthwhile task in writing Anwen's life story and had been blessed by having time to spend with her. She had much to be thankful for and to look forward to.

When she opened the door to her house and was greeted with silence, followed by the soft thud of Mouse jumping down off her bed and coming to greet her, she did not feel alone, as Flo had feared. There was so much of value here, such creative fire, natural beauty and rich history – her own amongst it. For now, that was enough, Elin told herself.

But before she slept that night, she texted Dylan both to apologise and to find out if Anwen had been right in thinking his companion was his sister.

Sorry the other day was so awkward, and if I annoyed your sister. I'm here indefinitely, so yes, let's meet. E.

This time, he did not reply to her message immediately, but she slept much better for having sent it.

THIRTY-FOUR

Elin was almost blinded by the sunlight streaming through her small bedroom window and directly into her eyes the next morning. It was going to be a hot day and for the first time, she understood the people who gathered most days on the pontoon near the lake, and swam in its clear, cold water. Would it make her feel as good as it seemed to make them feel? Their shrieks as they went in and blue-lipped shivers when they came out made her conclude that she wasn't brave enough to risk finding out today. Opening her phone, she saw she had two messages. The first, from Dylan, was kind and reassuring:

> No worries. Cara was twice as rude as you were. She's just a bit possessive of me. I actually think you two would get on and it sounds like you both need a friend. Off to Cardiff for a few days, but in touch when back. D.

The second, from Eva, Anwen's carer, was deeply concerning:

> Anwen is not good this morning, but I have to leave now to get to the next person. Sorry I didn't tell you before. Please come quick.

"Didn't tell me *what*?" Elin said aloud. "Shit. I knew something was wrong."

Within half an hour, Elin was at Anwen's cottage. She opened the front door to a dark, still-curtained room, a sinkful of dirty dishes and the unmistakeable whiff of dog poo. Smot, cowering under the kitchen table, did not emerge to greet her. Eva had clearly been too preoccupied with Anwen to let her out.

"It's OK, sweetheart. I'll sort this," Elin murmured, as the dog shot out of the open front door.

Going upstairs, Elin was hit by another unfamiliar yet instantly recognisable smell, a sweetness she remembered from her father's last weeks: illness. Anwen was asleep, her white hair fanned across the pillow and her mouth open to reveal almost no teeth. For the first time, Elin realised that Anwen wore dentures, as they were beaming at her from inside a grubby glass by the bed. Her breath was laboured, noisy, rattling with phlegm; she looked so old and frail that Elin decided not to wake her up before she was ready.

Tiptoeing out of the room, she went downstairs to deal with Smot's accident and clear up. The table was strewn with sketches, letters, photos and documents that Anwen must have been looking through last night. The old woman was intensely private, and had not known she would be unable to put them away this morning, so here they lay, next to an empty black metal box. Elin hesitated for only a few seconds before sitting down at the table to read them. These papers could contain the parts of Anwen's story that she would not tell her, and she wanted, needed, to know. Regret would have to wait this time.

One letter was from *Ysbyty Gwynedd*/Gwynedd Hospital in Bangor with an appointment with a Dr Bethan Elis-Williams to discuss Anwen's recent MRI scan and treatment options. The banner above the letter read URGENT: YOUR ATTENTION REQUIRED in red type. When Elin's brain had processed this, she realised that Eva must have taken her for the MRI scan when she'd been away for weeks in Bath for her mother's wedding. Why had neither woman mentioned it? Alarm bells began to ring very loudly indeed.

There was also a very dry letter from her solicitor confirming their recent discussion about minor changes she had made to her will, and Elin remembered Anwen's concern that some of her work would not be on public display, but secreted in private collections, after her death. These changes were probably to ensure that never happened, but Elin could not waste time wading through the legal jargon. Next, she found letters from admirers of her work who sugared their praise with offers of marriage and a few very ardent, almost pornographic, letters from an art dealer in Argentina called Juan. Beneath all of this, tucked inside a brown envelope, was a small black and white photograph. Elin struggled to make sense of the faint image at first: two stocky men standing a little apart, both with slicked-back hair, alike, but with different bone structure and both solemn-faced and staring straight ahead of them. One of the men she felt she knew somehow, but not like that, not so *young*. They were standing behind a plumpish woman with a sweep of blonde hair, a burning cigarette in one hand and a blank expression on her face. On the very edge of one of her knees sat a small baby, its face partly shadowed by a wide-brimmed sun-bonnet and its tiny pink arms like the sticks small children give the first people they draw.

"Oh my God, that man on the left is *Dad*," Elin whispered, looking more closely. "And so the other one must be his brother Dafydd, who *does* look a bit like me, just as Emlyn said when he first saw me. And that woman has to be a young Anwen, but a lot fuller of figure than she is now. But who is the baby?"

Possibilities ricocheted around in her head so fast it was hard to breathe. There had not been any other babies for Llion and Barbara after her, though she now knew that they had lost two before her. Anwen had never mentioned having a child herself, which meant that Barbara was taking the photo, so was the baby her, or her long-dead younger sister? This sad vignette asked more questions than it answered, but Elin knew it had to be important to have been hidden for so long.

As the dull thuds from upstairs became the slow tread of feet on wooden stairs, Elin stuffed the picture under all the other papers, but she deliberately placed the one from the hospital right on the top of the pile. That, they needed to talk about. When Anwen appeared in the doorway, her eyes went straight to it.

"Yes, I do have something to tell you," she said. "But first, I need a cup of tea and a cigarette."

THIRTY-FIVE

The next hour felt like the slowest of Elin's life. She let Anwen talk uninterrupted, as there was no need to prompt or question her: the truth flooded out of her without hesitation or distress, and she stopped only to light one cigarette from the glowing butt of another. She had known for months that she was very ill, as her weight had plummeted and her cough worsened, but, "We were too busy, you and I, making up for lost time. I hoped it would just sort itself out, which is the approach I've adopted all my life to things I don't want to think about."

She'd ignored her worsening symptoms even after going to the hospital with Eva for X-rays, tests and scans, and seeing the faces of the medics around her in the blue-curtained cubicles.

"They all knew, after those first X-rays, that it was lung cancer, but they insisted on running the whole gamut of tests before confirming the obvious," Anwen said. "Horrible business, all of it, but it does help focus the mind."

"So, Eva has known for ages, has she? Why didn't you tell me, and worse, why did you tell *her* not to tell me?" Elin said, her sadness mixed with a hefty dose of resentment.

"I didn't want to spoil the precious time we had together. I knew I was ill, you knew I wasn't well, but what would have been the point of baring all and casting the shadow of death over our second chance to be with each other," Anwen replied, a plaintive urgency in her voice that Elin had not heard before. "Once it was said, it couldn't be unsaid, and I didn't want to risk you not wanting to stay if things were going to… get difficult."

Suddenly, the old woman's need to write her life story, to catalogue her work, to prepare her legacy as she wanted it to be presented to the world, made complete sense. It was both her farewell and her last opportunity to be the centre of attention. When, eventually, Anwen stopped talking, sat back in her chair and took a few stertorous breaths, Elin took her chance to speak:

"But there's good treatment, Anwen. If there wasn't, surely the consultant wouldn't want to talk to you?" Elin said. "Please, at least *try* to live as long as you can. What will I do without you?"

"You will be fine. In fact, you will do great things, I know it," Anwen said firmly, but when she saw Elin's tearful face, she went on in a gentler tone. "Look, I don't see the point in talking about 'treatment' if they can't do anything to save me. I refuse to have chemotherapy, which is all they'll suggest. I don't want any of the dreadfulness my dear friend Non had to endure, when the person I had loved for over fifty years effectively died weeks before she *actually* died." She shook her head vehemently. "No, that's not for me. I will take enough painkillers to ease things but not enough to make me an incoherent idiot. My wish is to drift away in my own home." She paused again, and her eyes met Elin's. "But for that to happen, I need *you*, I'm afraid."

Wiping her eyes, Elin could not stop herself from saying what she said next:

"Is that why you were so glad when I came back? Because you need me to help you die?"

Anwen's face became thunderous. "No! You must never think that my joy in seeing you was *need*. I had no idea what faced me when we first saw each other again last year and if I need to hasten my end, I'll do it myself, thank you very much." A fit of coughing followed, which saw Elin gently patting her back as Barbara had always done to soothe her. "Ha, that won't help much, sadly. Cancer doesn't respond to kindness."

"We do need to speak to your consultant, whatever you say, so I'll arrange an appointment with her," Elin said, her voice full of resolution. "We'll go together, and explain how you feel about... what happens to you. And I promise I'll do my best to make sure it's as you want it to be."

"*Diolch, cariad*/Thank you, dear. Do what you think best. I'm tired now, so I think I'll go back up to bed, but stay for a while, if you can. I like to know you're here."

Despite the sadness of their situation, she had never felt closer to Anwen than she did at that moment, watching her brace herself to climb the stairs again. When she saw her slip her cigarette packet in her dressing gown pocket, she said:

"Might be worth quitting those, you know. Better late than never."

The old woman turned to face her. "Never is better than late, I say," before heading upwards, very slowly, one stair at a time.

The hopeful sunshine of the morning quickly dimmed and ominous rainclouds had crept across the sky by lunchtime. Elin sat with Smot at her feet and Merlin on her lap as the room darkened around her. She checked on Anwen regularly, and telephoned the hospital and made an appointment with the oncology consultant for the following week, explaining what had happened and apologising to the secretary for the delay.

"You'd be surprised how many people put these letters in a drawer and hope it will all go away," the woman said. "It never does."

By 3 p.m., Smot was restless. The sky was menacingly dark now, presaging a downpour, but Elin needed to get out of the gloom of the cottage, and away from thoughts of cancer and death. Anwen had been right, it would have spoilt their time together, to have known what lay ahead.

With each step she took down through the soft green canopy of trees and towards the lake, she remembered how it had been in the farmhouse, when her father was dying of the same disease that would soon take Anwen. Barbara had been dutiful, but it had been punishingly cruel to watch a strong man reduced to a haunted shadow of himself and to hear him groan in pain when the medication was waning. Elin had come home to share the burden for his last weeks, and exchanged her selfish lifestyle for the hushed dread of imminent death; she had not known what to say, or how to *be*. Would the same heavy pall soon descend on *Cân y mynyddoedd*? She shivered at the thought of it.

She had come home, like the cavalry, to rescue a struggling Barbara, but who would save *her* if it all got too much this time? Anwen had friends, but she had not seen most of them for a long time and they, too, were elderly. She could and would not ask her mother for help and advice, as she was happy now and it would be distressing for her to be reminded of cancer's cruelty. Flo and her other mates had busy lives and were hundreds of miles away and Dylan had a career to forge. This was too much to burden him with, surely? And yet, more than anything, Elin knew she needed a *friend* right now.

The face that swam into clear focus was not one she would ever have anticipated, but it was the only person who might begin to understand what she now faced: Dylan's sister Cara. She had nursed her dying mother, and hadn't he said that she seemed to have a gift for it? And hadn't he also told her, "*It sounds like you both need a friend.*"? Before the doubts about Cara's reputation crowded in, she texted him:

> Yes, I do need a friend. Anwen is dying of lung cancer. Please send me Cara's number if you still think we'd get on and she might be willing to help me. E.

A few minutes later, her phone rang and Dylan's name

appeared on the screen. Heart pounding, it took her almost a minute to muster enough courage to pick up.

"Hello, Dylan. Sorry to..."

"No worries. I haven't got much time now, but I wanted to speak to you, tell you how sorry I am about Anwen. Texts aren't enough for things like this." A pause. "I looked her up after I'd met her in her garden. She's an amazing person, and I'm not surprised you've always remembered her or that you came back to see her again."

"I had to, and now I'm so glad I did, because now, she's... dying, Dylan, and I can't bear it."

"Oh, Elin, I wish I was there. It's where I should be, with you. I have known that from the moment we met."

Elin, who had at first been thrilled to hear his voice, now shook her head in irritation. This was not the time for this kind of confessional outpouring.

"I just can't think about that, about us now. I'm sorry, because I know you want answers, but..."

"...I don't expect what you can't give."

"Thanks. I think I need to get through this with Anwen before I think about anything else. She and I share something I can't quite understand, but has sort of threaded through my whole life. Does that sound crazy?"

"Not at all, and I understand you needing to be with her and nobody else right now. I'll send you Cara's number, but I just wanted you to know that I am here for you and always will be." A pause, an in-breath. "I've been hurt in the past, like you, but you are the first person who made me feel that life could be good again."

Silence.

"I know and I feel the same, by the way. Bye."

They both hung up and a few seconds later, Dylan sent this text:

Cara's number is 08992 783991. Her bark is worse than her bite. X

Elin was glad that he'd sent her a 'X', not a heart emoji or a meme; just a simple, age-old symbol of love. They had the whole of the future to talk about what they felt about each other, and where that might lead. For now, Anwen was her only priority.

She would message Cara first, out of courtesy, but whatever the response, she would go to her late parents' smallholding and talk to her in person. To make herself vulnerable, and *ask* for friendship, did not come easy, but perhaps Dylan was right, and Cara needed a friend just as much as she did.

THIRTY-SIX

Cân y mynyddoedd became a hushed place, and the long hours were punctuated only by tending to Anwen and ensuring she was comfortable. Eva was within weeks of having her baby, and the new carer, Nia, was less friendly. Within a few days, Anwen had told her to "go away and never come back". This left Elin in sole charge, her only respite her walks with Smot while the old woman dozed. These precious hours only partially refilled her reserves of energy, and of sympathy, as Anwen became more irascible and her needs more constant. The old woman said she did not fear death, but feared *dying*, which was hard to listen to, day after day. Elin was more than thankful for the absolute necessity of walking the dog.

When she was outside, there was always something new, something small to make life seem brighter and more hopeful. The buttercups on the lower slopes almost glowed in the sunshine, a carpet of hopefulness. The hawthorns that clung to life in even the most exposed spots belied the vicious prickles they hid on each branch behind their ripening berries. Elin vividly remembered bringing Barbara a small posy of hawthorn twigs covered with creamy blossom, only to be scolded and told to take them outside immediately as local folklore said that they brought bad luck.

These memories, and these daily doses of nature, were a salve to Elin's beleaguered soul and a welcome counterbalance to what she knew lay, not too far, ahead. She had messaged Cara, saying:

> Hi, Elin Pugh here. Dylan thought we might get on, and I need your advice. An old friend is very ill indeed. Can I come and see you soon?

A thumbs-up emoji had been the only response, which was not as encouraging as Elin had hoped. She decided to go and ask her advice only when they knew the exact prognosis after talking to the oncology consultant.

In that strange, long week of waiting, Anwen slept for a large part of each day. Elin was often ready with a list of book-related questions when she woke, questions she answered willingly as they both sat in a fug of cigarette smoke. Both women sensed that time was shorter than they'd hoped. The main events, from childhood to adulthood were soon all in order, her foreign travel, her visits to other galleries, other studios and museums included and all her awards and achievements listed and dated. It became clearer and clearer, however, that the links, the emotional *cement* between these solid blocks, were the only things still missing. They were essential if there was to be any sense of a life well and fully lived in the book. Anwen had to tell Elin about the people she had loved and who had loved her, but this, she still remained reluctant to do.

"I told you, there are some things I can't talk about yet and there may well be holes you need to fill in... after I'm gone," she repeated. "Trust me. All will be well, I promise."

Life was effectively on hold for both women until they had seen the consultant in *Ysbty Gwynedd*/Gwynedd Hospital. Despite Elin refusing to give up hope of treatment, it finally evaporated when Dr Bethan Elis-Williams confirmed the fact that chemotherapy was the only option on offer, but that it would do little good. Speaking in almost robotic tone, the consultant said that provisions for palliative care could be put in place when the need arose, and she saw no reason, as things stood, why Anwen could not stay at home throughout her illness but that the logistics of home care could become more complex as the scenario progresses. She gave an apologetic shrug afterwards and Elin was unsure if it was for the jargon or the facts. Anwen had understood neither.

"I can pay, if that helps with the... logistics," Anwen said.

The consultant, her voice a little warmer, but worn with disillusion, said, "It might, to be honest."

The week after this doom-laden conversation was incredibly busy. Elin organised a specialist palliative care nurse to come once a day to help check and administer medication and to give her a couple of hours' respite. This helped, but each of Anwen's gut-wrenching coughs reminded everyone that she was dying a little more each day, which was dreadful. The airbed was lumpy and uncomfortable, and the old woman often called out in pain in the small hours, needing both drugs and comfort, so Elin was tired, but it was more than that. She was struggling to cope with watching someone die again. She needed to go and see Cara and ask if she could offer any guidance on how to endure the unendurable without going under yourself. She texted:

> Hi again, Cara. Can I come over tomorrow morning please? E.

When she received no reply, she decided to go anyway.

THIRTY-SEVEN

The lane up to the smallholding where Dylan and Cara had grown up was only just wide enough for a car. A tangle of trees, brambles and weeds, neglected and overgrown, hung over the top of the stone walls on either side of the lane, forming a narrow tunnel of green. The cottage itself was small and squat, huddled into the hillside behind it and shadowed by a wall of conifers twice as high as the rooftop. Yellowy-white smoke curled from the chimney even though the sky was blue and cloudless, but Elin could see that this place was never warmed by the sun as it was permanently in the conifers' shade.

Three bony goats grazed on the slope to one side of the cottage, their bells clanking wearily as they tugged at tufts of grass. They completely ignored Elin as she walked towards the door holding a bunch of peonies, and knocked. When there was no response, she waited, glad she had sent a message first so that Cara would be expecting her. She knocked again. Again, no answer. Eventually, the door opened very slowly to reveal Cara dressed entirely in black, arms folded and unsmiling. She resembled a wild animal, wary, poised for attack.

"*Helô*/Hello," she said. "Welcome to Shangri-La, or Shitsville as my brother always calls it."

Elin, instantly wrong-footed, was reminded of her first visit to Anwen's cottage when she had been greeted similarly frostily. Perhaps this was a North Welsh custom she had not come across in childhood – making visitors feel very unwelcome. It was not one she would cultivate if she stayed here.

"Hi, I did message to say I would be coming today. I'm Elin," she said, holding out her hand, and the flowers.

"Sorry, I don't always reply. I know who you are. Dylan told me about you. Come in, and sit down," Cara replied. "Thanks for the flowers. They're lovely." Her tone was formal and her words stiff and unfamiliar, as if her mouth was unaccustomed to talking. Anwen had said she had a reputation for trying to stay away from people, but Elin wondered if Cara had even less contact with others than she did, and was even lonelier.

The door led straight into the main room of the cottage, a large space that served as kitchen, dining room and lounge, judging by the eclectic mix of furniture. All of it had seen better days, and dated from the 1960s, so Elin assumed this was exactly how Dylan and Cara's parents had left it. It was a bright day, but even with all the lights on, the room still felt funereally dark. As no tea had been offered, a North Welsh custom she *would* have expected, she began to explain why she had come as soon as they had both sat down. Her voice wobbled as she began the spiel she had rehearsed, aware she had not come on any ordinary errand.

"I'll be as brief as I can. So, as Dylan may also have told you, I grew up in Nant Ffrancon and moved back to live in Bethesda recently, and am now caring for my elderly friend who is dying of lung cancer," she said, taking a breath. "I'm really sorry if this upsets you, but Dylan said that you had nursed your mother through cancer, and I'm feeling, well, a bit at sea with it all." She waited for a reassuring word, or even sound, but when none came, she went on. "I helped nurse my dad until... the end, you see, and it was so hard. I just don't want to get it wrong, for her, or for me, if that makes sense. All my friend wants is to drift away, she says, but that's easier said than done."

"I understand. Death rarely comes when we want it to," Cara said. "My mother begged for it for months, but it only made things even more painful for both of us that I couldn't offer it to her."

There was a long silence, in which a fat bluebottle bounced between a grimy window on one side of the room to a mirror on the other, looking for a way out. There was none.

"Tea?" Cara blurted.

"Err, yes, thanks. That would be great."

As Cara walked slowly to the kitchen end of the room, Elin looked around her quickly. She took in the rows of classic novels – Austen, Dickens, Flaubert, Trollope and her own beloved George Eliot. She also noticed that the walls of the room were all covered with pieces of paper stuck up with masking tape, all at different heights and angles. She could not make out much detail, but could see that each white sheet had a small, darkly coloured area in its centre, as if nothing further was necessary. When she leant slightly nearer one wall, and the images swam into better focus, they were incredibly detailed pictures of things from around her mountain-side home – a sprig of purple heather, a twig furred with lichen or a perfectly-drawn camomile daisy. Was this strange young woman an artist too? If so, she would find plenty to discuss with Anwen, which was good. They all needed a lighter topic of conversation than death.

When Cara approached with two cups of tea, she had the light behind her, so all Elin could see was an outline. All in black, with hunched shoulders and in soupy gloom, she resembled a carrion crow as she slowly put the fine bone china cups down, her thin fingers lingering over each one as if terrified of dropping them. Her mother's cups, and precious, obviously. Elin sipped her tea, hot and strong, and tried again:

"I know it's a lot to ask, but I wondered if you had any..."

"Hints on dealing with death so that at least one of you survives it?" Cara cut in, and for the first time, Elin heard her laugh, though it was more an exhalation of air and made very little sound. "What a strange skill I seem to have mastered – helping people die. A rare calling."

Elin was glad of the lack of light in the room as she blushed to the roots of her hair. "But it *is* a calling, you know. And Dylan said you were so good with your mum, however hard it was. He said it was as if you just knew what to do." A pause, another across-the-room dash by the trapped bluebottle. "And he also thought we could be friends."

Suspense hummed in the room as Elin waited for a reply, *any* reply. She did not know how to interpret Cara's silence, or what to make of her now getting up and walking to the far side of the room before standing silently by the window with her back to her. Eventually, she spoke, still facing outwards:

"I want to help you, and I will, and thank you for thinking we could be..." She stopped, and wrapped her arms around her body in a sad, self-hug. "But, you see, what I mean to say... if you take him away from me, how *can* we be friends?"

In that moment, all the fleeting impressions Elin had formed of this young woman finally made sense: her clasping her brother's hand in the pub; her sitting staring up at him at the London gig; her scowl, urging him to keep walking down the woodland path rather than stop and chat. She was unusual, yes, but she was mainly terrified of losing the one person in the world who cared about her: her brother. Very slowly, Elin walked over and put both her hands on Cara's shoulders before very gently turning her around. Cara was still trembling and her face, framed by her lank dark hair, looked as if it had been drained of life, like a vampire's victim. Before this could go any further, Elin knew she had to dispel the fantasy this girl was creating in her head about her and Dylan being intent on leaving her completely on her own in the world. Only then could she ask for her help with Anwen and, perhaps, for her trust and then, for friendship.

As George Eliot had written, and Cara might remember if she knew her works as well as her bookshelves suggested:

"What loneliness is more lonely than distrust?"

Elin spoke firmly, aware that each word was important.

"Cara, remember that your brother and I have met three times in our lives, the last of which was when you met me and my friend on the mountain, which was hardly a meeting at all. I think we understand each other's way of thinking, and like the same things, but I don't know where my future lies, and neither does he right now," she said, adding, when she glimpsed Cara's face, "I think that's something you find difficult to accept, don't you?"

Cara nodded. "I do, yes," she murmured, adding, her voice suddenly very forceful, "But I do want him to do well, to be a success!"

"Of course you do, and so do I, which is why I want you to believe that we haven't really talked about... getting together, but if we *did*, I would never get in the way of his relationship with you."

"Perhaps you wouldn't, but *I* do! I know I do, I hear what people say about me and how he's got to look after me like a child," she said, so quickly that the words all but formed one sound. Her voice was lower when she continued, almost a whisper. "But he's always been there for me, through everything, and we've only ever had each other. Even when things at home were at their worst."

"I get that," Elin said, stepping back a little, alarmed by such a sincere but terrible outburst. This unique sibling relationship had been forged in fire and suffering, it was clear. "I grew up in a miserable household too, so I understand more than you might think."

Cara sighed. "Then I'm sorry for you. Isn't it sad, that we lived so near each other, but never met? Dylan said that to me when he first met you, and he's right."

"Yes, we could all have been friends years ago, but do believe me when I say that you don't need to feel threatened by me now, or ever."

A silence, in which the only sounds were their breaths, in and out, in and out.

"But you like him and he likes you, even loves you. You could love him back, couldn't you?" Cara said.

These words, said with such openness, struck home, and Elin

could only answer with similar honesty. "Yes, one day, perhaps, but as I said, I hardly know him. His path lies elsewhere and mine probably does too, and we have always known that."

Now, Cara laughed again, but this time, it sounded happy. "Ironic, isn't it, that we both want him to stay here, but we also want him to go away?"

"Bloody ironic, but that's the way it is. You must believe that I will never take him from you whatever the future holds." It mattered, really mattered that Cara understood this. Elin reached out and took her hand. "So, why don't we take this opportunity to be a friend to each other, and see Dylan as, well, sort of the link between us, the *conduit* that made that happen rather than something we compete over?"

A few seconds passed, and gradually, she felt Cara's body relaxing under her fingertips as she began to breathe more easily. "Do you think you can do that?"

"Yes, I think so. And I will help you with your friend too. I want to pass on what I learnt with Mum's illness, but I worry you'll expect too much. I only did little things, like putting some wildflowers where she could see them, turning her pillows, playing her favourite music, making sure there was air from the mountains in her bedroom. Silly things that couldn't change the outcome."

"No, but those things show someone that you love them."

"I also used to forage for herbs and flowers I picked from around here, and made teas or tinctures that soothed her," Cara went on, less shyly, "but I'm self-taught. I dreamt of training properly once, even found a homeopath to teach me about remedies and how to use them, but Mum got ill and... well, it will never happen now. She was called Anna you know, my mother, and she was a wonderful person."

Moved, Elin could see how Cara's reputation as a witch might have begun in a small community like this, and how talk of potions and spells had taken hold of people's better judgement. But she was simply following an age-old tradition and delivering a gentle, natural form of healing that deserved more respect and understanding.

"Don't give up on your dreams yet," Elin said. "I haven't."

"Then I hope your dreams include my beautiful brother," Cara replied with a smile.

THIRTY-EIGHT

Just over an hour later, Elin felt as if she had known Cara for much, much longer. The more she relaxed, the more of herself she revealed, but it was obvious that her greatest skill was in making others feel comfortable. Somehow, she got Elin to trust her enough to tell her all about her childhood, her disastrous love affairs and the sense of being adrift in life, including some things she had told nobody else, such as how Antoine had dismissed her like a servant he no longer needed once he had met Chloe, her wealthy and beautiful replacement. When she had told her how Barbara had sent her away to school, telling her to be grateful for an "exit plan", Cara had nodded vigorously.

"Sounds like she was just like my parents, shunting their failures down the line and onto us to sort out. Remind me never to do that if I have kids!"

"Will do, if you do the same for me," Elin said. "But I want you to tell me about *you*, Cara. Even the bad things, the sad times, if you see it as reassurance that you've got competition in the how to screw up your life stakes!"

Cara laughed, but this time, the sound filled the room with its sheer musicality.

"Look, we all have them – dubious problems and dodgy pasts –

so I never want you to feel you're on your own again, OK?" Elin said. "I know how that feels."

"*Diolch*/Thanks, Elin. I believe you, and I will tell you things when I need you to know them, as my... friend," Cara replied, sipping her tea like a bird. "I've never, ever had one of them before, apart from Dylan of course."

She opened a drawer next to her chair, and pulled out a huge photo album. Beckoning Elin over to sit by her, the two women leafed through the yellowed pages, Cara gave a little background about each photo. At first, there were two rosy-cheeked children with Anna, their mother, sitting in a suburban garden, smiling happily as their father snapped away, but as they progressed slowly through the album, Elin saw them all change. Gradually, Dylan and Cara became the sad young people sitting alongside a now-haggard Anna in the final photo, taken here on the same smallholding. As time passed, she saw Cara's bright eyes fade a little more and become ringed with tiredness and Dylan's open expression harden into one of sullenness with every photo she saw. It was like a time-lapse movie, showing the death of hope in a family, a process truly terrible to witness. When Cara finally closed the album, Elin could only put an arm around her shoulder in sympathy. She wondered how many years it had been since this young woman had spent an afternoon chatting about her life and sharing her memories with anyone? As she had vowed to Anwen, she vowed that Cara would never feel that alone again either.

"I meant to ask, what's your friend's name, the one who's dying?" Cara asked, once she was calm again. "Dylan never told me."

"You probably didn't hang around long enough to find out!" Elin said with a wry grin. "She's called Anwen Jones. She's an artist – quite well-known. You may have heard of her."

Cara clapped her hands. "*Heard* of her? Of course I've heard of her. I love her work, and I always knew she lived not far from here, but as the local weirdo, I've never dared enquire exactly where, let alone go and visit her."

"Yes, she said she'd never spoken to you, but I think you'd get on well. And she's far from mainstream herself," Elin murmured.

Cara pointed to some of the sheets taped to the walls. "I draw, too, as you can probably see, but just the plants and flowers I find. Nothing in her league."

"Me too, but also, nothing in her league. Anwen is really good at encouraging people, though. She did that for me when I was a little girl, so don't be scared when you first meet her. She's very... *frank,* shall we say, and I must warn you that her cottage is rather basic."

"I look forward to meeting her properly more than anything, and look around you. I think I can handle 'basic'."

When Elin left the smallholding a little later, both women felt sure that they had laid the foundations of a friendship that would change their lives forever.

THIRTY-NINE

Cara came to *Cân y mynyddoedd* several times the following week, despite having to take a bus and then the long walk up to the cottage as she refused to allow Elin to fetch her. Bearing the huge responsibility of her friend's care was tough, so Anwen eventually permitted Nia, Eva's replacement, to return as Elin was clearly very tired. When she even apologised for being "a little less than reasonable", Nia's face was wreathed in forgiving smiles and peace was restored between them. Elin was very glad of her help, but she was truly delighted to see Cara whenever she came, especially as she never came empty-handed.

Once, she brought a bunch of buttercups, camomile daisies and Lady's smock she'd picked on her way up from Llanberis. The next time, she brought some goat's cheese she had made herself. Elin loved it, telling her that every mouthful somehow tasted of the *ffriddoedd*/mountain pastures – rich, but slightly bitter. Dylan had been right, she decided, his sister was a gentle, generous soul and her presence made Elin feel as if he was alongside her for the challenges every day inevitably presented. Now, she could understand how desperately Barbara had needed her help when Llion was dying, as it was a gruelling ordeal to endure alone and left deep and lasting scars.

Anwen was a little guarded in her reaction to Cara at first, but this had been anticipated, so the young woman took it in her stride. Nevertheless, Elin did not leave the two women alone until, one afternoon, Smot had such a terrible tummy upset that she had to ask Cara to take a drink up to the old woman whilst she dealt with the fallout. When she had not returned twenty minutes later, Elin went upstairs to find her friend perched at the bottom of Anwen's bed, leafing through one of her sketchbooks.

"These are so beautiful," she murmured. "You have such breadth of vision, Anwen. I can only ever focus on the tiny details, like the veins in a petal or the vanes of a bird's feather when I draw or paint."

Anwen looked happy and relaxed, her face almost glowing at this thoughtful praise. "We can look at the same things, but see them differently. Think of Redouté, and his beautiful paintings of plants and flowers. Detail matters, you know."

"I don't know anything about him, but I'll find out," Cara said in a reverent tone. "I think flowers and herbs are such gifts from nature, don't you? They are the source of wonderful stories and healing powers that we know so little about."

Anwen's face told Elin that she was now fearing a potion coming her way, but she said nothing to Cara, which was a rare display of tact. She was much quieter these days, as speaking was becoming more difficult, and her breathing more laboured. The palliative care nurse warned that the decline could continue on this trajectory or take a more rapid downward turn without much warning. This alarmed Elin, reminding her of her father's agonising deterioration, and she was more grateful than ever for Cara's calm presence. Elin made sure she texted a concerned Dylan to let him know how things were, and was more open in her choice of words. In her last message, she even reciprocated his concluding 'X':

Your sister is helping me enormously. Thank you for trusting me enough to befriend her, because we ARE friends now. She misses you so much, and so do I. X

When he didn't respond as quickly as usual, she told herself he was busy with work, but she *felt* a little like a snail that retreats into back its shell. Had she been foolish to even begin to trust him with her feelings? She dared not believe it.

Within a week, Cara had taken over more and more of the daily care of Anwen, a task she undertook with a patience and quiet efficiency than Elin could never have matched as she found it too painful. The old woman did things for Cara that she had refused to do for her, so Elin stepped back from almost all hands-on caring duties and focused on getting the final draft of the book as near ready to submit to a publisher as she could. *Cân y mynyddoedd* was a place of quiet industry, as the tap-tap-tap of Elin's keyboard melded with Cara's gentle humming as she made some soup or a ginger cake, Anwen's favourite. It was also a place of waiting.

If it was sunny, the old woman sat outside in an old deck chair and watched the butterflies dance around the rampant buddleia and the swallows dip and swoop above her cottage. One afternoon, Elin heard her mumbling and rushed out in case she was trying to call her, but could not muster the strength to do so. As she approached, she realised that the old woman was speaking into the tiny Dictaphone she had given her so that she could add recollections or observations when they struck her. When she saw her coming, Anwen stopped speaking, struggled to find the right button to turn it off and then secreted it in her pocket.

"Do not sneak up like that. You'll be the death of me," she said, before coughing explosively at her own wit.

Elin saw terrible pain on the old woman's contorted face. Subtly, she checked the morphine level in her driver to see when she could safely have another shot. Not yet, so distraction would have to suffice.

"Were you filling in some of those mysterious *lacunae* for me on that machine?" she asked. "You promised me you would, remember?"

"Yes, yes, I remember, but you have to be patient with me. My life has not followed a straightforward path, and my story won't either."

But as Elin watched her eventually fall into a doze, she hoped that Anwen would be granted enough time to keep her promise.

One evening, the old woman was very agitated, and reluctant to be taken upstairs for the night. She said she wasn't hungry, or in pain, and finally, she admitted that she wanted to discuss *something important*; the subject surprised Elin enormously.

"I had heard nothing good about Cara, poor girl, and I was dreading being poisoned in my bed, but she's a treasure," the old woman wheezed, and wriggled herself upright in her chair. "She has the ability to make someone feel cared for without forgetting who they are, or were, before they were old and ill. That's a rare gift indeed."

"I'm glad you like her as much as I do," Elin said, trying to suppress a tiny niggle of jealousy. Cara had known Anwen a matter of weeks, whereas she...

Anwen spotted this at once, as ever. "Oh, please don't be jealous! You are a marvel, but putting me to bed, getting me dressed, helping me on and off the commode – well, those are things I don't want you to do anymore, as I can see you find them hard. Cara is a born carer and organiser, but your gifts lie elsewhere, as I've told you."

Elin smiled. How did this old woman manage to see into her heart so easily?

"Thank you, and I think you're right," she said. "She's a bit of enigma, is Cara."

"I see another myself in her, someone who doesn't fit the mould, which discomfits people," Anwen said firmly. "You must *make* her see a future, and find out what's going on in her head too. And please get me a cheese and tomato sandwich while you're at it."

Buttering bread in the kitchen, Elin thought a little more about Cara and her lost dreams of helping and healing people naturally, dreams she had watched ebb away as the years passed. Again, some of George Eliot's words rang true:

"...despair is often only the painful eagerness of unfed hope."

Anwen ate, and five minutes passed in companionable quiet until they resumed their conversation exactly where she had paused it, a habit that had taken Elin some getting used to (especially when the "pauses" were several hours, or even overnight).

"And I believe that you and I met this young woman for a reason. I needed to find someone I can help, you need a friend, and so does she. Once I'm dead, you both run the risk of losing each other again. Don't let that happen."

"I won't do that, I promise."

"She intrigues me, but I think I'm beginning to understand her," Anwen went on. "She's not allowed herself to trust anyone except her brother for so long that she's forgotten how to. It took you a while, I seem to remember."

The old woman was right, yet again. Elin remembered her former self, the woman who allowed herself to be jettisoned by Antoine, bullied by Sadie, kept at a safe distance by her mother, used by Theo and, yes, been fearful of Anwen. What a long, long way she had come in such a short time; it made her proud to realise it.

"Perhaps I'll suggest an outing, just the two of us on one of Nia's longer shifts here with you," she said. "Cara loves flowers, and nature, I know that much."

Anwen nodded enthusiastically. "So, take her up to walk around *Llyn Idwal*/Idwal Lake. You might even spot a *Lili'r Wyddfa*/Snowdon Lily. If they still survive up on the top crags around Idwal, they'll be blooming now," Anwen said, her eyes misting. "He picked one for me once. It was silly, and it's a criminal offence now, but he said I was worth it."

Elin hardly dared breathe. This was important. Was this Dafydd, who had been someone her old friend had loved and then lost? He was the heart of Anwen's story, she was certain and without finding out the truth of their story, the book she was writing about her friend would, like poor Maggie Tulliver, "flutter, but not fly".

FORTY

At first, Cara was reluctant to commit to a daytrip with Elin, though tempted by the possibility of seeing a Snowdon Lily. She was only, finally, swayed when Elin asked if they could begin their walk at *Wern Farm,* her old home.

"That was one of the walks I often did with my dad, and it would mean a lot to me to do it again with you."

"OK, I'll come. I've always loved that tiny road that threads along the bottom of Nant Ffrancon, and now I know *you* lived in *Wern Farm,* I will love it even more," she said. "It's for sale at the moment – did you know that?"

"Yes, I did," Elin replied sadly. "It was a tough life for my dad, trying to eke a living out of such unforgiving land, but I can't bear to think of the place not being cared for as it deserves to be. If it doesn't sell, and isn't rescued soon, it'll become a total ruin and my father and grandfather's lifetime of work will all have been for nothing."

Cara nodded in sympathy.

"So many hill farms fail when the family line ends or it becomes just that bit too hard to survive. I wish I could save it," Elin said urgently.

Both women were sitting on an old stone bench in the cottage garden, watching the sun slowly set. Reaching out, Cara took one of Elin's hands. "Listen to me, I hear what you're saying, but I don't think a building and a pocket of land is worth sacrificing your life for. It was your father's fate, but it needn't be yours, remember. I wish I'd done things differently myself on that score."

"But you still can!" Elin cried. "You could sell up, use the money from the smallholding to go to college and train as a homeopath, or see the world if you want to. I know Anwen wants you to do at least one of those things, if not all of them!"

But Cara smiled and shook her head. "No. I belong here, so whatever I do has to be in these hills that bred and moulded me, and near the water, be it the lake or the sea." She paused. "I think you and Dylan feel that too, if you're both honest with yourselves. He told me that, in fact – he said that home *called* you both, in a way. I think it's an omen."

Elin stood up quickly. She was hot, and Cara was so direct, so intense that it was too much at times, and this was one of those times. She was already tense because she had still not had a reply to her last message, telling Dylan that she missed him. Cara's earnest words irritated her even further.

"Let's not make this all about me, and give the old omens and *hiraeth* stuff a rest, please," she said brusquely. "Yes, Dylan and I talked about the bond we have with home, but we also said it can feel more like a tether. I came back for myself and for Anwen, and I like living in Bethesda right now and have no idea where my future lies after she dies, end of."

"I understand," Cara said.

But she looked so hurt that Elin was wracked with guilt. Her reaction, her tone, had alarmed her, too, and their exchange replayed in her head repeatedly as they sat in silence. She knew she should apologise, or at least explain, but doing so might expose her to the possibility of more questions about Dylan. She went inside to check on Anwen instead.

. . .

Wern Farm looked forlorn when they pulled up in front of it the following morning, and the outbuildings even more dilapidated. Swallows were still nesting in the barn, as they had done every year of her childhood, but she saw them zoom in and out of a large hole in the roof of the farmhouse, too, and wondered what the house was now like inside if it was as open to the elements as this. Just as she was toying with the idea of peeping through the ground floor windows, she heard Cara say:

"Look, now it's for sale by auction to the highest bidder on the day. They're obviously desperate, the people that bought it from your mother."

For a few seconds, Elin pictured herself in the auction room, bidding with money she hadn't got for a farmhouse she didn't really want. Shaking her head to dismiss this unhelpful fantasy, she marched off at a rapid pace. Cara's face showing her bafflement at her friend's unpredictable behaviour and ever-changing moods, but she was used to it. It reminded her of Anwen.

The route up to *Llyn Idwal*/Idwal Lake was not arduous, but the pathway of roughly interlocking stones meant looking at *them* rather than looking up at the scenery was necessary to avoid tripping up. Taking step after step, slowly and carefully, dissipated any remaining tension between them and both women had soon forgotten their ill-tempered exchange. Instead, they focused on breathing in the stunning landscape laid out around them. Only when they reached the edge of the lake were they fully able to take it in, the jagged peaks that formed a dark rim around the glassy water and the sheer perfection of a cloudless blue sky. There was no one else in sight and the only other living things were the two birds of prey who circled the upper slopes, their eerie cry echoing off the rocks like hungry ghouls.

"I have come up here all my life, but it always takes my breath away," Cara murmured. "It puts everything into perspective, feeling this *small*, doesn't it? I can forget all my problems looking at all this."

Elin could only nod in agreement. She, too, was deeply moved. Anwen had been right yet again, this was the perfect place to bring Cara to get her to open up a little more. When they set off on the stony path around the lake, they passed the spot where Elin could almost see her father standing and skimming stones over the water. The memory was searingly painful, but she had come here to remember him as well as trying to find out more about Cara, so she made no effort to hide her tears: this woman understood grief more than anyone. They walked arm in arm in companionable silence for twenty minutes before sitting on a boulder to enjoy the view and drink some water. Elin began by asking some gentle questions.

"My dad, who used to bring me up here, died almost ten years ago. How long is it since you lost your mum?"

"Four years," Cara replied. "A long time, and yet I've done nothing with all those hundreds and hundreds of days."

"You've survived them, and in many ways, that's enough."

Cara sighed. "But is surviving *living*?"

"No, but I know exactly what you mean. I felt like that in London, stuck in a job I hated, pining for an arrogant man who'd kicked me out of his life without a thought when it suited him," Elin replied. "But since I've been here, it's as if my life's begun again, like it's a blank page I can fill with anything I want to."

"Then I envy you. It feels as if my life stopped too when Mum died," Cara said sadly. "I miss her desperately."

"So is that why you stay on the smallholding, because you and she were once happy there?" Elin asked gently.

Cara hesitated. "No, I don't think so – not completely anyway. The time she was ill was awful, but we become very close I suppose. Overall, the whole 'move to the country' venture was a disaster, as my brother has probably told you."

"He did. The place 'chewed them up and spat them out' were his exact words, I seem to recall," Elin said.

Cara smiled grimly. "Mum was devastated when Dad left her,

and never really recovered, but it had always been her dream to live somewhere remote and beautiful, so when he went, it became her sanctuary from the world. Nobody visited, nobody asked questions, or judged her and I've inherited that isolationist tendency, I think. For years, I've walked in the hills or swum in cold water to calm my body and mind. I don't know how to *be* around people."

Looping her arm through her friend's again, Elin said, "Yes, you do. Anwen and I think you're wonderful."

Cara laughed. "Thanks! You know, once I thought it was love, a partner, that my life was lacking, but now I'm not so sure if that's what missing."

"I understand. I used to think I could only feel truly whole if I had a partner, someone to *complete* me I guess, but I'm not sure anymore either and I can't risk being hurt again."

"I suppose we have all lost someone."

"I know, and Antoine was years ago now, but I'm still raw."

A long pause alerted Elin to the possibility that Cara's next response would be significant, when it came.

"Is that why you're still a little scared to get too close to Dylan, or let him get close to you?"

This time, it was Elin that hesitated. This was a question she had been asking herself ever since she'd heard Dylan singing last year in the pub, and even more frequently since she had made herself vulnerable in her last message and still received no response.

"It's one of several reasons, I think. Antoine destroyed any self-confidence I'd managed to build up, telling me how needy I was, how messed-up, how he needed space to be himself. Space to go and screw someone else, more like!"

"That's tough, but it happens, or so I've read," Cara whispered.

"I know, but after I'd met Dylan, and he was all I thought about, I heard about Alys' death. The love of his life, Gwenda in the pub called her. That's a hard act to follow, especially for someone like me who *expects* to be rejected."

"Ah, now I understand. Yes, he loved Alys, and he was lost

when she died, but that's in the past now, just as what Antoine did to you is in the past," Cara said, taking Elin's hand. "I think you and Dylan just need to find out what you both feel rather than running scared, because he's just as terrified as you are." She paused. "Will you see him, talk to him? He's coming back soon, and for quite a while I think. Things aren't working out the way he'd hoped down South. It's all been really difficult for him, deciding what to do for the best, what will make him happy."

Elin did not answer. She sensed that Cara had chosen her words very carefully indeed. She got up and began walking up the scree-covered slope behind them to give herself time to think. She was sorry about his disappointment, but was seeing Dylan again face to face too much of a risk for her to take? A voice inside her head was telling her it was, a voice she wished she had listened to in the past, when she had let herself be fooled by a man unworthy of her trust. The last thing she needed was another disastrous love affair just as she was beginning to see what the future could offer her. But seeing Dylan, hearing his voice and accepting that she felt helplessly drawn to him could mean commitment, belonging and love. She would only know, if she was brave enough to find out.

"I'm not sure," she mumbled, because she really, really wasn't. "Let's go."

But Cara was not so easily deflected this time. "Don't run away from me. Promise that when Dylan comes home again to see me next week, you'll *talk*. That's all I'm suggesting."

When Elin finally turned around, she was smiling. "OK, you win. We'll talk, but only if you promise to let me help you break out of your self-imposed exile. This has to be a two-way street. Do we have a deal?"

"Deal, but only if you also promise to try cold water swimming with me."

"Now, that's pushing it," Elin replied with a grin, adding, "But for you, I'll think about it."

The two women laughed, and both hoped that this was the first of many such honest conversations. As they scrambled over the rocks and nearer the huge, open sky, Elin was thankful that she had got to know the young woman beneath the reputation. Cara deserved a second chance in life just as much as she did.

FORTY-ONE

The ascent up the ridge that leads on up to *Twll Du* (Black Hole, or Devil's Kitchen as it was known locally), was challenging, but Cara had done some research, and discovered that the Snowdon Lily was only to be found only on the most inaccessible spots up in the mountains, if at all. The women had to concentrate on finding safe footholds, so conversation dwindled as they focused on their feet.

"Did you know that Charles Darwin did a lot of research here?" Cara said when they neared the top, gasping for breath. "He must have been a whole lot fitter than me!"

They sat on a huge boulder to recover, and surveyed the scene laid out before them in all its splendour once more. The lake, that had looked so vast when they'd walked alongside it, now nestled like a mirror in a frame and beyond, a second, *Llyn Ogwen*/Ogwen Lake, stretched alongside the tiny ribbon of the main road far below. The only sounds were of a distant gull, cruising the skies before heading homewards to the sea, and the light, warm breeze that caressed their faces. Elin felt goosebumps rippling along both her arms. This, again, was the song of the mountains, its notes differing slightly from those she had heard with Anwen, and with

Dylan, but the same perfect, peaceful pitch. She turned to Cara and said:

"Can you hear it, the song of the mountains? It's never the same, but always says the same thing, if that makes sense. Dylan and I heard it together once."

"I know. He told me," Cara said. "And yes, I hear it."

"Anwen said it always tells us something important, but we have to listen very carefully, to know what that is," Elin replied.

"Well, I hear it telling us that you're doing the right thing in agreeing to talk to Dylan, and we're doing the right thing in helping each other find the right path in life," Cara said with uncharacteristic certainty.

Elin grinned. "Agreed. I just wish it could be a bit more specific about where to find those bloody lilies!"

The two friends were not experienced enough or equipped enough to venture even higher, and they knew it. Llion, her father, had always told Elin to be careful in the mountains and be aware that they posed great danger if not treated with respect as the weather could change in minutes and clear pathways simply vanish in the mist. Walking downhill was easier and their pace faster, so they almost missed the tiny clump of white, star-like flowers and their spidery leaves hidden in the mossy lee of a large boulder. The blooms were so delicate, so modest in their beauty, but Elin could only guess what harsh weather the little plant had witnessed and what brutal winters it had endured to survive here. When she crouched down to take a photo of the flowers on her phone to show to Anwen later, she saw that she had several missed calls, but there was no signal here to return them. A niggle of unease began in her belly, but up here she could do nothing, whoever needed her to.

As they walked down to the lake once more, she wondered if this was where the man who had loved Anwen had picked her a Snowdon Lily as a token of his devotion. Had it been Dafydd, her father's brother? It seemed likely, as they were so rare and few would know the landscape well enough to find them. That had not changed a jot since then. For these mountains, thirty years was a mere millisecond. Elin was happy, certain that Anwen would rejoice that the fragile flowers had remained safely hidden through those long years, whatever life had thrown at her.

It was almost 5 p.m. by the time Elin returned to *Cân y mynyddoedd*, having dropped Cara off at the smallholding. It was still sunny, so she was surprised not to see Anwen in her habitual deck chair, with Smot guarding her from the safety of its shade. But when she went inside and saw Eva, she knew something was wrong. She was still on maternity leave, but had come anyway, bringing her month-old baby girl with her.

"Anwen is very bad today. Nia called me, and I came and I try to call you, but I guess no signal in the mountains."

Nia came downstairs and into the room. "I think she needs to go into hospital, Elin, but she refuses to go. I can't be responsible if she..."

In the past, Elin's instinct would have been to allow Nia, the professional, the medic, to take charge, however wrong it felt to do so. This time, she listened to what her instincts told her, and they gave quite different advice.

"Eva, go home with little Rosa. Nia, I'll take over now, and take full responsibility. Thank you both, for everything."

Elin could hear Anwen's laboured wheezing from the bottom of the stairs as she went up to her bedroom. The old woman's face was ashen pale, and she was struggling for breath. It was frightening, but it had happened before, and Elin knew they both had to stay calm if the episode was to pass. Checking her morphine level, she released another dose into Anwen's bloodstream, stroked her hair and gave her a sip of water, which soothed her slightly. After a few minutes, a little colour had returned to her cheeks and she seemed anxious to speak.

"Please don't try and talk yet," Elin urged. "I'm here now."

But the old woman's eyes had a wild look as she tried to control her breath enough to say a few words.

"I have things to say. Things I want to tell you."

"They'll have to wait until you feel stronger or I'll have to take you into hospital."

The old woman grimaced, and waited a minute or two before saying, in a pleading, almost child-like voice, "But the book! You said you need to know what goes in the *lacunae*! I want to tell you now."

"Not yet. It's not the right time," Elin said.

"But I may not get a better one at this rate," the old woman said. "I wanted to tell you myself, not leave you to find out after..."

A violent fit of coughing overtook her, and when it finally ebbed, Elin watched her drift in and out of sleep as the morphine did its work. Pulling the covers up over her chest, she found a half-eaten croissant and the Dictaphone amidst the sheets, the latter covered with greasy fingermarks and still recording.

"You love this thing, don't you? Goodness knows what's on it – white noise I expect, because you've pressed all the wrong buttons!" Smiling, she turned the machine off and lightly kissed the old woman's forehead and whispered, "We saw the Snowdon Lilies, Anwen. They are still there, strong and defiant, just like you."

An hour later, with Anwen deeply asleep, Elin finally went downstairs. Her rucksack was on the floor where she had dropped it, her sweater thrown over a chair. She'd felt so happy when she'd come through the door but now, a gnawing fear lurked inside her. If Anwen was that breathless and distressed again, she would have to go into hospital, or a hospice, if a place could be found, and she would not want either option. She would not be able to see her suffering and be powerless to ease it, but her old friend would never forgive her if she did not die in her beloved cottage. It was a risk to trust morphine to help her over these crises, but she had no real choice and the very real possibility of having to give her too much to speed her death terrified her. Would Anwen ask her to if she was unable to do it herself? And would she be able to, if so? Cara had faced the same dilemma with her mother Anna, and it had been almost unbearable.

Going out into the night, the sky was clear and tiny stars sparkled like grains of sand across the thick blue-blackness. Looking up, she remembered once again what Dylan had told her about the Kalahari bushmen asking the stars for guidance, and listening, waiting to their response. Lifting her face towards them, she murmured:

"Show me what to do. I need your help now, more than ever."

But she was greeted only with silence.

Going upstairs to check on Anwen one last time before bed, she found her still sleeping with her body curled up like a baby and one hand under her cheek. Relaxed, her face was transfigured from the gaunt, haunted look her illness had given her and Elin could see the beautiful young woman she had once been.

Death had spared her that night, but it would not do so for much longer.

FORTY-TWO

For the next few days, Elin barely left Anwen's side. She knew that the old woman had been so close to telling her the missing parts of her life, the links that led from the passionate young artist travelling the world to the regret-ridden old woman in bed brimming with secrets she now, finally, wanted to share. Elin had to stay close, and to wait. Cara quietly cared for them both in the background, Eva called each day to see how Anwen was and Nia did her job with such calm efficiency that Anwen's face radiated gratitude, despite her illness. These women formed a protective shell around the old woman, but it was Elin who she wanted more than any of them and hers was the face that calmed her in the small hours, when she awoke in darkness and in pain.

Late one afternoon, as the sun streamed through the window Cara had opened, and the air rang with the spectacular birdsong that only precedes dusk, Anwen pushed herself upright in bed and braced herself against her pillows as if in preparation for delivering a formal lecture.

"*Reit 'ta.*/Right then. I am going to tell you some things now, and all I ask is that *you don't say anything at all*," she began, pausing to take a deep, rattly breath. "If I stop, I may never start again. I need to get into the flow of it, as I seem to have lost that of late. Can you promise not to interrupt me?"

Elin nervously nodded her assent.

"Good. The first thing I want to tell you is that I have left you everything in my will, and it's a *lot*."

Elin shouted, "*What?* Don't do that! I don't want to be forever in your debt," but she covered her mouth immediately when she saw Anwen's furious expression. She had promised not to interrupt.

"Well, it's what *I* want, so it's happening. I've left you three paintings too, two of the places you, Llion and I loved when you were little and one that I did when you were a baby, when I... I..." her voice crackled and she stopped to cough. Eventually, she went on, "I don't want them shut up in some museum, or in some rich collector's safe. I've told my lawyer to make sure that doesn't happen."

Still shocked, Elin could only murmur her thanks, rather than articulate them.

"But, as you've probably guessed, the bequest comes with conditions," Anwen went on. "Firstly, I insist you use some of the money to buy *Wern Farm*, and convert it into a centre for all the artists in the area. You've met the best of the bunch – I saw to that." Again, she paused and took a breath. "I would like you to offer each of them the chance to exhibit some of their work and even offer occasional workshops to show people their skills before they are lost forever, if they wish to. What these makers do will only be preserved and passed on if people *see* them in action, as you did. You don't have to commit to running it, or staying here if you choose not to, but I am asking you to set the wheels in motion. That's where your skills lie – appreciating beauty and the people who create it, and making them feel *seen*. Can you do that?"

Elin nodded, but said nothing as she did not trust herself to say the right thing. The old woman was right in her analysis of where her talents lay, she had realised exactly the same herself over the past weeks and months, and was proud of her newfound ability to accept who and what she was. But she would need so much advice, help... and reliable builders. Who could she ask for any of those things? Those were doubts for another day.

"Secondly, I want you to help Cara find what she wants to do. I've left her money as well. It may be training as a homeopath, doing up the smallholding she's clung to like a limpet since her parents' death or breeding obscure breeds of goat – I don't know what she wants but whatever it is, it's her dream and nobody else's. Do you agree to help her?"

This time, Elin was glad to agree with a broad smile and a very vigorous, but silent, nod.

Placing an open hand on her chest, Anwen paused for a long while, to regain both her breath and some strength. Talking at such length, and with such firmness, was depleting her limited reserves and she looked extremely tired. Once more, Elin waited, hoping that her friend was at last going to tell her what she had wanted to know about far more than money or plans for an arts centre – her lost love, the mysterious man who had brought her a Snowdon Lily from the mountaintop.

"Thirdly, I want you to see Dylan again."

This time, Elin found not replying very difficult indeed. She was both disappointed, and ever-so-slightly offended. She had felt the same when Cara had pushed her to committing to talking to Dylan. Who she loved or didn't love was her business, and nobody else's. Anwen saw her irritation immediately.

"I've seen that look before, when you were a very stroppy teen. Listen to what I have to say before you dismiss me," Anwen urged, leaning forward and wagging her finger. "We may only have one chance at real love, love that changes us and then changes itself as it accompanies us through the years. I squandered mine and I don't want you to do the same."

Elin had to respond. "Have you been conspiring with Cara, for goodness' sake? She made the same point, and I agreed that I will meet him, talk to him. But I hardly know the man and I'm not sure how I feel about the parts of him I *do* know."

"Nor will you, if you don't take a risk, be completely open and find out if you can love each other!" Anwen snapped. "I know you're frightened, and I know I warned you off him, but all I ask is that you try, once, for my sake. You told me you wanted to love, and be loved, remember, so it's time..." Her voice dwindled again, overtaken by coughing, and the morphine driver despatched a top-up dose. "The rest will have to wait, but leave my phone here please. I need it. Tomorrow, I will tell you the rest. Yes, tomorrow..."

Closing her eyes, she drifted into sleep in seconds. Elin sat and watched her breathing gradually settle into a calm rhythm until the room was dimmed by the slow fall of dusk. Her thoughts raced, but she sat quite still as the reality of what her future could now hold descended on her slowly like a soft mantle. She would have money, which could change her life and many others in ways she could only begin to imagine, but she would not have her friend alongside her. Her guidance, her support, would come to an end very soon and it looked like she would be alone again unless she took a huge leap of faith, and of trust.

Occasionally, her own phone pinged, but she did not look at the message previews. Many locals were aware of the situation, so the supply of kind messages was as constant as the casseroles, soups and crumbles. Elin marvelled at the closeness of a community that did not hesitate to rally around one of their own, however irascible Anwen had always been. They did not see her as the unlikeable oddity she perceived herself to be at all: she was strange, different, *unique*... but she was still one of them.

Going down to the darkened kitchen, she let Smot out and began washing a lettuce in the sink when she glimpsed her face in the glass of the window. Even in the limited light, and more tired than she had ever felt, she could see that she had lost her city pallor, and her hair flowed like a rippling tide over her shoulders; she looked beautiful. Loving someone entailed vulnerability and trust, but if she did not follow Anwen's dictum and *try*, she could face as lonely a life as the old woman had lived. Drying the dishes slowly, she remembered some words George Eliot had written that had puzzled her once, but now, made sense:

"*It will never rain roses: when we want to have more roses, we must plant more roses.*"

To be loved, she had to dare to love and accept the risks. She hadn't taken his hand that first day, but now, as she stood looking at her true self, the woman she had become since coming home, she wanted to more than anything in the world. Fumbling to text Dylan before her resolution faded, words danced before her eyes, tangling and weaving until she had drafted countless messages, countless times. At midnight, totally overwrought, she sent:

> Hi. Haven't heard back from you, but Cara says you're home next week. It would be good to meet again. E.

The words were bland, and she could not bring herself to add an 'X' this time, but hoped he could decipher the code with which she so often hid her true feelings.

FORTY-THREE

When a text from her mother pinged into her inbox early the following morning, Elin visibly jumped. Cara was kneading dough at the kitchen table, her face so whitened with flour that Elin was reminded of a portrait of a mercury-daubed Queen Elizabeth I.

"Nice or nasty message?" she asked Elin.

"Puzzling, certainly. It's from my mother, Barbara. She wants me to ring her asap, which is even more puzzling as I never hear much from her these days."

Going into the garden, Elin dialled her mother's number. When Barbara picked up almost immediately, she suspected things were not good.

"Everything OK, Mum?" she said, knowing they couldn't be.

"Yes, yes, fine, dear," came Barbara's usual clipped tone, but there was a slight wobble in it this time. "But I need to come home, to, er, sort something out. If that's all right with you, I mean."

Elin's heart sank. There was obviously trouble in paradise.

"Sure, er, I mean yes, of course. I'm living up at Anwen's at the moment, as she's, well, she's terminally ill, Mum, with cancer, so she can't be here on her own."

"Cancer is a terrible thing. Are you coping with all that? I mean, it's hard, being with someone who's... well..." Her words guttered and died.

"Dying? Yes, it's tough, I remember and I know you do too, but we're OK," Elin replied, rescuing her mother. "There's a few people here calling in every day as well as me; Nia, the replacement carer, the specialist palliative care nurse, Manon and Cara, a friend. We make a great team," Elin said, her thoughts darting around like minnows in a stream. This was all very strange, but what perplexed her most was her mother's apparent lack of surprise at the news. Did she already know about Anwen's illness? She had long since cut all ties with North Wales, and Elin had not told her about it.

"That's good at least. I was completely on my own with your father," Barbara said mournfully.

Elin had to resist reminding her that she had come home from her travels to help specifically so that she would *not* be on her own and that it had been hard for her, in many ways. What would be the point of doing so now? When the silence between them lengthened embarrassingly however, she wondered whether to ask how George, her husband, was, but that seemed gauche if the marriage was already foundering. She decided to go straight for the fundamentals instead:

"When do you think you might be coming, so that I can meet you at the station?"

"I'll be arriving in Bangor at 6.25 p.m. today. Does that suit you?"

Suppressing a strange yelp, Elin said, "Yes, fine. See you then," before both women hung up. Turning to Cara, eyes wide, she mouthed one word: "Help."

During the half hour drive to Bangor that afternoon, Elin had no idea how she mirrored, signalled or manoeuvred and got there safely. Cara had agreed to cover the evening with Anwen, but Barbara would be in need of support for considerably more than a few hours if her newfound bliss had indeed crumbled. When her mother stepped off the train, she looked thinner, paler, but still very well-groomed; being a lady who lunches was obviously suiting her, so why on earth had she come back here, to a place she hated? Taking her mother's arm and her small suitcase, she led her to Anwen's old Renault 4.

"God, I remember this old banger," Barbara said. "I can't believe it's still drivable."

"Many people would say it's not, but it gets me where I need to go," Elin replied. "Let's go home and you can fill me in on what's been happening in Bath. When you're ready, of course. No rush," she added, squeezing Barbara's arm in case her mother was masking deep trauma with pleasantries. That had been her modus operandi for years.

Barbara smiled politely, and said, "I'm fine," very unconvincingly.

The drive home was a quiet one, as Barbara registered sights that had been a part of most of her adult life with a nod or a slight lean forward. She smiled at Bangor City Council's efforts to spruce the place up with garish hanging baskets, but she looked up at the sunlit hills and slate slopes that formed the backdrop to Bethesda with a wistful sigh.

"It's all still here, just the same as when your father was alive, which strikes me as amazing when everything in my life feels like it's been shaken like one of those snow globes you used to love as a girl," she murmured.

"I remember, but the mountains have been the same for about five hundred million years, so they're not going to change in a few months, thank goodness," Elin replied, watching her mother closely. Such esoteric musings were very out of character.

Fortunately, Barbara approved of the transformation Elin had wrought in her house, though her facial expression was particularly mobile when she saw the bright yellow kitchen cupboards. Having had so little notice of her return, Elin had not even had time to tidy up, but when she saw her mother sink into one of her old armchairs and close her eyes without seeming to notice that she had removed her lurid floral cover and draped a colourful Indian kantha over it, she could breathe again. So far, so good.

When, later, they sat down to some pasta and a jar of sauce, Barbara seemed unusually animated, even a little hyper, but certainly not heartbroken. Her daughter was becoming desperate to ask why she had come, but biding her time still seemed the best plan, so she bided it.

"This house feels much happier now. You've made it so light and bright," she exclaimed. "I love all the colours! It was always rather drab, but I didn't have the vision to lift it like this. It's wonderful, dear."

But in twenty minutes, this frothy façade had slipped and Barbara had started gently criticising how Elin had organised her cupboards. It was time for the truth.

"Mum, why are you here?" Elin said gently. "Has something happened?"

"No, nothing's *happened*, you silly girl. Everything's all right, if very different to my life here. I just needed to come back, and to see you. It's been too long, and there are things I need to do," Barbara said, picking lint off her cardigan. "And I want to see Anwen, before..."

"Really?" Elin blurted, surprised. "You were never the best of friends, Mum."

"Things change when a person is near death," Barbara replied.

Elin resigned herself to the familiar game she and her mother always played, one in which honesty was very rarely one of the rules of engagement. "Well, it's nice to see you. I do need to go back up to Anwen's for the night, but I'll be back in the morning, once the carer arrives, and I could take you up there if you like," she said, full of doubt that Barbara *would* like. "Will you be OK here, on your own?"

Barbara turned to her and said, "Of course I will, silly."

But as Elin drove away, she could not stop wondering why her mother wanted to see Anwen so badly, and what she had come to do, or "sort out". Unlike her, Barbara was not a complex soul, but she had clearly kept some secrets very close: the babies she had lost, and the mysterious photograph of her father and his brother standing behind Anwen with a baby on her knee. She was a woman who had spent her adult life playing a role she did not fit, and she was very good at it.

The differences between them were a familiar train of thought, one Elin had revisited many, many times as a child, but that evening, as she drove through this place where she finally felt some degree of peace, she recalled some words of George Eliot's that had always helped her accept their differences:

"Souls have complexions too: what will suit one, will not suit another."

Barbara was who she was, and nothing would change that now, whereas *she* was still a work in progress, discovering, learning about her true self as she had never done before. Elin vowed to adopt Anwen's attitude and hope that her mother would reveal her secrets *when the time was right.*

FORTY-FOUR

The leaves on the trees begin to crisp and brown in late August in North Wales, as summer begins to draw to a slow close earlier than it does further south. Beach days are possible, and the sea is almost warm, but there is the imminence of change in each breeze, so it's wise to take a jumper as well as a swimsuit. On the morning after Barbara's arrival, each blade of grass dripped with dew, and it took Elin a few tries to get the Renault 4 to start to drive home to Bethesda.

"Mum?" she called. Silence. Walking into the kitchen, all her senses were assaulted by the smell of spices, one that took her back to her childhood when Barbara had creamed, mixed and whisked to vent her frustration, baking cakes that would then moulder in the tin as she was a poor cook and often left out a key ingredient. That morning, she was astounded to see that her mother was wearing a lavender silk shift dress, a lot of make-up and had borrowed her earphones, and was now jiggling to an unheard song. It was all very surreal. She tapped her lightly on one shoulder.

"Oh hello, dear. Just enjoying a bit of a boogie while I make us a ginger cake." She pushed her glasses to the end of her nose. "I thought we could take it up to Anwen. She always liked it, and she said her appetite's not bad, despite everything."

Elin was speechless. So it was true: the two women had been in touch very recently *without her even knowing about it*. Barbara had always been so disparaging of Anwen, and jealous of her close relationship with her only child. The disregard had seemed mutual, too, so this was the last thing Elin could ever have predicted and she was at a loss how to react to it. Saying the wrong thing could be worse than saying nothing at all, so she erred on the side of caution. This was all becoming more surreal by the minute.

Driving her mother to Llanberis after lunch, her brain ran through possible permutations and probable outcomes of the two women meeting face to face after all this time, even if they had communicated with each other in some way beforehand. Neither was renowned for their tolerance, sensitivity or understanding of others, so this reunion could go one way or the other. "The other" would not be good at all.

The day was now one of bursts of hot sunshine interrupted by periods of cloud, so Anwen was back in her deck chair in the garden, but cocooned in two old Welsh blankets and topped with a dozing Merlin. For a few seconds, she did not seem to recognise Barbara. When she did, her eyes vanished into folds of wrinkles as she beamed at her, but she did not look remotely surprised.

"*Arglwydd mawr*/God Almighty! You look like a waxwork under all that make-up, Barbara *fach*/dear! What have you done to yourself?" she said.

Elin flinched. Her mother was bound to be offended at this and present the brittle side of herself that had so often been her default. Barbara did indeed twitch a little, like a bird ruffling its feathers before settling, but then she went towards Anwen and gave her a brisk hug.

"Nice to see you, too, Anwen. I see your manners haven't changed."

Anwen cackled, which induced a bout of phlegmy coughing

that saw Barbara patting her shoulder gently until she calmed down.

"Life has put both of us through the wringer, but we're still here, if slightly *flatter* than we once were," Barbara said.

"Flatter, but still fighting, because that's what we do," Anwen said, when she could speak. "And that's more than many are doing at our age."

"We should hold our heads up high, given all we've been through," Barbara replied, sitting down with a sigh.

Anwen dismissed this whiff of self-pity with a snort.

"Elin is helping me write my life story, you know. It's nearly finished, just a few gaps she needs me to fill in – the important stuff, of course. The juicy bits, the last gasps as it were."

Barbara made an effort to smile, but Elin saw a flicker of concern in her eyes. Anwen carried on, oblivious.

"It's amazing to realise how many things we've done, you know, when you corral them into order as we've been doing. *Millions* – some good, some bad, some in-between and… a few, well, a few that you would give your life to be able to undo."

Again, Barbara looked worried, as if she feared what Anwen would say next. Perhaps luckily, any revelations were curtailed by another lengthy coughing bout. Again, Barbara patted her back, but the atmosphere was still far from friendly. "Frosty" was the only word that sprang to Elin's mind.

"Shall I make us a *panad*/cuppa?" she said, as it seemed the most obvious thing to do and might make this meeting more convivial. "Mum's brought you some ginger cake we could have with it, Anwen."

Awkwardly, Barbara produced the rather lopsided cake, saying, "Your favourite, I seem to recall."

Anwen mouthed "thank you", but the veneer of gratitude was thin indeed.

There was no love lost between these women – so why were they both here? Elin wondered. As the kettle slowly boiled and she cut the cake into slices in the kitchen, she tried as hard as she could to make some sense of this bizarre reunion. The only clue seemed to be how much of the past they both shared. These now-old women had a decades-long relationship, one that had begun in their youth, before Llion had married Barbara, so it was founded in a time she knew nothing about. Despite their mutual dislike, this commonality had created an indissoluble bond, one she could both see, and feel today, even if it manifested itself in well-aged contempt. Anwen had never liked Barbara, and her mother had certainly never liked Anwen, so Elin asked herself again and again what on earth had brought her mother here today, bearing ginger cake? Flummoxed for a satisfactory answer, she was almost relieved when her phone buzzed in her pocket. When she saw it was Dylan, her belly performed several quick somersaults.

> Sorry didn't have time to get back to you properly. Was sorting things out. Am back in town, working in the pub for a while, so we can talk. Time to suit you, as I hear your mum's in town. D. X

Flushed with girlish happiness, Elin smiled. The phrase "in town" belonged to New York or London, not Llanberis, and his concluding "X" made her guilty at not having put one in her last message. Part of her wanted to jump in the car right now and go and meet him, leaving these two cantankerous old women to slug out whatever was between them. Anwen had urged her, all but *told* her, to meet him again, so she would understand, and Barbara, well, she would have to lump it.

When she approached the two women with a tray of tea and cake, their animated conversation stopped immediately, as if the plug had been pulled and they both looked at her guardedly. Elin, annoyed at this obvious rudeness, decided that she had had enough of massaging their egos for today.

"Right, I'm going to meet Dylan for a couple of hours so that you two can catch up, or whatever it is you need to do. You've got my number if you need me."

There was a short silence before both women exchanged an unsurprised look.

"Glad to hear it. Give him my best wishes, *cariad*/dear. We'll be just fine," Anwen said gaily.

Stomping off towards the car, Elin heard Barbara hiss, "Is Dylan the nice young man you mentioned? I hope she cheers up a bit if so," which made Elin even crosser.

It was only when she reached Llanberis that she realised she hadn't replied to Dylan to let him know she was coming. She went to the pub, but when Emlyn told her that he was not due at work until an hour later, her mood plummeted and her courage begin to fail. She faced a dilemma: go back and endure Anwen and Barbara's company whilst they said whatever it was they had to say, or be brave enough to go for a dip in the freezing lake as Cara had been urging her to do and hope it balanced her mood before she met him. It was supposed to make you feel great, and full of energy, after all – so many women raved about its power to both calm and uplift.

It was not a difficult choice. Today, she would embrace the cold water for the first time; it was by far the more palatable option.

FORTY-FIVE

There is a tiny, gravelled beach on the far side of *Llyn Padarn*/Lake Padarn that only walkers know about. Llion, Elin's father, had brought her here many years ago. They had picnicked beneath the trees as swallows flew millimetres above the lake to snatch tiny sips of water, and father and daughter had skimmed stones, as they always did. Most lake swimmers congregated around the pontoon near the town, or in the Lagoons which were a favoured spot for paddleboarders, but as she had no bathing costume, Elin knew she would have to swim in her underwear, somewhere very secluded. It could only be the spot she remembered from childhood. When she reached it, happy memories flooded back and her breathing calmed in seconds. Now, it was just her, a warmish breeze and the water, with the mountains reflected in its silver-mirrored surface. She could barely even see the gaggle of tourists on the far bank, which meant they could barely see her. In that moment, she decided to do what she never thought she would be brave enough to do: skinny dip.

Peeling off all her clothes and laying them carefully on a rock, her feeling of defiance grew. She had come so far and learnt so much since coming back to Wales. Nobody, not even two infuriating old women with a mysterious mutual grudge, could stop her now. She picked her way over the stones and then felt soft, silty mud squidge cold between her toes, another memory so vivid it made her smile. The water was cold, very cold, but as it reached her knees, her thighs, her belly, the tension of the morning ebbed away and she surrendered her body to something that had seen the millennia come and go without alteration: this pure, cold water, these mountains, this place. She swam, and with each stroke, she felt as if she was leaving the wounds of her past further behind – her miserable schooldays, her heartbreak after Antoine's betrayal, her father's death, her mother's lack of true warmth and her own deep, unfulfilled yearning to love and be loved. Each of these things were valid and had happened, but as she pulled her body through the water, she told herself again and again that the sequence of her life was not complete. She had more, much more, ahead of her and what came next was her choice alone. Perhaps the best really was yet to come.

Next, she did something she would never have believed she could actually do until this moment. She tilted her head right back so that the water soaked her neck and scalp and hair, and let herself produce the strange, primeval howl that the bitter cold induced. It was a release, a *freeing* she had waited too long to experience, but when she heard a similar sound echo hers, she jerked her head up in shock. Dylan Williams stood on the bank, howling back at her like a demented wolf. Gulping furiously, she trod water for a few seconds as her brain processed what she'd just seen and done. It told her with alarming clarity that she was in the middle of a huge lake, completely naked, behaving like a madwoman and that the man she had come here to meet was watching and mocking her. Logically, this was disastrous, her brain whispered, but her heart yelled that she had never felt so exhilarated in her life. With this man, and only this man, she could be *herself*... but that did not mean today was the day for him to see her naked.

"What the bloody hell are you doing there?" she exclaimed. "I need you to go away right now, Dylan. I have nothing on."

The howling wolf now metamorphosed into a man bent double with laughter.

"Jeez, my mother used to walk around the house naked all the time, which was a lot for a teenage boy to handle," he said. "A naked you will be a breeze."

"I don't care what she did! Go away! I mean it!" Elin shouted from the water. She was getting tired of treading water, and this was not how she'd wanted this meeting to be. "Please, Dylan, go away a *bit*, at least. Over to that tree, perhaps."

Still laughing, Dylan walked away and stood with his back to her as she staggered out of the water and, realising she had no towel either, brushed the water off her body with her hands with long, sweeping movements. Yanking on her clothes before she was fully dry was not easy, but within five minutes, she said:

"Right, I'm decent now."

"That's a shame," he muttered as he turned to face her, still smiling guiltily. Elin took in his kind face, his rich brown curls, his sharp, angular nose that had always reminded her of a beak. Somehow, she did not care one whit that her hair stuck up around her head in tufts or that damp patches had appeared over both her wet breasts where she had pulled her T-shirt over them. For a few seconds, she allowed herself to feel, to *know* that this man wanted to be with her more than anyone on earth, but when he came nearer, instinctively, she stepped back. There was danger here. There was risk.

"I would have preferred to be better dressed, nice as it is to see you," she said in a strange, brisk tone she hardly recognised as her own. Floundering, she babbled on. "So, are you on your way to work? I didn't think you'd come this way. I went to the pub to see you, but... anyway, you're going to be late at this rate, and I really do need to get back to Mum and Anwen now. They might be tearing each other's hair out by now."

She began walking quickly along the footpath around the lake, back towards the town, and Dylan, looking crestfallen, followed her, but as they neared the pub, he gently pulled one of her arms and stopped her.

"I didn't mean to embarrass you. I always walk that way to work, but that's not important. Don't you want to hear *why* I've come back to Wales?" he said, his face both hurt and hopeful. "I'll give you the abridged version if you're in a rush."

Elin blushed at her own rudeness and could not meet his gaze. "Sorry, I... I mean, Cara said that you were coming back to... for a while..." Her words dwindled to silence. She wanted, and did not want, to know why he was here.

He turned her body to face him and took both her hands in his. "Elin, I came back for several reasons, but the main one was you. You must know that, because I told you how I felt about you on the phone," he said, as she looked at the sky, at the floor, at anything other than his face. "I know how scared you are of making yourself vulnerable again, and I get that, I really do. It's taken me years to get over Alys' death, to believe that it wasn't my fault."

Elin wriggled like a fractious toddler. She did not want to hear about the love of his life who had died in a tragic accident, not right now, anyway.

Dylan went on, his eyes fixed on hers as if pleading:

"Believe me when I tell you that it's taken me months to feel brave enough to say this to your face: I think we belong together, I truly do."

At that moment, a family of noisy tourists passed them, dragging a cocker spaniel behind them, trying to do a poo. This funny vignette lightened the mood for both of them and gave Elin a few seconds to think; her reply was important, and she knew it. She had to be strong, and think clearly.

"Thank you for saying that, but I sometimes I feel like that poor dog, never free to decide for myself where I want to go or what I want to do, and it feels awful," she said. "I know there is something amazing between us – I felt it the first night you sang in the pub, but I don't know if I want to *belong* to anybody right now, and I have other things in my life that demand my energy and commitment, and so do you. We both have to be honest here."

The tourists had now come back to pick up the poo, arguing over which of them should do the honours. Elin waited for them to move on and Dylan looked down at his feet in silence, still holding on to her hands. Only when the family and their dog had gone, did she continue.

"You see, Anwen wants me to convert *Wern Farm* into a space for local artists. She's going to leave me the money to do it too, but it's a huge project, and I just think having a relationship... I'm not sure..."

"How would being with me mean you can't do that?" Dylan cut in. "I *want* you to do it, and I've got plans too – a friend works in a recording studio near Caernarfon, and I am going to record my first album there rather than sell my soul to those bloodsucking vampires in London. We could still be together *and* do all the things we want to do."

Elin hesitated, like a wild animal wanting the reward but sniffing danger. "Good, that's really good, but my mother's up here as she's been summoned by Anwen to 'sort something out' before she dies and, I, well, everything feels so *overwhelming* at the moment," she blurted, all composure gone and tears not far away. "Bear with me, and wait a little longer."

Dylan sighed. "I hear you, and I understand, I really do. But I'm falling in love with you, Elin, so waiting is hard," he said, fixing her gaze on his face. "I am going to be here for the duration, so let's see how things go, for both of us, shall we? I don't want to add to your stress, but before you go, let me at least tell you how grateful I am for what you're doing for Cara. I've not seen her this happy for years."

"I almost forgot! Anwen has told me to make sure she has money to do what she wants to, but you mustn't tell her yet, not until... you know."

Dylan nodded his understanding, and Elin could see him struggling to manage his feelings as much as she was. A few feet from them, a grey heron landed at the water's edge, its legs folding beneath it with perfect synchronicity and its huge wings folding like a velvet cape around its slim body. Its sudden, silent presence made them both pause, and take a breath.

"So, it seems we all have a lot to look forward to," Dylan said, as they watched the bird stab the shallows in search of food. "You know where I am when you're ready. I'm not going anywhere and, I think, neither are you." Slowly, reluctantly, he let go of her hands and walked away.

As she watched him cross the road, she did not call him back, or run after him, but she wanted to. Only when he had vanished into the pub did she realise what had just happened: he had told her he loved her and she had offered him nothing in return. Anwen had warned her not to waste this chance, but taking it was so very, very hard.

She remembered a conversation in *Daniel Deronda*, one of George Eliot's finest novels, words that had rung so true after Antoine's betrayal of her trust:

"I shall never love anybody. I can't love people. I hate them."

"The time will come, dear, the time will come."

FORTY-SIX

Elin got back to *Cân y mynyddoedd* only an hour or so after she had left, but it felt like a lifetime. She found her mother and Anwen still sitting outside, but neither was speaking and the atmosphere was verging on the arctic. Barbara got up as soon as she saw her, her face tired and drawn.

"I'm ready to go now, if that's all right with you. The nurse is inside, so Anwen will be fine." Pulling on her cardigan, she added, "I would be grateful if we could visit your father's grave later, if you've got time, but I'll get the 8.17 a.m. train home tomorrow morning."

"Gosh, that's a flying visit," Elin said. She was disappointed, even hurt, but not surprised. She had no real idea why Barbara had come back at all, but had not got the energy to press her into telling her now. "I'll take you back to the house, and then we'll go to Nant Peris church, but I'll just see that Nia knows I'm going. Won't be a minute."

"I think I'll walk down to the town and wait for you in that little café," Barbara said, turning to Anwen, who was slumped in her chair looking utterly exhausted. She gave her a farewell peck on the cheek, and murmured, "Goodbye, Anwen, and thank you... again," before vanishing into the trees. Elin wondered how long her mother's heels would last on the path down to the town.

She went straight to Anwen and put her hand on her forehead, checking for a temperature. "Did it not go well, seeing Mum?" she asked. "I can't say I'm surprised. I really think you need to go inside and lie down. You look wrung out."

The old woman turned her head slowly, and again, Elin could see pain in her eyes. Had the morphine worn off sooner than usual? If so, it did not bode well, but cancer had its own timetable, and waited for no one and nothing.

Helping her old friend into the cottage and then into bed, Elin tried to be gentle as she held her bird-like arms and Nia administered more medication. Anwen was asleep within minutes, but Elin sat beside her bed watching her face. She did not see the relief that morphine usually offered her, the old woman was sleeping a troubled sleep, as if beset by waves the drug could not calm. Had Barbara said or done something to upset her, brought up some decades-old quarrel, or was this the next phase of the disease, as she had been warned it could be? As she left the cottage to meet her mother, Elin knew that she had to ask Barbara questions about what she and Anwen had talked about that she would not want to answer.

A brief visit to Llion's grave early that evening confirmed to Elin that Barbara felt next to nothing for her husband of over thirty years, which soured the mood between them even further. A light drizzle meant sitting outside for a simple supper of salmon, samphire and local new potatoes, as Elin had planned, was impossible. Instead, mother and daughter made awkward, sporadic conversation whilst they ate in the kitchen and the most animated thing in the room was Mouse, yowling for their fish skin. Elin did not taste a mouthful of the food as she knew exactly what lay ahead and that it would take real courage to see it through.

"Mum, since I've been back here, Anwen has told me a few things I need to talk to you about it before you leave," she began.

Barbara's hands went up to pat her hair – a nervous gesture Elin immediately recognised. "Oh really? I wonder what she can have said."

"She told me that you'd had two babies before I was born. Why have you never told me that?" Elin asked, as gently as she could.

"Why would I tell you? It happened, as you say, before you were born."

"But is that why you didn't have any more children after me? Did you lose more babies? I would have loved a brother or sister."

Her mother looked at her, anger flashing in her eyes. "If you must know, we never had any more children as we slept in separate rooms, your father and I. There was precious little love between us by that stage."

Now it was Elin's turn to flinch. Of course, her parents had existed, but never truly *lived*, together in the farmhouse, a difference Cara had pointed out to her. How could they make love and thus, perhaps, have more babies if they never slept in the same bed? Suddenly, she thought she saw why she had been kept at a distance, sent away to school, never allowed the closeness she craved from a mother. Her heart thudded as she said:

"Is that why you never loved me, Mum? Because your other babies had died?"

Barbara stood up and a strange, gulping sound followed. Elin assumed it was Mouse choking on a fish bone, but when she saw her mother's shoulders shudder, realised she was weeping. Even in *Wern Farm*, however miserable she had been, Barbara had never wept. Mortified, Elin went to hug her from behind, laying her head between her heaving shoulders. For a few moments, neither woman spoke, but when her sobs had subsided Barbara turned around and Elin saw how old she looked beneath the recent finesse of wealth.

"No, my dear girl. That's not the reason. I have always loved you, in my own way. Never doubt that, whatever else you think of me," Barbara said.

A lump rose in Elin's throat. "But why were you always so formal, almost *cold* to me, as if you couldn't bring yourself to show me you loved me?" she stuttered. "I'm like that now, too – restrained, slow to trust anyone. I *hate* being like you!"

When she could speak, Barbara's voice shook with emotion. "I'm sorry, Elin, truly I am and I wish I could change things, but I can't. All I can do is stand here and reassure you that I loved you all the more because you were the only child I was given and I'm sorry for the way I behaved. I can only hope that one day you will know that's all true, even if it's not today."

"I hope so too," Elin replied, trying with her whole heart to believe it.

Knowing she had this once chance, Elin risked asking one more question she needed an answer to. She doubted that Anwen would ever answer it now.

"Can I ask about Dad's brother, Dafydd, the one who died on Tryfan?" she said. "Were he and Dad close?"

Barbara sighed deeply. "I knew you would ask about Dafydd one day. Yes, they were very close, but very different. Life dealt them both the wrong hand. Your father hadn't wanted to run the farm after we were married, but Dafydd did, desperately. And he wanted Anwen, too."

Goosebumps rose on Elin's arms, and she shivered. "So Dafydd and Anwen had loved each other, and it was him who gave her the Snowdon Lily? I knew it had to be him," she said.

"Please don't tell her that you know. It would distress her too much."

"She won't tell me anything about that part of her life, but I think she knows that I suspect they were in love. If I am going to finish this book and make it as good as it could be, I need to know personal things, the glue that sticks the facts together. Can you help me, Mum?"

"I don't think it's my place. Some secrets are hers, and if she wants to keep them, that should be her prerogative," Barbara said hesitantly. After a moment or two, she went on, "Yes, they loved each other, but... things happened, and Anwen wanted more than Dafydd. She wanted success, praise, prizes, all the stuff that you will already have in your book because she *has* told you that."

Elin nodded, but there was more: she felt it.

"But how did he die, up on the mountain with Dad? Was it really an accident? I think Dad blamed himself, as he was so upset."

"They quarrelled about... something else, a decision that had already been made and was for best for everyone, but his death was a terrible accident, yes. They dared each other to jump between the two rocks at the top of the mountains, as they had done as boys, young men, to see who was the *best* if you like, but Dafydd fell, and died the following day in hospital," Barbara said, with a calm air of finality that Elin knew spelt the end of the conversation. Possibilities ricocheted around in her head. Had Llion also loved Anwen more than he had Barbara, and had an affair with her, making the brothers quarrel so fatally? Or was their argument about the farm, or finances? Deeply frustrated, she wondered if she would ever find out now.

"Just one more question, please, Mum, then I'll leave you alone," Elin said. "I found an old photo, one without you in it, so you must have taken it. It's of Anwen sitting outside her cottage with a baby on her knee, and Dad and a man who must be his brother standing behind her. Was the baby my sister, the one who was ill and died so young?"

Barbara flinched, and her face crumpled in distress. "Oh, please stop bringing up painful memories. Why can't you just leave the past in peace? I don't know what photo you're talking about. Good night."

She went upstairs to bed, leaving Elin both upset and absolutely convinced her mother was not telling the truth.

. . .

Elin took Barbara to Bangor the following morning, but when they parted, it was unlike any previous farewell. An almost palpable tension hummed in the air between them, and unsaid words waited to be spoken.

"I know coming back has revived some memories you'd rather forget," Elin told her. "But I hope you sorted out whatever it was you came for."

"Yes, I did, and I'm glad I came," Barbara replied crisply. But then she took one of Elin's hands in hers and looked her in the eyes, saying softly, "And don't follow my example anymore. Be yourself and give yourself, fully, as I could never do and know that you are truly loved. Please, for me, do that."

"Thanks, Mum," Elin said, deeply moved. "I'll do my very best."

And as she watched the train pull out of the station, she believed that, although life had disappointed her, Barbara would always love her, in her own way.

FORTY-SEVEN

Anwen died a week later, in her bed, with Merlin curled up on her feet as he had been almost every night of his life. Her final days had been quiet, as she had drifted in and out of wakefulness only long enough to register someone plumping her pillows or offering her a sip of water. There were no dramatic scenes or tearful outpourings and no sharing of any of the secrets she had promised to tell Elin. They did not talk much, did not mention Dafydd, and all the other *lacunae* in her life story remained unfilled. Anwen's conversation with Barbara had been the last one of her life, and what they had discussed remained between them.

Elin could not find it in herself to be angry, as at least she now knew that Anwen *had* loved and been loved, but she resigned herself to submitting a biography that would lack any detail about her relationships. She would not mention Dafydd, as Barbara's version of their love affair still felt incomplete and as such risked raising more questions than it answered. Out of respect for her old friend, that secret would remain just that, secret.

In the days that followed Anwen's death, Elin surprised herself by not succumbing to the incapacitating grief she had expected to feel.

She was sad, very sad, but this death had approached gently, getting a little nearer each day and slowly enough for them all to feel almost able to welcome it, when it arrived. It had been just as Anwen had wanted, which consoled her enormously.

The funeral was held in the same church she and Anwen had visited together, and where Llion and Dafydd were buried at different ends of the same graveyard. Flo came up from London, and held Elin's hand hard as six local men had carried the flower-laden coffin out of the church and into the graveyard and she sobbed uncontrollably. There was a small coterie of people from the art world who stood apart in their finery, but most were familiar faces, dressed in their best suits and frocks, including Emlyn, Gwenda, Ifor the postman and Geraint, the stonemason. The men all doffed their caps at Elin. They were of Anwen's generation, and had watched one of their own become famous and inhabit, for a while, a world very different to theirs. They had heard rumours about her, perhaps some knew details about her past that were best not known, as old Ifor had suggested to Elin. Perhaps they had envied some of her glamorous experiences and the wealth that they would never have, but despite that, they were here today, to honour her, because she had come back and because she had loved her homeland as much as they did.

The great artist, the award-winning doyenne of exhibitions and galleries around the world, was laid to rest next to Dafydd's grave beneath an ancient yew tree which had sprinkled the ground with its fine, needle-sharp leaves. Elin read the simple Welsh words on his gravestone, and knew they were the truth:

DAFYDD PUGH, DYN CARIADUS, FE'I GARWYD YN ANNWYL./DAFYDD PUGH, A LOVING MAN, WHO WAS DEARLY LOVED.

It was fitting that, as the fashionable mourners from the art world slowly dispersed, only Elin and Cara stood by her grave at the end. Her will, to be formally read the following week, would, they knew already, give them opportunities they could never have had if they'd never loved Anwen Jones. She had also bequeathed them their friendship, which all three women had known was for life and beyond it.

Elin could not face the colossal task of clearing Anwen's cottage immediately. She got rid of the perishables in the fridge and made the place secure in case squatters moved in, but beyond that, her days were empty. She had to wait for the will to be read for the next phase of her life to begin, but it was hard to realise that her main purpose in returning home had gone forever: seeing Anwen. Her mood dipped rapidly and she ignored messages, saw almost nobody and went nowhere for over a week. Cara, ever caring, saw the possibility of depression on the horizon and tried to persuade her to go to the *Noson Lawen* in the pub on the last day of August, the end of the summer season.

"You told me to get out there and see people, so it's time for you to follow your own advice for once," she said.

Elin was hesitant, though she knew Cara was right. Many of the people who would be there had known her family since childhood. They would not stare, ask questions, but behave with respect and dignity and simply accept her presence amongst them now as they had always done... and probably buy her a drink. But she also knew that Dylan would be the main act, as ever, and she knew that he was still patiently waiting for her decision. Could she love him as he loved her? He would expect to know, now that Anwen was gone.

He had come to Anwen's funeral, and she had felt his support emanating across the aisle, but he had not broached what would happen next since their meeting at the lake, for which she was deeply grateful. Billed as "our upcoming superstar" on the posters around Llanberis, Elin knew that he had started recording his album locally, which reassured her that he was not pining for her in a damp garret. She felt sure that she would know what to do when the time was right, just as Anwen always said, so she agreed to go and hear him sing.

She got the bus to Llanberis, planning to get a taxi back as the last bus home left ludicrously early, at around 8 p.m. Without thinking, she found herself choosing her outfit carefully, and applying make-up to her tired, tear-weary eyes. It was important to enjoy the small things in life, Anwen would have said, and good company and good music were amongst the best of those small things. She left a £10 note on the kitchen table for Gwilym, who'd promised to feed and check on all three pets (as Merlin and Smot had both moved in with her since Anwen's death). Everything in her life had transformed since she had come here, under a year ago, and she was conscious of a future full of creative fulfilment and, if she chose it, love. Excitement fizzed through her body as the bus rounded the corner and she climbed on board.

The journey to Llanberis from Bethesda was long, as it entailed changing buses in Betws-y-coed, but the route was spectacular. It wound its way through mountains, past stunning waterfalls and within feet of black-hooved sheep who watched the traffic pass with yellow-eyed disinterest. When Elin reached the pub, it was already busy and Emlyn and Gwenda could only wave at her from behind the bar as she looked for Cara, who would surely be there to support Dylan. She scoured the crowd for her, but she had to look twice at the stunning young woman in a bright red dress and matching lipstick to realise it was her.

"Don't we scrub up well?" Elin said, marvelling at the transformation in both of them since the last time they had met, at the funeral. "You look wonderful."

"So do you," Cara replied. "But you always do."

Half an hour later, as Elin was beginning to relax and enjoy chatting to people, a ripple of applause and a few whoops told them that Dylan was coming onstage. She felt a lurch in her belly when she saw him, his hair in his usual loose ponytail and his cheekbones highlighted by the overhead spotlights.

"He looks pretty wonderful too, don't you think?" Cara whispered, nudging her. Elin rolled her eyes.

The acoustics in the room were good, but the sheer amount of people soaked up a lot of the sound, so the two women moved closer to the stage between songs to hear better. They were almost in the front row when Dylan spotted them and a huge grin spread across his face, like a little boy promised an ice cream. When Elin coyly beamed back at him, Cara made an enthusiastic thumbs-up.

He sang song after song with such effortless ease that the crowd watched, almost mesmerised by his pure voice and the musical skill on show. Some songs were in Welsh, but most were in English. All had their own mood, and described a place, a feeling it was easy to imagine and lose yourself inside. By 10 p.m., his voice was beginning to sound a little croaky, so he said:

"OK, this is the last one for tonight. It's a new one, written for someone who... means the world to me. I hope she likes it."

Elin shuffled from foot to foot, feeling as if hundreds of eyes were boring into her. Everyone *knew*, because nothing was private here, but she felt only their good wishes. Both she and Dylan were one of them, and they all cared about their happiness. As he began to sing, she looked up and saw his eyes looking directly into hers and this time, she did not look away.

> "Sometimes I've thought I'd never have
> Anything better than I had before,
> But now I know that loss can lead
> To the greatest joy of all."

Elin smiled at him. Here was a good man singing about her, to her, a man who felt things as she did, and who yearned to be loved as much as she did. How many chances at such a love would she have in her life, she asked herself? She could almost hear Anwen's answer: "only one". As the song drew to a close, it made the decision for her:

"Can you trust me to break your fall?
Will you let me take your hand?
If you will, we'll listen to the mountains' song
Together, us two, 'til the end."

Elin did not get a taxi back to Bethesda. She went back to the smallholding and she and Dylan spent the night outside, swaddled in blankets, watching shooting stars blaze across the sky and listening to the song that, even in darkness, filled the mountains with its mysterious sound as it had done for thousands of years.

FORTY-EIGHT

Elin was incredibly busy for the next few months, and autumn arrived without her noticing the changes around her as she would have wanted to. She was organising repair works on *Wern Farm* and meeting architects, builders and local craftsmen to help her draw up a plan to convert it into the arts centre Anwen had envisaged. Everything was locally sourced, using local tradespeople and Elin made sure the artists and makers in the area were fully involved in the plans from the outset. Most of them were on board to give demonstrations, run classes or give talks about their work, but all of them were full of encouragement about what Elin was doing and offered their advice and support freely.

But when she *did* have some time, going up to *Cân y mynydd-doedd* to begin sorting through Anwen's belongings was the last thing she wanted to do. The memories of her friend and the time they had spent together was still too vivid to consign them to the past by sweeping the cottage clean of any evidence that they had ever taken place. They had, and she treasured them. Those months had been, literally, life-changing for Elin and she was not ready to "move on" or "draw a line under them" as her well-meaning friends in London advised her to do. It was Dylan, with whom she spent every free moment, and knew she would spend all the days to come, who gave her the nudge she needed to begin the task.

"You will do it with love – even the difficult things, like taking her junk to the dump. It won't lessen what you shared, or what you felt for each other, but it's got to be done and she wanted only you to do it. Her will said as much, remember?" he said. "And you need to do it before we have a home of our own and you end up filling it with all the hideous knick-knacks from Anwen's cottage because you can't bear to part with them."

"I know," Elin replied. "She crammed so much stuff into such a small cottage!"

Dylan nodded. "I'd offer to help, but I think it's a one-woman job, and that woman is you. Be ruthless. The hardest part is starting, my mum always said."

"I do wish you'd stop being so bloody wise," she said, kissing him on the nose.

"You're only marrying me for my incredible wisdom," Dylan replied.

"Well, it certainly isn't for your money," Elin retorted, flashing the second-hand engagement ring he had given her, bought from an antique shop in Menai Bridge. When she had seen it, her response was now destined for inclusion the best man's speech at their wedding at Christmas:

"It's lovely, but a bit tarnished – just like me I suppose."

And so she was braced for the task ahead, but it was with a still-heavy heart that Elin finally opened the door of *Cân y mynyddoedd* one morning and the familiar, if faint, smell of cigarette smoke overlaid with mildew and damp assaulted her senses. Every surface was covered with dust and dead flies and a few silvery snail trails went from one side of the quarry-tiled floor to the other. Ivy had found a way through the window they had left open a crack to keep the place aired, and was now reaching, blindly, out into the room. A pigeon cooed from its nest on the chimney, echoing down the flue so loudly that it sounded as if it was in the room. Nature was reclaiming the cottage, and Elin wondered, for a few seconds, if that was exactly what Anwen would have wanted. Should she simply shut the door and go? It was only when she'd reminded herself that this could be a new home for someone who needed one in an area where they were all too scarce, that she was able to walk purposefully towards the Welsh dresser on one side of the kitchen and start work.

For the whole of that morning, she packed away grease-coated china and battered saucepans ready to donate to charity, threw away half-squeezed tubes of paint and moth-bitten cardigans and put the very few things she wanted to keep in a box – the chipped teapot in which she had always made them a *panad*/cuppa; the Welsh blanket that had kept Anwen warm in the deck chair and the unfinished painting of the heron. These things seemed so little, but said so much.

Elin was hugely thankful that Anwen had already sifted through mountains of papers, letters, photographs, newspaper articles, reviews, exhibition programmes, plane tickets, bank statements and greetings cards before she died, in preparation for her book. There still seemed to be huge amounts to sort through however, and by noon, she was tired a) of inhaling dust and b) feeling like a voyeur into the minutiae of another person's life. It was only when she discovered a small leather suitcase hidden under the chest of drawers in Anwen's bedroom that she felt her energy return. She knew at once that her dear friend had collated the things it contained, so that Elin would find them. When she opened it, she was trembling so much that her fingers fumbled as she lifted out diaries, crisp-edged photographs and even more letters and postcards from all around the world, from all kinds of people Anwen had met, and men who had cherished her. She had almost married a Peruvian musician, been engaged to an Italian leather merchant and spent a year living in a yurt in the then-Yugoslavia with a man called Luka. The little Dictaphone was there too, still smeared with greasy fingerprints, though Elin was quite certain Anwen had not recorded anything intelligible on it for the final weeks of her life as she had been so weak, and she had already listened all to her voice notes before then. It was here because it had been a gift that had meant something to her, freeing her to say things she could not say in person.

No, it was the other things in the suitcase that held the secrets, Elin was sure, and would fill in the *lacunae* in her life with things Anwen had wanted her to unearth now, when she was gone, because she had not been able to tell her them in time. Finally, she knew she could write a book that would do her friend justice, as the complicated person she had been, one who had known love more than once in her life. There, safely hidden, was the photograph of the Pugh brothers and Anwen with the baby on her knee, taken, she was still certain, by Barbara. Finally, right at the bottom, Elin found a homemade card with a faded, pressed wildflower on the front.

"A Snowdon Lily," she murmured. "The one Dafydd gave you."

She opened the card, and as she read the faded handwritten message, she felt colours, senses and objects blur, and the room all-but dissolved around her.

> Dwi'n dy garu, mi fyddaf bob amser, a byddaf yn trio dallt dy benderfyniad i beidio â chadw ein merch. Bydd fy mrawd yn gofalu amdani, dwi'n gwybod.
>
> I love you, and always will, and I will try to understand your decision not to keep our daughter. My brother will care for her, I know.

It was signed, simply,

> Dafydd

As tears streamed down her cheeks, so much that had not made sense for her whole life began to form a pattern, a sequence that Elin could track and understand. Her uncle Dafydd was her biological father, and Anwen, her biological mother. They were not married, as Anwen had refused marriage, feeling her destiny lay elsewhere, so she had given her to Llion and Barbara to bring up on the farm. She let this fact wash over her like one of the many mountain streams of her homeland, first icy, then bearable and finally, almost uplifting in its chill purity. Amidst everything Elin felt, there was no bitterness towards Barbara and Llion. They had done the best they could, hindered by unhealed wounds, regrets and unforgotten tragedies. As to how she now regarded Anwen, she was not so sure. Yes, she remembered the soft-sung lullabies, the visits to the beach, painting together, picnics in the garden, all happy snapshots in what had been a long, bleak childhood, but a child needed consistency and love and, for all their flaws, Llion and Barbara had tried to give her that when Anwen had decided she could not.

As she closed the door of the cottage that afternoon, Elin felt calmer, surer of the path she had to take than she had in a very long time. Finally, she knew who she was, and she was strong, but there remained unanswered questions that would trouble her forever if she did not ask them.

FORTY-NINE

Elin told nobody what she had discovered. She stayed at the house in Bethesda, telling Dylan and Cara that she was working on the last draft of the book about Anwen's life before submitting it to a publisher. In reality, she was sitting inside with the curtains half-closed doing nothing but stroking the cats and letting Smot out when she needed to go. How could she tell Barbara that she knew the truth? How could she ask her for more detail without risking their fragile relationship finally imploding? Only as she faced that possibility head-on did she realise how little she wanted that to happen.

Yes, her childhood had been far from happy, but now, at last, she understood why: her adoptive parents had wanted children desperately, but had had to settle for adopting her when Anwen chose her work, her career, *herself* over marriage and motherhood. She had regretted that selfishness later, and now Elin saw the subtext beneath the old woman's concern for her future, the huge bequest in her will, and her irresistible need to keep her lost daughter close as she neared death. Hadn't Barbara asked her to tell Anwen that she was "glad her wish has been granted, and you are back with her at last"? How incredibly difficult that must have been, and how *unselfish*.

A phone call to Barbara about this was unthinkable, a text or email equally so. She would have to write a letter and hope that by being completely open and *forgiving*, her remaining questions would be answered. It was brief, and simply worded:

Dear Mum,

This is not an easy thing to tell you, and I want you to know that I love you, and always will, but I need to know some things that you have never shared with me. Anwen left proof that she was my biological mother for me to find after her death, and I have found it. I want to find out exactly what happened, but only you can tell me.

Please, Mum, let me know in whatever way you want to, when you feel you can. I know it won't be easy, but I also know you will do what's best for me, and that is to tell me the truth, all of it.

With love, Elin

Barbara did not reply, or contact Elin at all, for almost a fortnight. When the postman delivered a crisp, white envelope one morning, she could not open it until the evening. Then, as the swallows chattered in the sky above her, she took it outside to watch the sun slowly set over the mountains and tore it open.

Her first surprise was at how long the letter was, as Barbara had never written more than a shopping list or a greetings card in her life. She could not help but smile wryly at some of her mother's efforts to sound formal, even *proper*, but as she read on, the letter's inherent kindness stayed with her long after she'd read the last word:

My dear Elin,

I have thought for a long time about how to reply to your letter, so here's the best I can do. I hope it's what you need, and you are right to ask for the whole truth.

You wanted me to tell you how me and your father (I hope I can still say that) came to adopt you, and bring you up in our home as our own. I am happy that you say you still love me, as I have always loved you. I will do my best to tell you what happened.

Anwen and Dafydd were lovers after she came back from her years of travelling. When she fell pregnant, she did not want the baby, but Dafydd would not let her consider an abortion. She only wanted to work, but Llion and I longed for a child after the two we had lost, so she asked us to take you in. We never did it legally, as Anwen always wanted you to inherit her money as her only child and I have your birth certificate which formally names her as your mother and Dafydd Pugh as your father. Let me know if and when you want to see it.

When I was in Wales recently, you asked me about a photo and I denied knowing about it, but I did. I took it on the day we took you home, when all of us were feeling such a mixture of emotions. Dafydd could never accept Anwen's decision to give you away and was very bitter when she wouldn't marry him as he had always loved her. It was decided that Llion would run the farm when he married me, as we hoped to have a family, but neither brother was happy about it and their relationship was a sour one afterwards.

Your father was angry, saying Dafydd was ungrateful for him sacrificing his dreams to run a farm he hated and bringing up, and truly loving, a child that was not his own. As I told you, they went climbing together on Tryfan one day, as they often did, and they argued bitterly about it... and Dafydd fell. It was an accident, a stupid dare born of bitterness and regret, but it ruined Llion's life. He believed his happiness in being given you had been bought at too high a price, and he never forgave himself.

I think I never felt I had earned the right to be your mother, and that's why I always held myself at a distance. I didn't dare get too close because I knew I was a fraud, and that you would find me out some day. Your father felt that too, and he refused to visit Anwen after she wanted to tell you the truth when you were a teenager. It was hard for him, but he couldn't bear to lose you, so he broke all ties with her. She never understood his decision, but she respected his wishes.

I came back to Wales that last time because Anwen called me to say that she wanted to tell you the truth before she died, and I had to beg her not to. She agreed, and said she would leave it for you to find in a way that only you would understand (not sure what that meant, I'm afraid). So you see, she was selfish in many ways, but in that, she was a truly generous soul.

I wish I had been different, and better. I wish it very much. Whatever you think now you know all this, remember what I told you, that I love you with my whole heart and always will. I was the best mother I could be to you, even if that wasn't a very good one.

I hope to see you again soon, and that you are still courting that nice young chap, the musician. Anwen said she thought he was made for you.

With love, always,
Mum

Elin sat quite still for a while after she'd finishing reading. She could only imagine the effort that had gone into writing this letter – her mother's struggle for the right phrase, the best words. In fact, she could almost *hear* her voice, feel her desperate need for forgiveness and she did not hesitate to give it, texting her:

> Mum, thank you for your letter. I understand everything now. See you soon. E. xx

She knew exactly what Anwen had meant in leaving proof that "only she would understand", and went upstairs to find the Dictaphone. Listening to Anwen's voice would be painful, but she did so, and heard the story Barbara had written in her letter for the first time in her friend's voice, croaky and cough-broken. She did not sound bitter, though there were many regrets expressed about opportunities lost and bonds that should never have been broken – that between her and her dear friend Llion and that between a mother and her child. Her concluding words were gracious and kind and, in time, it was those that Elin chose to remember most:

"I was the woman who gave birth to you, but in my eyes, and I hope in yours, Barbara was your true mother, the woman who cared for you as a mother should, and as I could not. I never thanked her enough, so make sure you do so for me please. And tell her you love her. All mothers need to know that."

"I did, Anwen," Elin said. "But I hope she already knew."

EPILOGUE

Elin and Dylan married on Christmas Eve and set up home in Barbara's old house in Bethesda until the new home they wanted to build outside Rachub, up in the foothills of Eryri, was ready. It was no surprise to Elin that the day of their wedding was bright and sunny without the snow and ice December conjured up, as the seasons made their own decisions up here. Barbara wore a muted pale blue outfit, because Elin felt she had finally earned the right to veto peach, and she insisted on giving her daughter away which felt completely right to both of them. It was a day of celebration followed by a party in the evening attended by many who were invited, and many more who were not. On the order of service, Elin chose to have some words from George Eliot printed, words that expressed exactly what she now felt about love, and being loved:

"*Blessed is the influence of one true, loving human soul on another.*"

The new arts centre in *Wern Farm* opened in January, and was called "The Anwen Jones Centre for North Welsh Creativity". Elin felt it was rather clunky, but was the name specified in Anwen's will, which nobody dared argue with. It was an immediate asset to the community, and helped ensure several traditional skills were passed on, and therefore kept alive. In March, Elin's 300-page biography of Anwen was published to considerable acclaim in the art world. It included everything she had achieved and most of the people she had loved, but Elin stopped short of sharing her own father's role in her story, or outing herself as the artist's daughter, both for Barbara's sake and her own. To know the truth herself was enough.

In June, Cara sold the smallholding for less than her parents had paid over twenty years earlier and bought Anwen's cottage, which she renovated and made into a centre for herbal remedies, yoga, meditation and a residential retreat for those seeking a quiet place in a busy world. She still had people coming up to the cottage to ask about Anwen Jones, the great artist who lived there before her. She was more than happy to tell them her memories, calling her old friend "the woman who changed my life, and that of many others." She never wore black again.

On October 21st, just as the sun was setting over Eryri, Elin and Dylan welcomed a baby boy into the world, and they named him Dafydd Llion. Barbara was a doting *Nain*/Grandmother who visited the family as often as she could, and the little boy adored her. Cara, his godmother, learnt to time her visits not to coincide with Nain's lest they become competitors for Dafydd's attention and irresistible smiles

By the following February, the Williams family's new home was ready, its rooms filled with light and colour, and the paintings Anwen had wanted Elin to have were given pride of place. Every morning, when she drew back the curtains, Elin saw the dappled mountain slopes laid out before her like an ever-changing tapestry and she was thankful for her new life, her family and for loving and being loved. Whenever she opened her front door, whatever the month, whatever the weather, the mountains greeted her with their song, breathtaking in all its permutations.

A LETTER FROM THE AUTHOR

Thank you for reading *The Cottage in the Clouds*. I really hope you enjoyed reading Anwen and Elin's story and getting to know Eryri a little, a beautiful part of North Wales that has been close to my heart since childhood. The mountains, where my story is set, are wonderful at making us realise how small we are and how huge the natural world is in comparison: we need to remember how precious it is and treasure it more.

If you'd like to join readers in hearing all about my new releases and some bonus content too, you can sign up for my newsletter.

www.stormpublishing.co/caroline-young

If you enjoyed this book enough to take the time to leave a review, that would be very helpful to other readers, and much appreciated by me. Even a short review can make all the difference in encouraging a reader to discover my stories for the first time.

Thank you for coming on this journey with me, and do stay in touch. I look forward to sharing more stories with you.

Caroline

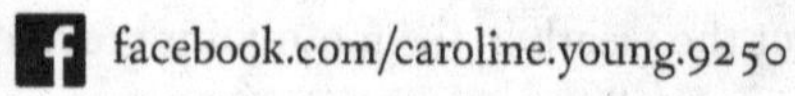 facebook.com/caroline.young.9250

ACKNOWLEDGMENTS

This is the first novel I have set anywhere other than the island of Anglesey, where I live and which I know very well. I love the mountains of Eryri, but let me apologise to those who know it far, far better than I do if any inaccuracies have slipped into my story. I hope I have managed to capture the *feel* of this spectacular place, at least.

I have, as ever, people to thank for their support, and they are usually the same people! Geoff, my husband, believes in me far more than I believe in myself. Idris Jones willingly checks my hesitant Welsh. Jane Walsh, in +39, a lovely café in Menai Bridge, where I live, displays copies of my books for customers to browse and, hopefully, order. My daughters Bethan, Rhiannon and Mari continue to tell me how proud they are of me, and their friends Niamh and Vic are my biggest fans, allegedly! Thank you to Felicity Brooks for telling me about her late aunt Eleanor Brooks, a renowned artist who lived and worked in Llanfrothen, and for letting me visit her incredible cottage there. It filled my mind as I wrote about *Cân y mynyddoedd*, so to see it was a gift indeed. Kate Smith, my editor at Storm, thank you once more for encouraging me to keep going with a story I doubted, and for saying kind things about it when I got to the end.

My most heartfelt thanks this time need to go to my eighteen-year-old Jack Russell, Daisy, who has sat in her basket under my desk as I have worked for many years, and who will not be doing so anymore. I will miss her more than I can say, and hope she knows just how calming and loving a presence she has always been for me, and how much I have appreciated her unconditional love all these years. Sleep well, Daisy May.

www.ingramcontent.com/pod-product-compliance
Lightning Source LLC
Chambersburg PA
CBHW011554190726
48287CB00010B/2890